MARIA MAROTTI

The Etruscan Princess

2021

A Captain Fusco Mystery Case

ISBN:9781792845185

For the loving memory of my late husband,

Jack Ceder

ACKNOWLEDGMENTS

In 2011, during a two month vacation in Brazil, I completed *The Etruscan Princess*. I had the time and the necessary concentration. My husband, Jack Ceder, had read the first chapter a few months before and liked it a lot. He told me, though, that he was not going to read chapter by chapter, as he had done with my other novels. He intended to read the completed manuscript. That was not going to happen. My husband passed away just a few months after our return to the States. His death marked the end of a 33 year marriage. With his passing I had lost my supportive reader. I put The Etruscan Princess in a drawer, and for years I never re-read it. For a while it seemed like my writing life had ended. My first acknowledgment goes to my late husband for his support.

Years later, as I was going through my files, I accidentally bumped into *The Etruscan Princess*. I started reading it and I was surprised. It engaged me. I knew I couldn't be objective, but I knew someone who could. I sent it to Mike Foley and asked him to give me his opinion. Over the years I had taken several writing workshops from Mike Foley, both in Big Bear and online. He was a writing instructor in Big Bear Lake and the Extension Section of the University of California at Riverside. He was also an editor and continues to write and publish. He read and edited my manuscript and, in no uncertain terms, he encouraged me to get it published. My second acknowledgment goes to him.

Finally, I want to acknowledge my partner, Thomas Robinson, for editing this book and for continually helping me get my computer to do what I needed it to do.

Table of Contents

Foreword

Astute California detective Nickie Fusco joins his fiancée Valentina, a professor who specializes in *film noir,* for a long-awaited trip to Italy. But the mysterious disappearance of Valentina's colleague and roommate transforms the dream vacation into a perilous journey. Maria Marotti guides the reader on an intimate and sensual voyage that crisscrosses the Italian peninsula, from urban Rome with its piazze and landmarks, its surrounding quaint villages, Etruscan ruins, and lakeside castles, to a bustling Naples and its sinister underbelly, to Venice's artisanal islands, and to the picturesque towns of the Cinque Terre. Detailed descriptions balance the fast-paced unfolding of harrowing events, and allow us to indulge with Nick and Valentina in the richness and diversity of Italian life, offering up sumptuous meals of *pasta all'amatriciana* and *parmigiana di melanzane,* serene vistas across Lago Bracciano and the glimmering Mediterranean, and the excavated treasures of Pompeii. Marotti's traveling narrative weaves seamlessly backwards and forward in time, heightening the drama while filling gaps in the lives of its unsettled characters and their tangled relationships. As we are dragged deeper and deeper into the case, we discover dark secrets and troubled pasts through the small-time kidnapping hijacked by the Camorra and the cold and calculated world of international art theft. This is armchair travel at its best: satisfying the appetites of both the uninitiated to Italy and the veteran Italophile. Informed by Marotti's nuanced and wide-ranging knowledge of Italian culture and peppered with her experience in the quirky halls of academia, the novel is perhaps most memorable for its transmission of a profound understanding of the fragility and generosity of the human spirit.

By Professor Bernadette Luciano
Head, School of Cultures, Languages and Linguistics
Associate Dean (International)
Faculty of Arts
University of Auckland (New Zealand)

Coauthor of Reframing Italy: New Trends in Italian Women's Filmmaking,. Purdue University Press, 2013

Author's Notes and Bonus

Thank you for purchasing my book. I hope you enjoy it. As an expression of my gratitude, I would like to give you "The Crying Game," which is one of my best short stories. Just email me at mariamarotti@gmail.com and I will send it to you

I have a favor to ask: after you've read the book: would you please leave a review on Amazon? Your doing that will make it possible for more people to enjoy my book.

You can find the book by doing a search for Maria Marotti The Etruscan Princess on Amazon, or you can find a link to it on my website: https://mariamarotti-author.com/booklinks.

Thank you!

CHAPTER ONE

THEIR BEST VACATION

A whole-face juicy lick, a paw tapping on his shoulder, and a soft growl – feels kind of comforting for Nick Fusco. During the first seconds, just before opening his eyes, he even confuses the face lick with a passionate kiss from his sweetheart, Valentina, rather than his dog waking him up. A moment later, though, the sad reality of Valentina's absence gives him a pang of disappointment. The dog's lick has just interrupted a delicious dream in which Valentina kissed him, after a big Italian-style outburst of rage.

"Just a second, Pippo," he yawns as he gets up. "I'm going to let you out."

Pippo follows him into the kitchen and then outside, where they both retrieve the morning paper laying on the garden path.

After the kettle filled with water for coffee is set on the burner, the first thing to do is to check the email. Valentina might have sent him a message. In Italy it's the afternoon when in Santa Abelina, California it's six in the morning.

Hi, hot lover, the message starts. Hot lover, Fusco chuckles remembering a few blanket fights over the right temperature in their

1

bed – Fusco always hot and Valentina always cold. Or maybe, hot lover as in passionate lover? And the memory of their lovemaking sends a wave of desire through his body.

I miss you a lot and not only the love, the sex, and your company, but also our fights, the message continues. *I have a problem, and I wish you were here to tell me what to do. Remember Caterina, my annoying apartment mate? Well, she's disappeared. I know, now you're saying, "good riddance!" But I'm actually worried. It has been six days and I don't have the foggiest idea of where to look for her. Could you possibly come over sooner than you'd planned?*

Oh, no! Fusco is disappointed. Not another case! He's a captain and a detective in the Santa Abelina Police Department. He's been looking forward to his vacation in Italy with Valentina and has no intention of spoiling it with a wild goose chase. This Caterina, whom he's never met, sounds absolutely horrible. Valentina, who is spending three months in Rome on a scholarship for her research in Italian film noir, has described Caterina as the roommate from hell. Rude, arrogant, pushy, competitive – you name it.

Sweetheart, he writes back ignoring the whistle from the kettle, *I hope you don't take this the wrong way, but when I read that Caterina had disappeared I thought that simply meant that we would have the apartment all to ourselves. I'm done with the Vessely case. I testified at the trial yesterday, and that's over once and for all. As you know, I was planning on arriving in Rome in ten days, but I might be able to get a flight sooner. I'll see what I can do. As for Caterina, I'm sure she's fine and did not have the good grace to let you know that she's going to be out of town for a while.*

"O.K., Pippo." The dog is nudging him requesting his breakfast. "I

2

got it."

I should check the internet for a flight to Rome, he tells himself as he sips his morning coffee on the deck and Pippo noisily chomps his kibble. *No way, I'm going to worry about this Caterina!* A vacation in Italy with Valentina. This is too big. A great opportunity. He isn't going to waste it snooping around. He would like to use this vacation to relax and win Valentina over. He wants her to marry him, to set a date. So far, she's been non-committal.

"Maybe," she'd responded to his marriage proposal. "What do you mean 'maybe'?" He'd felt deeply disappointed. From his perspective, they'd lived happily together for almost a year. "We don't fight all that much, do we?"

She'd laughed in her wholehearted way. "No, I'm not worried about the fights. I love you." She'd looked straight into his eyes and had squeezed his hand. "Marriage is the problem for me."

"That it didn't work out once doesn't mean that it won't work out this time around," he'd alluded to her divorce four years before.

"I don't know, *Amore*, let me think about it." She'd shaken her head, but then she'd given him her luminous smile. "I'm totally committed to you. I want you to know that and believe it."

She'd accepted the ring he'd bought for her and had worn it ever since.

A solid wall of fog covers his view of the ocean in this "June gloom" morning. He misses the sunshine and the coastline view from his deck – both of which Valentina seems to have taken away when she left for Italy four weeks ago.

Why don't I go and have lunch at Franca's deli tomorrow? He needs to arrange for Pippo's stay with their friend during his Italian vacation. It's always fun to chat with Franca, anyway. And she might have some pertinent information about Caterina, who has replaced her in the European Studies department after she'd resigned a year ago.

Oh no, not Caterina again!

He catches himself thinking about her disappearance, as he gets up and heads back inside, ready to start the day.

The tram in Piazza di Torre Argentina makes the ancient building shake as it turns the corner of via Arenula. *It must be the five o'clock tram.* Valentina yawns and turns around trying to fall asleep again. It's too early to get up, but the many thoughts rushing through her mind don't let her relax. She wishes Nick, her partner, were here. She could turn around and hug him. And everything would be all right again.

The past four weeks have been quite different from what she'd expected. Despite all the turmoil brought into her life by Caterina, she'd been able to focus on her research on Italian film noir. She had met some of the people whom she'd planned to meet and found most of the research material she was looking for. She missed Nick every single day, actually every single moment. Not that she ever doubted her feelings for him, or his feelings for her, for that matter. The thing is that she's not ready to get married. Not only did she have a negative experience in her previous marriage, but she also doesn't see the point.

She can't have children. The thought saddens her and makes her turn over in bed as if she could chase away the grief by simply moving around. The one thing she wants most her body will not give her. Ever since she's met Nick, the desire for a child has increased. *We do have a great relationship, though—child or no child.* She stretches and

4

throws away the sheet. Nick will be here soon.

Why is she so tense? Shouldn't she feel relieved that her unpleasant apartment mate, Caterina, hasn't been around for a week? It had all started on the plane over. Just as she was settling down on her seat on the Los Angeles-Rome flight, Valentina had noticed her, striding down the aisle. She knew who she was. Caterina Pedersoli, the Italian lecturer who had replaced her friend, Franca De Giusti, could never pass unnoticed. Rather tall, thin, with long curly light blonde hair and those enormous, slightly elongated dark eyes, Caterina commanded everyone's attention with her self-possession, imperious ways, and exceedingly hyper energy level.

Caterina had settled on the seat next to Valentina's, without noticing her. Valentina had smiled and greeted her. Caterina had nodded back – no smile, no sign of recognition. When Valentina had introduced herself, and tried to remind her of their previous acquaintance, Caterina had said that she didn't recall ever meeting her before. It didn't get any better. Any attempts at conversation had been thwarted by Caterina's rude interruptions, sarcastic and patronizing comments – all of them uttered in halting Italian.

"You're a film noir expert? Isn't it totally *passé*? You're a friend of Franca? I haven't heard a single good comment about her. Your boyfriend is a cop? Oh, that's a new one! You've been a lecturer for ten years? That's all over for you, then! Why even do research?"

The worst part was still to come. The university agency in charge of finding rentals for visiting scholars had paired them up in the same apartment in an ancient building in downtown Rome. It was an excellent location, close to the libraries, the bookstores, the stores, theaters and restaurants, right at the border of the colorful Roman

Jewish ghetto. However, sharing it with Caterina had been very trying. One couldn't even ignore her because her lifestyle encroached on Valentina's – late hours, noisy guests, loud lovemaking with a varied array of men, and to top it all, dirty dishes in the sink.

Why am I even worrying about her disappearance? Valentina grabs her robe as she gets up. The six o'clock bells of the nearby *Chiesa del Gesu`* are tolling for the first mass of the day. She opens the wooden shutters and lets the soft light of the early Roman June morning into the room. She looks down toward the square. A few cabs are driving by through the still deserted streets. Later, the traffic noise will be deafening. *I need to check my computer and see if Nick has answered my email.* She heads toward the kitchen, ready to start the day.

"*Two suppli` di riso* and an *insalata caprese*" Fusco orders. He can't resist the fried delicacy made of balls of rice in a thick bread-crumbed crust. Since he has entered Franca's deli, aptly named, *Ricordi Italiani*, the delicious scent of the *suppli`* has been tempting him. *A little heavy, but irresistible.* He balances it off with an order of the more delicate Insalata caprese—buffalo mozzarella, basil, olive oil and tomato salad.

He has come here mainly to chat with Franca, Valentina's best friend and former colleague at the University of Santa Abelina. The food is an added bonus, he has almost to remind himself. Franca's deli brings out the glutton in him.

Franca spots him, seated near the window and immediately makes her way toward the table.

"Hey Nick!" She smiles, giving him a peck on the cheek. "Getting ready to fly to Rome?"

"Yeah… I testified yesterday. It looks like they're going to let me go now."

"I read it in the paper. I'm next—on Tuesday of next week." Franca settles in the seat opposite to him.

She'd been framed as the murderer in the Vessely case. Fusco feels that he should stick around in Santa Abelina until Franca has testified. He had been the detective assigned to the case. He'd solved it, but the murderer, a university employee and the victim's wife's lover, had taken off for Mexico before Fusco had managed to arrest him. A few months later, in a joint operation with the Interpol, Fusco had caught him in Cancun, just as he was planning his final escape to Cuba.

"I have a flight reservation in ten days, but Valentina has asked me to go there sooner. I'm still trying to find a flight. It may be another week. I may still be here for your testimony."

The Vessely case had been an unusual one. Leslie Vessely was a powerful and highly-placed university administrator who'd been found strangled in the European Studies department. The murder weapon was a bike guard chain that belonged to Franca. She was at the time a lecturer in the European Studies department and the head of the lecturers' union—a long-time antagonist of the victim. Obviously, she'd immediately become a prime suspect. Despite pressures from all sides—even his chief and a state senator—Fusco had discounted all suspicions surrounding Franca and conducted an investigation, which had rapidly led him to the culprit. During the unfolding of the case, he'd started going out with Valentina, Franca's best friend, and had later developed a good friendship with Franca and her husband Bill Evergreen.

"What do you hear from Valentina?" Franca asks him.

"Do you have any time now? There's something I want to ask you."

Franca looks around assessing the situation. It's one thirty and the lunch crowd has partly dissipated. She nods. "Sure, shoot!"

"What do you know about Caterina Pedersoli?"

Franca giggles, quite amused. "You mean the sexy dragon lady – or rather kid – they hired to replace me? Not much except that Rupert fell for her, head over heels."

"No kidding!" Fusco chuckles. Rupert used to be Franca's supervisor in the European Studies Department. Fusco then had the opportunity to have a couple of chats with Rupert – a very nervous and almost terrified man. "Where did you hear that?"

"I had lunch with Gloria a few months ago and she complained about that. Apparently, old Rupert only has eyes for Caterina. He's already campaigning with the faculty to have her promoted to ladder faculty. Anything to keep her!"

"Do you know that she ended up sharing an apartment with Valentina in downtown Rome?" Fusco doesn't know whether there has been communication between Franca and Valentina during the last month.

Franca nods. "I heard. Poor Valentina! I only met Caterina briefly. She's annoying—very presumptuous and arrogant. Her spoken Italian is passable but very halting and Gloria complained that her written Italian is ungrammatical. Not my problem anymore!" Franca still needs to remind herself that she's out of there, Fusco notices.

During the investigation and after it had been proven that the murder weapon belonged to Franca, the European Studies faculty had wasted no time in suspending her. She had taken it very hard and decided to leave academia for good and pursue one of her passions in life—cooking. She'd opened a very successful Italian deli.

"Well, Valentina emailed me this morning – very worried. Apparently, Caterina has disappeared and she doesn't know where to look for her."

"Oh, dear Valentina is such a sleuth and always so generous!" Franca smiles, certainly remembering Valentina's sleuthing during the Vessely case when she was trying to prove her friend's innocence. "I wouldn't worry. Caterina must have gone out of town. Rupert is in Rome right now. She may be showing him a good time." And she bursts out laughing.

Fusco laughs, too, and attacks a delightfully oily *suppli`*.

The roar of the traffic subsides as soon as Valentina leaves behind *via Arenula*, the main throughway separating the two parts of the Roman Jewish ghetto. She makes her way into the narrow *via dei Giubbonari*, where the prevailing sound is that of an incessant human chatter rising over the vroom vroom of the fast moving motorcycles.

"Are you interested in a nice handbag, or maybe a suitcase?" The Jewish shop owner points to the leather goods inside the window, and without waiting for an answer, he continues: "The latest fashion, excellent prices. We have a great selection inside…"

Valentina shakes her head, and gives him a faint smile. "No, thanks," she cuts him short.

By now, she knows better. If she followed him inside into the dimly lit store, even for a few minutes, it would be like having been swallowed up by the mythical Jonah's whale—with no hope of being regurgitated, except with two unwanted bags hanging from her arm. Today, she's in a hurry. She's already wasted enough time at the Police, reporting Caterina's disappearance.

After sitting for an hour on a metal chair in a busy waiting room with half-discolored walls, she'd been admitted into a police *ispettore*'s office.

"You said that your apartment mate has disappeared?" The officer was an older man, short and bald with a friendly paternal smile. "How do you know that?"

That was the problem: how did she know? Did gut feelings account for anything?

"Most of her clothes and her suitcases are still there, in her room. She never mentioned to me that she was going out of town. I have a feeling that something might have happened to her." There. She'd said it.

"How long has it been since you last saw her?" The smile had left the *ispettore*'s face. He was now looking straight into Valentina's eyes, probably questioning her motives.

"I haven't seen her in a week."

"Have you talked to other people who might know her?"

"We don't really have common friends and don't share activities, "she sighed as the memories surfaced—that unpleasant month of apartment sharing. "However, yesterday, they called from the language school where she teaches twice a week. It was the second time that she hadn't showed up for her classes."

At that point the *ispettore* appeared slightly worried. *At last!* Valentina thought. Romans never seemed to show concern. They looked at you with a spunky and lazy half-amused smile, which seemed to invite you to take it easy. The many layers of history, which one could observe in the Roman forum and even in the nearby piazza di Torre Argentina, impacted the collective consciousness of the city, making its citizens both skeptical and semi-absent.

"I need you to give me a precise description of your apartment mate." The *ispettore* sat at his typewriter and started to pound the keys, drawing a report.

When it was all said and done, it had taken two hours. The morning was mostly gone and it didn't make much sense to go to the library for her research work.

So now, as she continues headed for piazza Farnese, where the language school is located, the deliciously titillating smell of freshly baked *pizza al taglio* captures her senses. She suddenly realizes that she's hungry. *I didn't have breakfast.* At home in Santa Abelina, she would sit down with Nick and eat every morning. In Rome, she's gotten out of the habit.

She walks inside the small *pizza al taglio* store. As she tries to decide which one to order – a small piece with thinly sliced mushrooms and a small piece with the eggplant and red peppers, or just one large piece with artichokes *alla giudia?*—she suddenly remembers. Caterina must have stopped at the *pizza al taglio* store at least twice a week for a whole month on her way to work.

"*Dica?* May I help you?" a curly haired Roman boy behind the counter expects her order.

Pointing to her chosen piece, Valentina asks: "Do you remember the American young lady – tall and blonde – who used to come here at least twice a week?"

The boy nods. "Yeah, the blonde who spoke Italian with an American accent… She was here yesterday."

"Yesterday!?" Valentina doesn't even try to conceal her amazement.

Valentina's surprise startles the boy. "Yeah, I think so, or maybe a couple of days ago…"

"I haven't seen her in a while," Valentina blurts out. "I was wondering…"

"Yeah, a couple of days ago…" the boy insists, handing her a pizza slice folded and wrapped up in coarse paper napkins.

Trying to keep the oil on her pizza from dripping on her clothes, Valentina continues headed toward piazza Farnese. The open market is in full swing. The statue of Giordano Bruno – the free thinker executed by the Inquisition in that colorful square more than four centuries ago – watches over the fresh fruit and vegetables and the loud vendors.

Valentina crosses the square, making her way through the stalls and taking in the fragrance of the fresh food – *Nick is going to love this feast for the senses!* –and then, rather unwillingly, she turns into the narrow and dark side street.

The entrance to palazzo Aldobrandi is dilapidated and very dark. It is a testament to the aristocratic family's financial demise. Once a part of the so-called black aristocracy—the noble families who were part of the close circles faithful to the Popes and admitted to the Vatican court —this branch of the Aldobrandis were caught in more recent decades in some financial troubles. That's why the palace was rented out to the office for the University of California's abroad program and its Italian language school.

The smell of mold in the dark marble stairway speaks of neglect. Yet the discolored frescoes on the walls and ceiling evoke the memory of more illustrious times. The first floor opens on a spacious hall, which has been turned into an office. The very large Baroque paintings on the walls clash with the modern desks. The only secretary seated at one of the desks appears busy and flustered. She pushes papers around as if she can't find what she's looking for. Her gray hair is frizzy and uncombed. As she approaches her, Valentina realizes that she's only middle aged, but extremely worn out.

"*Buon giorno,*" Valentina greets her. "I'm Caterina Pedersoli's apartment mate. Someone called from here and left a message yesterday."

The woman stares at her, her eyes widening. She shakes her head nervously and bites her lower lip. "I don't know anything."

This is odd. Luckily, Nick will be here in ten days. Valentina has a feeling that something is really wrong.

Valentina stares into the void and then stares at the woman – frizzy hair and frazzled manners, hands twitching as she moves papers around on the desk. *This can't be happening!* First, the boy at the *pizza al taglio* who insisted he'd seen Caterina yesterday and then this receptionist denying knowledge of anything. The situation is getting stranger by the minute.

"Who left the message on our answering machine, then?" Valentina tries again.

The woman sighs, shakes her head with a nervous tic, and shrugs her shoulders. *Speaking of body language!* Valentina realizes that she's not going to get much out of her.

"Can I see the director of the center, please*?" I'd better get to the bottom of this one*, she reasons.

The frizzy lady smirks with unexpected mirth. "Professor Novak is not available right now."

Novak!? Oh, Jesus, not her again! Valentina realizes that she hasn't followed campus politics at Santa Corona ever since she'd left that campus for Santa Abelina three years ago. She completely missed Laura Novak's reincarnation as director of the exchange program in Rome from her previous life as Santa Corona's most annoying provost.

"She'll be back this afternoon at three," the receptionist adds, busying herself with Novak's schedule. "Actually, I'm not sure she'll be able to see you today. She has only fifteen minutes in-between appointments at three thirty."

"That's fine," Valentina hastens to squeeze herself into that little window of opportunity. "I'll be back this afternoon."

You won't believe what I've just found out, she writes in her mind in the text she intends to send to Nick in a few minutes. As she crosses again *Campo dei Fiori*– the market still in full swing, the fragrance of fresh produce hitting her nostrils and the incessant loud chatter of vendors and buyers surrounding her –she imagines Nick and Pippo happily snoring in their bed at this time in California.

I don't remember, she writes in her mental text, *whether I ever told you about this supercilious administrator who didn't let me give a talk on film noir when I was teaching in Santa Corona. She said she wasn't sure about the quality of my preparation since I was just a lecturer, despite the fact that I'd been teaching courses on film noir for seven years. Well, my luck or my karma (as Franca would say), she's now the director at the exchange center and she's possibly the only person who can give me some information about Caterina.*

Back in the large hall, at three thirty in the afternoon, waiting to be admitted in the presence of the mighty director, Valentina recalls the phone call she received just half an hour before.

"Don't you think you're wasting too much time on this Caterina gal?" Nick hadn't minced the words. He'd called her as soon as he'd read her text. He still had his nasal *just woke-up* voice.

"Maybe," she'd admitted. "It's the strangest thing. I haven't seen her in almost a week and yet the pizza boy says she was there yesterday and at the center they act as if they haven't tried to contact her."

"O.K. Fine! Go talk to the director and then put this thing to bed. Speaking of bed…I can't wait to share the bed with you. Pippo farts too much and snores too."

"Pippo snores? Serves you right!" she guffaws.

A door closes in the hall interrupting her train of thought. A woman walks out of the director's office headed toward the stairs.

"Professor Novak is ready to see you," the frizzy receptionist – her hair even frizzier and more messed up— announces sullenly.

The enormously large objects in the room – the late Renaissance dark furniture, the giant baroque paintings on the walls, and the extremely high ceilings decorated with gold — hover over Laura Novak. In her office in Santa Corona, as Valentina recalls it, Novak had surrounded herself with small-scale furniture– a tiny desk and chairs, a love seat – better suited to her diminutive size. The ample ambiance of the Roman office dwarfs her.

"Have we met?" Novak addresses Valentina without getting up. She looks down on her notes. "Snupia? So you're Italian. Sicilian, maybe."

"I taught film for a number of years at Santa Corona," Valentina sits down on the chair across from Novak's desk, even though the director hasn't invited her to.

"We're quite strict in our requirements." Novak admonishes her. "You would need a *laurea* in Italian from an Italian university. Gabriella and Cecilia, the two girls who teach here, that's what they

15

have. And with your Sicilian accent…"

"There must be a misunderstanding here." Valentina stops the flood of senseless words, trying not to get too annoyed. *What's this thing about calling the two teachers girls?* "I do have a degree from an Italian university, but I'm not interested in teaching here. I'm here to inquire about doctor Caterina Pedersoli, who also teaches here, even though she doesn't have a degree from an Italian university."

Novak is taken aback. She stares at Valentina, squinting her beady eyes behind her thick lenses.

"That's a special case. Pedersoli is already teaching at one of our campuses, Santa Abelina, if I'm not wrong."

"You're not wrong," Valentina smiles, quite amused by Novak's confusion. "I'm not here to apply for a job. Caterina Pedersoli is my apartment mate and she seems to have disappeared."

"And how can we help you?" Novak looks annoyed. "We don't monitor our teachers' private lives."

"And thank god for that! But I found a phone call from the center on my answering machine. It looks like Caterina didn't show up twice this week to teach her classes."

"And why are you worried about that?"

"I'm not worried about professor Pedersoli missing classes, I'm concerned about her disappearance. I was with the police this morning."

Novak springs up from her chair. "The police? Are you out of your mind?"

Valentina stays seated. "I was told that if a person disappears for a week, it is time to let the police know."

"They won't do anything about it." She sits down, almost finding comfort in the idea of police negligence. "In this country…they have their hands full with the mafia, as you certainly know, being Sicilian and all."

Valentina gets up, walks swiftly toward the door, and as she reaches for the doorknob, she turns around facing Novak. "I don't know whether they'll do anything about it or not. And maybe, Caterina will show up after all. But if she doesn't and the police decide to do something about it, they may show up here."

As she walks down the semi-dark stairway, Valentina can't repress an uncomfortable feeling. Novak's defensive behavior is suspicious to say the least. *Nick is right, I should let it go.* She walks out in the warm afternoon sun as the sound of car horns greets her back into Rome's traffic.

"Flight attendants prepare for landing!"

Finally! Fusco stretches his cramped legs, yawns, looks out the plane window, and sees a giant urban sprawl on one side and the green waters of the Mediterranean on the other. He hasn't been in Rome for five years. The only other time he'd visited here was with his late wife, Melissa. She already had cancer at the time, and it had been her wish to see Rome before she started chemotherapy. The memory of that vacation is clouded with sadness for Fusco, but it also has a touch of sweetness because they enjoyed their stay and it was their last trip together.

The plane circles over the ocean and the coastal towns of Ostia and Fiumicino, and starts the final descent to the *Leonardo da Vinci*, International Airport. *In less than half an hour I will see Valentina again.* The thought chases away any sadness. A five-week separation is more than he can handle. They've planned a wonderful vacation.

You're right. She'd written in her last email. *I've let my imagination get the best of me. Caterina isn't worth worrying about. People like her always manage to come out ahead. Whatever the director of the exchange center needs to hide is none of my business. I can't wait to hug you. And I promise – unlike Pippo— I won't fart or snore in bed.*

Pippo. Fusco had taken him to Franca's house yesterday. The dog had seemed happy to see Franca. He'd wiggled his tail vigorously and landed a big wet smooch on Franca's mouth.

"I'll take him for walks on the beach every morning," Franca had scratched Pippo behind the ears. "And you're going to get along with my kitty, young boy! Agreed?" And Franca had shaken Pippo's paw. Pippo had looked at her with a puzzled expression.

Then when the dog had noticed that Fusco was walking toward the door, getting ready to leave, he'd become agitated—moaning and wiggling his body. Franca had distracted him with a freshly baked cookie. Well, Franca's lovely house and spacious backyard is certainly better than the dog hostel. "Don't forget your humble origin—the pound," Fusco had admonished Pippo.

I can't wait to kiss my Sweetie. Fusco is now in line at the passport checkpoint at Rome's airport. *They make it quite easy to get into this country.* He notices the perfunctory way in which the officer looks at the passports. *And if you're a European, you basically walk in and out at your leisure.* A crowd of African immigrants is in line in front of him. They talk to each other in their languages – totally unintelligible to Fusco. They wear colorful costumes and carry heavy bags full of merchandise they must plan to sell in some market. They don't seem concerned about passing the checkpoint. *They must live here,* Fusco ponders. After the Africans move beyond the passport officer, the line speeds up with new impetus. *Have they lost my luggage?* Fusco always fears that. However, that too goes smoothly. *Good omen*, he thinks as he lifts his suitcase and rolls it toward Customs.

"Anything to declare?" An officer picks up his custom declaration without waiting for an answer. He yawns and motions to Fusco to head toward the exit.

An ocean of faces welcomes him outside. For a moment, he is taken aback. How am I going to find Valentina here? But a second later, he sees her hand waving for him– the stone of the engagement ring he'd given her shining in the midday light. And then he sees her face – her radiant smile, beautiful dark eyes, and luxuriant curly hair. *She's wearing the dress I like* – a flowery print with a flowing skirt.

They kiss—their lips touching, their tongues searching – and hug with the insatiable passion built up in more than a month's separation. They kiss in the large hall, in front of everybody watching them. And they are still hugging and kissing on the escalator. Their bodies glued to each other.

"Where are we going now?" Fusco asks when they reach the upper level.

"To the train that takes us to town," Valentina explains. "We'll get off at the pyramid. From there, we can either take a cab or a bus. It won't be far."

They hold hands–Valentina rolling his suitcase and Fusco carrying his backpack on his shoulders. They are now striding along inside the covered overpass. The roar from underneath makes him turn toward the floor-to-ceiling windows and look at the heavy traffic below in front of the arrivals –cabs, buses, cars, and passengers loaded with luggage crossing the street headed toward the parking buildings. Then, he looks at the sunny and hazy Roman sky. The air conditioning hides the impact of the summer heat – high temperatures at midday.

"Oh!" Valentina's sudden exclamation takes him by surprise.

"What?" Fusco sees her gesture toward a car in the street below.

"That woman…Caterina!"

Jeez! Not her again! The irritation almost makes him speed up inside the covered hall, leaving Valentina a few steps behind. However, when he turns around, Valentina's frozen expression halts him. "What?" he repeats and faces the window and the street below.

A blonde, extremely thin woman is getting into the back seat of a car. A man is right behind her, glued to her. He seems to push her inside. The woman appears to resist. When she eventually gives in to his pressure and bends her head to squeeze her body inside the car, Fusco notices a dark object in the man's hand. As he squints to get a better look, he hears Valentina whisper in his ear.

"A gun! Did you see the gun?"

CHAPTER TWO

ONE FILTHY ROOM

By the time the cab stops in front of Valentina's apartment building, it's almost five in the evening. The color of the sky is starting to change to a pinkish hue and a soft breeze is lifting the heaviness of the heat and pollution.

"Here we are," Valentina opens the cab door and hands the money to the driver after the man has taken Fusco's bags out of the trunk.

As he steps out, the first thing Fusco notices is the tremendous size of the main door and then the clamor of the traffic. The building, too, seems ominous – a gray mass of stone, several stories high. Exhaustion hits him suddenly, now that the journey is over and the much-coveted moment of intimacy with Valentina is close, very close, just beyond the tall main door. *Have I suddenly aged?* The terrifying thought strikes him as Valentina swiftly unlocks the door, pushes it open and then turns to face him.

"You must be exhausted," she looks at him with tenderness in her lovely dark eyes. "Twenty-four hours without sleep, a long flight. You didn't need another case."

Damn right! He doesn't need another case in his summer vacation to Rome. He didn't need to see what he saw four hours ago at the airport – Caterina pushed inside a car with a gun pointed at her back.

"A nice shower, something good to eat, you'll feel better," she promises, as they cross the threshold.

Fusco follows her inside a dark hallway as the door slams with a thud behind him. The glimmering light of a courtyard and the sound of water gushing from a fountain take him by surprise. Suddenly the thought of the promised shower and good food energizes him. *I might still make it.*

In the elevator they kiss. He holds her soft body against his as the ancient elevator, clanging and swaying, makes its way to the fourth floor.

Everything is well again. *Life is good.* Caterina is just another crazy broad who has gotten herself entangled in some shady business. Nothing he can do about it.

They shower together – the water is just a trickle. *Why can't Europeans figure out the fine art of American showers?* Even so, all is well. And all is actually wonderful as they stretch still wet on the bed and find each other's bodies, remembering and reacquainting with each other—a month's separation is such a long time.

Later, in front of the food – *pasta alla amatriciana* is nourishment from the gods—his inner cop reemerges.

"We need to search her room," he says with a last glimmer of energy, before sleep defeats him.

At the airport, they'd rushed to the police station. Nothing could be done to stop the car that had taken Caterina away. There was no way to know in which direction the car was going – where they were taking Caterina and why. The only thing he knew was that it was at gunpoint. Why at the airport? What was she doing at the airport? Was she trying to run away and they'd found her there? And who were *they*? What did they want from this academic woman spending a semi-academic vacation in Rome?

The Italian cop – the *commissario* of the police station at the airport – was rather young. Tall and lean, his dark hair slightly thinning in front, he'd addressed Fusco in a hesitant English, which wasn't much better than Fusco's Italian. He'd actually shown some camaraderie toward Fusco when he'd heard that he was a cop, too, and called him *collega* (the Italian for colleague). He was also bewildered. The only thing he could think of was a drug connection.

"Have you noticed anything strange?" the *commissario* had asked Valentina. "Was she on drugs?"

"She might have been. She impressed me as exceptionally hyper… some strange personality traits. We didn't spend much time together. We both were out a lot."

"Have you searched her room?"

"No! Of course not! I just noticed that her suitcase and clothes were still there."

The room – they have to search her room.

"The cops will be here tomorrow morning, I'm sure. But I need to know." As he mumbles that, his eyes are closing and he knows that sleep is defeating him. "I'll take a nap and then I'll search the room."

As he stretches out on the bed and pulls the sheets over his body, he hears Valentina open the door of the room across the hallway. *She shouldn't be doing that. She's such a sleuth.* Sleep hits him like a tall gray wall collapsing over him.

Suddenly he wakes up feeling totally rested. He opens his eyes and in the semi-darkness of the room, he discovers Valentina's body next to him in the bed. She's asleep on her side, facing him, one hand cupping her face and the other hugging her pillow. He hears her breathing quietly and all he can think of is how happy he is to have her back.

The traffic has subsided. Buses and trams have stopped for the night. *It must be four*, he guesses as he crosses the room on his way to the bathroom. He turns around before the threshold and notices a digital clock on Valentina's night table. *One o'clock! Damn!* The realization surprises him. What now? What is he going to do? He can't wake up Valentina, just because he wants her company. *The room!* He suddenly remembers—Caterina's room and the Italian cops who are coming tomorrow morning, first thing, and yesterday's messiness.

He opens the door cautiously, wearing kitchen gloves on his hands. He closes the door slowly behind and then turns on the light. The flash startles him, hurting his tired eyes. A second later, the disquieting turmoil inside the room assaults his senses. An animal scent overpowers him. Dirty lingerie is strewn on the floor. The air is stuffy, hot from the accumulated heat for days and days. *Those wooden shutters must have stayed closed for over two weeks.* Open books, papers, jewelry lay around all over in extreme untidiness. The drawers of a walnut bureau are pulled out revealing more papers, lingerie and disorder. *It looks like someone went through this room and searched it.* A disturbing thought flashes through his mind. Valentina must have searched the room, while he was asleep. *No, she knows better than that!* He looks around wondering where to start.

"You're up!"

He hears Valentina's voice even before he realizes that she's opened the door. "You can't sleep. The first few nights jet lag is pretty brutal."

"Did you go through this?" And he notices that she's covered her hands with a scarf.

"What do you mean?" She seems surprised. "I was in here last night, but I didn't touch anything."

"Someone must have searched this room while you were gone."

"Really?" Her eyes and mouth open in terror. "I just assumed that she's very untidy."

"No," he shakes his head. "Even a very disorderly person doesn't have open books and papers and lingerie strewn all over the floor."

"What about the dirty lingerie?"

He knew she'd notice. "They might have emptied her hamper, looking for something."

"You know, I might have found a lead."

There she goes again, my lovely sleuth! Fusco makes a funny face. "Where did you find it in all this mess? And you said you hadn't touched anything!" He chuckles, amused, but he notices that she's serious. "So what's this lead?"

"Let's go to the kitchen." She opens the door, the scarf protecting her hand. "I can't breathe in this room. And the smell makes me want to puke."

As they sit at the kitchen table, Fusco feels hungry. *Too early for breakfast, not even two o'clock.*

"Yesterday morning, before I started for the airport, I was looking

25

around for my day-planner," Valentina explains. "I looked for it near the phone on the table in the hallway. I opened it and only after a few minutes I realized that it wasn't my day-planner, but Caterina's."

"And...did you read it?"

"Sort of...The name of a place recurs a few times throughout her last notes, two weeks ago – Calcata."

"Calcutta? India?" *What is she talking about?*

"No, no." Now, it's her turn to laugh. "It's a small town north of Rome – an artists' community."

"Let's go there." She may be right, he reasons. This might be a lead. "The people who kidnapped her might come from... Calcata. I mean she might have met them there and they might have taken her back there."

Valentina yawns. "You don't mean let's go now, do you?"

"Yes! Why not? We can beat the traffic." He feels awake and hungry. A little breakfast, a cup of coffee—and he's ready to go.

"No way!" Valentina yawns again and shakes her head. "You're in jet lag. I'm not."

She gets up and heads for the bedroom. "Why don't you try to sleep some more?"

Sleep some more? *That's the problem.* Fusco follows her, resigned to waiting a few more hours.

Several hours later, when Calcata finally appears on a hilltop, it looks like the promised land after a long journey—the noon sun illuminating a Medieval Camelot, placed on a steep and high rock foundation. Totally unexpected, the sudden appearance changes the mood of the day. After several woodsy hills, canyons and clay quarries, quite a few miles off the main northern road, the town seems to call Fusco. Maybe this hilltop community holds the secret of Caterina's messy Italian vacation.

"Do you think that they might keep Caterina captive in Calcata?" Valentina had asked him as she was cuddled up in his arms at about two thirty at night. Another yawn and she'd fallen asleep without waiting for his answer.

There was no answer. *How do I know? Maybe, maybe not.* Still, it was well worth a visit. He'd gotten up again to check Caterina's day-planner. In one of the last entries, he'd also noticed she'd scribbled *Mickey Mouse* and then *RV,* next to Calcata. Then the word *quarry* recurred twice. What the hell did these words mean? Maybe RV stood for a recreational vehicle, which she might have needed to go visit the quarry. However, Mickey Mouse didn't seem to have any relation to anything. Was it someone's nickname?

He'd gone back to bed, and quite suddenly and unexpectedly, he'd fallen asleep. The insistent sound of the doorbell combined with the smell of strong espresso coffee and the sun shining through the cracks of the wooden shutters had woken him up just as suddenly and unexpectedly. He'd jumped.

"What's going on?"

It had taken him a few moments to realize that he was in Rome. Valentina had just opened the door of the apartment and was talking with some men. They were speaking Italian and at such a distance he couldn't make out the conversation. *Who were they?* He'd run to the entrance hallway.

The two men looked respectable. One was young, short brown hair, with an innocent and concerned expression. The other one, who looked in charge, was middle aged, bald, short and skeptical.

"Oh, this is my fiancé, captain Fusco from the Californian police," Valentina had introduced him, and had seemed to be slightly embarrassed by Fusco's attire or rather lack of one. In the hurry and confusion of the moment, he had run to the door wearing only his underpants. "He arrived yesterday from the States and was with me when we saw Caterina Pedersoli being abducted at gunpoint at the airport."

They shook hands with Fusco. Valentina had already been to the police station and had talked to the older man, *ispettore* Del Pozzo, about Caterina's disappearance. He didn't seem pleased about the recent development in the case. To Fusco the policeman's expression seemed to say: *What did I do to deserve this crazy American chick?*

The policemen went into Caterina's room. Fusco and Valentina left looking for a car rental.

"Do the words, *Mickey Mouse, RV* and *quarry* say anything to you?" Fusco had asked Valentina as they were driving north on the Cassia way.

"No. Why?" She'd given him an inquiring look. "Where did you read them?"

"In Caterina's day-planner, next to Calcata. I thought you might have heard her mention something."

"I'm sorry to say, but after the first week, I disconnected from her."

"What about the first week? Did you hear her mention Calcata?"

Valentina hesitated, her attention temporarily taken by the road signs. A large one, leading to an overpass, read Mazzano Romano, and a smaller one, pointing in the same direction, read Calcata.

"How big of a place is Calcata?"

"Rather small—just a few thousand people living there. At some point it must have been some kind of ghost town. Then, artists and eccentrics moved in. Now that you ask me, I recall her mentioning Calcata once. I guess she spent a weekend there."

CHAPTER THREE

A TOWN ON A HILL

As they drive up toward the town's entrance – a Medieval stone portal – they realize that cars are not allowed inside the town. Quite prominent on the way up are signs indicating that Calcata is part of the "slow movement." They park and walk in. The silence and the clean air are the first things they notice, as they cross a square bordered by houses, on one side, and by a terrace over a deep canyon, on the other side. They look down. A path leads to the bottom of the canyon. At least, that's what the signs say, and one has to trust them, because the bottom is invisible in this forest — incredibly thick, totally untouched by humans. Another sign attracts Fusco's attention. It offers a four-hour walking tour inside the forest all the way to the old *cava*.

"Cava?" he asks. "What's a cava?" He notices Valentina's triumphant expression.

"It's a quarry. Wasn't that one of the words she wrote next to Calcata?"

The walking tour is not available today and their chances of getting lost in the midst of the thickest forest they've ever seen are pretty high.

They opt for their own walking tour of the town—no other kind being offered. A wide stone stairway opens at the other end of the square and it leads to an arch and a dark alley beyond it. Before embarking in this exploration, Fusco turns to the right of the stairway and notices a restaurant placard, placed right in front of a small entrance. Jet lag is making him hungrier than usual and the frugal Italian breakfast didn't quite hit the spot.

"Do you want to have lunch already?" Valentina sounds surprised.

She seems never to be hungry. *What women won't do to stay thin!*

"Well, let's at least look at the menu." He tries to act indifferent. She's accused him of being a glutton more than once. "We may consider it in a little while."

The menu is quite attractive with lots of vegetables, pasta dishes, and no meat. Of course, *Ristorante Vegetariano*, it reads on top of the door – Vegetarian Restaurant.

"*RV*," Valentina whispers in his ear. *She got that one, too.* Fusco feels a bit humiliated by Valentina's cleverness. However, he's also relieved that they're getting somewhere.

Now, they have to go in, no matter what. They walk down a rickety wooden staircase and find themselves in a large room.

"Welcome," the cook, at work at a wooden stove, doesn't even turn around. "Sit wherever you like," he yells after them. He's totally intent at his creation, stirring a sauce, licking the spoon to taste it and then putting it back into the sauce. *Hygiene isn't a high priority in this place.* Fusco makes up his mind to go along with the experience. No choice anyway. As they walk by, he notices that the cook, his back still turned, holds a joint in his free hand. The smell of marijuana is unmistakable. That might explain his uninhibited behavior.

They sit at a table next to a window looking down into the woodsy forest canyon. They wait patiently to be helped. No waiter is in sight and only another table in an adjacent small room seems to be occupied. It's a weekday after all.

"Does the slow movement mean we have to wait forever to be helped?"

"It may." Valentina seems to go along with it better than him. "Everything is supposed to be made from scratch and we're supposed to eat slowly... and..."

Before she finishes her explanation, the cook turns around and approaches their table. He's a man in his thirties, with a long beard and hair and an earring. He looks at them with a beatific smile. He wears a white T-shirt with Mickey Mouse printed on its front.

Fusco kicks Valentina under the table, and their feet meet in the middle as she tries simultaneously to do the same. *We got there together this time. Sexy!*

"*Buon giorno!*" Mickey Mouse doesn't carry a menu. "What would you like to eat today?"

"Do you have pasta?" Valentina seems to be hungry now. Success helps digestion.

"Yeah! I just finished preparing a wonderful sauce with fresh tomatoes, black olives, capers and local mushrooms" and Mickey Mouse turns around motioning to his creation sitting on the stove.

"No!" Fusco interrupts him. *Like hell I'm going to eat sauce with spit!* "Pasta is too fattening!" That doesn't come out right.

Valentina looks at him amazed. She must not have seen the cook lick the spoon.

"When did you ever worry about that?" she whispers. "Did I gain weight?"

Oh, I'd better stop this train wreck! Fusco shakes his head and kicks her again under the table. "What else do you have?" he turns to the waiter.

"I made a potato casserole. The thing is that I burned it. I'm sure I can scrape two good portions from the top."

"That's O.K. Let's start with that."

Mickey Mouse walks back toward the stove muttering to himself: "I don't know why I always burn the potato casserole. Actually, I do know. I like to scrape the burnt potatoes from the bottom and eat them."

Of course, now Fusco has to whisper to Valentina why he doesn't want her to eat pasta today. Her only reaction is: "Well, at least the food isn't poisoned. He tasted it and didn't die."

Now, he wonders, what does this pothead hide under the meek smile and the scattered behavior? *How are we going to approach him?* Fusco and Valentina exchange a knowing glance. They don't even need to talk.

As Mickey Mouse serves them two scrumptious plates of potato casserole, Valentina smiles and asks: "Do you happen to know Caterina Pedersoli?"

The beatific smile is gone. He stares at them. He looks scared. *Interesting!*

"She recommended your restaurant to us," Fusco reassures him in his hesitant Italian, pretending not to pay attention to the cook's alarmed expression. "We don't know her well—just an acquaintance."

It works like a charm. The beatific smile is back on.

"Oh, you're American, too!" Mickey Mouse exclaims. "I remember

Caterina—blonde, skinny, tall, very lively! She came to eat here a couple of times."

As he walks back toward the stove, he mutters: "She sure likes pot!"

As the men help her go down the stairs, her legs are shaking. Then they make her stretch out on a soft surface on the floor – a mattress, maybe. And they leave. The stench of humidity is the most disturbing and revealing trait of the place. With her head entirely covered, Caterina can only guess her whereabouts. A cellar? Some kind of dungeon? *I hope there aren't any rats here. I hate rats!*

"Don't worry! You're going to be O.K.," the big man with the gun and the gruff voice had told her on the way over. "Your father will pay. He wouldn't let his little girl suffer."

Tears had coursed down her face. She'd better keep her mouth shut and not tell them the truth. Her so-called father might not pay for her ransom. She was not his little girl, not any more.

She now hears some steps approaching, but they are different steps, not the big man's--lighter ones.

"I'm going to take this hood off now," a man's voice says. He sounds muffled.

She's on a mattress. At first, she can't see her surroundings. Her eyes are unaccustomed to the light, even the semi-darkness of the cellar. Then she sees the man, but his face is covered by a ski mask. He's not one of the two men who kidnapped her. Of course not—that would be too risky for them. He's slimmer and shorter than her captors. His accent is Roman. She notices the slightly nasal sound of his voice. The big man sounded Southern.

34

As soon as her eyes are able to focus again, she moves her head around. It's some kind of basement, with small high windows, which allow a faint sunlight to seep through. *It must be early morning.* This means that many hours have gone by after the kidnapping. She's lost her sense of time. Her mind is fuzzy as if she just woke up after a night doing drugs. The realization brings with it a memory. After they'd pushed her into the car, shortly after they'd left the airport, she'd felt a prick on her arm. They must have given her a dose of some heavy sedative.

Her gaze moves down to her feet. They're chained. *That's why they are so heavy.* She doesn't feel like moving anyway. That's unusual for her. Normally, she can never stay still. Even when she teaches her classes, she's constantly moving, from the blackboard to her desk, to the lectern, back to the blackboard. The memory of the Caterina who taught, the Caterina who used to be, brings tears to her eyes. Will there ever be that Caterina again? *Will I survive this one?*

"Here is your food," the man with the ski mask pushes a bowl with some milk and bread in it toward her.

If the bread is unsalted, I will know whether we're North of Rome. Yet, she doesn't feel like eating. She extends her hand and reaches for a small piece of bread. It's warm. They must have bought it in a bakery in the area, just out of the oven. She tastes it. *Unsalted!* Now she knows: north of Rome—but where? It could be Northern Lazio, or it could be Tuscany. Who knows?

It is also hard to guess how long it took to get there after they'd left the airport. She doesn't even know when they got here. It might have been yesterday afternoon, or nighttime. Her mind was so confused, so dopey. She almost wishes that it stayed that way. *To sleep...perchance to dream…* Instead her mind is going back to its usual pattern, jumping around, speeding away as a wild horse on a racetrack. No medication and no drugs to keep it from crashing—nothing to prevent it from remembering.

She eats some more bread and its fragrance brings back a long lost memory. The bread she used to eat at the farmhouse was unsalted—the bread from her childhood.

Once upon a time—that's how fairy tales start. *My grandmother used to tell me fairy tales when I was a child.* A sunny courtyard, the sounds of animals wandering freely, the stone farmhouse—with her eyes closed, it all comes back.

"Catherine," her grandmother called her. This was long before she changed her name to Caterina, long before she claimed her mother's last name, Pedersoli. "Catherine! *Vieni qui!* Come here! I want to tell you a story."

She was a blonde and dark-eyed child, with thin long legs. She resembled her Belgian father a bit. It was a sunny afternoon. Her Italian grandmother, *nonna* Tina, had finished washing the lunch dishes and was ready to sit down under the shady porch and tell her a story. The smell of the wisteria vines was so pungent. It was one of the first smells she'd ever noticed. Every time she smelled it, no matter where, she was reminded of the farmhouse, of the Italian vacation, before they moved to the States, before everything changed.

"Once upon a time," nonna Tina would start. Her hands used to smell like soap, as she brushed Caterina's hair away from her forehead.

I wish time had stayed still. She revisits that time before her life had changed. She feels now that she has to hold on to her memories if she wants to still know who she is.

Now, the man with the ski mask comes back. He brings her a pot. They must have thought that if she eats she may need to eliminate it. Then he leaves again.

Where am I? Calcata? That's where she got herself in trouble.

They get to the lake before sunset. A soft breeze ripples the surface of the water. An idyllic peace pervades the small town. Fusco and Valentina park their car in the main square, with the intention of taking a walk before dinner and letting the afternoon in Calcata sink into their minds.

"Franca told me about Trevignano," Valentina tells him as they walk, holding hands, along the lake promenade, "but I've never been here."

"It's amazing how different this is from Calcata, and yet so close— only a few miles away."

Fusco can't let go of the images of Calcata. That afternoon they spent a few hours walking around in the hilltop community, combing the place in search of possible clues —one cobblestone alley after another, all leading to terraces over the precipice. The problem with Calcata was that inside a small space it contained hundreds of semi-deserted dwellings—weekend houses, artists' studios, closed antique stores, and zillions of deep dank cellars. *Could any of those locked-up houses be a hiding place for Caterina's captors?* And then there was that dark, huge, deep forest canyon, visible from each and every terraced viewpoint of the town. *How could anyone find her down there?*

"The difference is that Trevignano is a place where human beings actually live," Valentina points out, almost reading his thoughts. "Some people work in Rome and commute and others have always lived here."

"What about the hills and the countryside surrounding this town?" Fusco motions to the woodsy landscape behind the lake. "Wouldn't that be a perfect hide-away for kidnappers?"

Valentina nods. She seems lost in thoughts. "What do you make of Mickey Mouse? Was he as stoned as he looked?"

"He was stoned all right. But he knew more than he wanted us to believe. He was covering up. The food was good, though, even though he spits on it."

The sun starts to disappear into the lake, painting the water a purple hue. A school of geese waddles to the shore, settling down on the pebble beach for the night.

A large castle is still visible on a distant shore right across the lake.

"That's the Orsini-Odescalchi castle, where Tom Cruise got married," Valentina points towards it.

"No shit! Are you hinting?" Fusco teases her. "You would like to have a sumptuous wedding in a Renaissance castle, wouldn't you?"

"What's this?" She laughs. "Another marriage proposal?"

"No way!" Fusco lifts her left hand and points to her ring. "I proposed once to you and I'm still waiting for an answer, remember?"

Valentina smiles, appearing slightly uncomfortable. "Just to change the subject, are you ready for dinner?"

"I thought you'd never ask."

The restaurant, too, is just as Franca had described it—a country house facing the lake, just outside town, with vines covering the area with the dining tables and a squad of cats lounging around, hoping for accidentally dropped food.

"My mother made fresh pasta today," the young owner announces. *Fresh pasta?* Who could refuse? The restaurant is clearly family-owned. The pasta-making mother has already appeared and so have the father and the two sons—all honest looking country people. "We also have *coregone*, the fish from our lake."

"We'll take it all," Fusco is hungrier by the minute.

"Grilled red peppers on the side?"

"Those, too!"

Valentina sighs making a comic face. "So now that we've ordered this gargantuan meal, what do you think we should do tonight? Stay in the area? Go back home to Rome?"

"I vote for staying here," and the disturbing memory of Caterina's room crosses Fusco's mind.

"Do you still think someone searched the room?" Valentina asks with hesitation. She holds her breath for a few seconds. He can tell she's quite scared by the thought of the intrusion.

"Yeah," he nods and then feels that he needs to reassure her. "They're not going to come back though—not with the police seals and all that. It's just that it wouldn't be pleasant for us to stay there with policemen coming and going."

"True," Valentina looks at the water. It's dark now, but the lights from the other lake communities glitter at a distance. "This is so great!"

"Do you know of a nice place where we could spend the night?" Fusco asks the waiter who brings their pasta.

"Yes, just half a kilometer down this way, there is a beautiful old villa—a small *pensione*. It's called *La Villa Incantata*. I'm sure they have room."

The Enchanted Villa? It couldn't be better—Valentina, Italy, a lake and an enchanted villa. *Tomorrow morning, we will wake up and all thoughts of Caterina will be gone.*

CHAPTER FOUR

THE ODD COUPLE

One of the two men is really big and has a hoarse voice and a Southern accent. Valentina recognizes the Calabrian way of talking and puts out her antenna. She knows immediately that this person is out of place. It's not only his size, but the shape of his large head and his expressionless face that give him away as the odd man around. The other one—shorter, slimmer and with a local accent from somewhere in the Lazio region—fits in with the people in Trevignano's main square. His dark eyes are lively and he gestures lightly as he talks. Had it not been for the proximity to the other bigger man, the smaller one would have gone unnoticed.

From the bench where she's seated, close to the newspaper stand, Valentina can only catch a few words. The two men stand next to the railing, close to the lake. And they talk, but curiously enough, they don't look at each other.

"A dangerous game..." the smaller man says. "...more money...hardly worth it..."

"Tough luck..." the big man responds. "...knew before..."

How am I going to get closer without alerting them? Valentina spreads out the paper, and very slowly crosses the cobblestone lake promenade, pretending to be totally absorbed by the book review page. She reaches the railing and leans against it, just a few feet away from the strange pair.

"A billionaire...we'll make him pay through the nose," the big man says. "A question of waiting a few weeks..."

"In the meanwhile, we're the ones running all the risks," the smaller man whines and gestures still not facing the man.

What an odd conversation! Valentina squints and pulls the paper closer to her face, pretending total absorption. These are not ordinary business men or cattle farmers discussing a deal. She wishes Nick were here with her, instead of still in bed, snoring happily away in *The Enchanted Villa.*

She woke up shortly after seven and Nick was up, on the balcony, contemplating the beauty of the Bracciano lake.

"I woke up at three," he kissed her and then yawned. "I'm starting to feel sleepy now. Damn it! Jet lag is a bitch."

"There is no sense in fighting it." She'd gone through a similar process when she'd come over from the States. "Why don't you just sleep a couple of hours."

"Wake me up at nine," he stretched out on the bed. "Please, don't let me sleep all day," he mumbled and fell asleep before she could answer.

He must be exhausted, she thought and went down to have breakfast in the large, old-fashioned dining room. Caffe-latte, warm bread, fresh butter and thick homemade jam—she had not had a breakfast like that since childhood when her family used to go on vacation in a *pensione* at the seaside.

Then she walked down to the main square to buy a paper, with the intention of returning to the villa and sitting under an oak tree and reading it. She was sidetracked by the calm beauty of the lake. The water was now blue and completely smooth. A small crowd of sunbathers and swimmers was already on the beach facing the villa. The geese were back in the water. *Why can't we just have a nice vacation?* Once she'd reached the newspaper stand, she'd sat down on a bench, with the intention of taking in the idyllic peace. That's when her eye had caught the odd couple.

"The Americans are working on the Belgian," the big man says now in his monotonous tone. "The thing will be solved fast."

The Belgian? Who's this Belgian now? They must be talking about something else—nothing to do with Caterina. She decides she'd better head back to the villa. However, something like a sixth sense keeps her stuck against the railing with the newspaper close to her nose. She's even holding her breath to make herself inconspicuous.

"Easy for you to say!" the smaller man's voice is now getting animated. He's the emotional of the two. "The owners may come back for summer. We'll need to move her. And that's your part of the job."

"No way. You should have planned this better." Now the big man sounds annoyed. "I did my part."

"Your part! It only took you a few hours. We're stuck here with that bitch!" The small man now turns toward the big one, with his back to Valentina. "No end of requests! She thinks we're her servants or something."

Could that be Caterina? It sounds just like her to treat her kidnappers like servants. Valentina smiles at the thought of her former apartment mate giving a hard time to people besides herself. Yet, given Caterina's dire circumstances, she can't help but admire her gumption—if she's the woman they're talking about.

"You're a bunch of pussies!" Now the big man faces the small one and grimaces in disgust.

"I would like to see you!" The small man's shoulders twitch. "Why don't you go see for yourself? I'm not going to beat her up. That wasn't part of the deal."

"The fourth kilometer you said." The big guy breathes out loudly, still staring down the other one.

"Yeah, and then a country road to the left." The small guy nods. "You know where that is."

"The Russian won't be pleased." The big guy walks away.

Valentina doesn't dare move, not until they've both left. Only then, does she lower her paper, just in time to see a car leave the parking lot in the main square. From where she stands it looks like the big man is driving away in a small car, which barely contains him. *What happened to the other one?* It looks like he disappeared. She scans the entire lake front area and detects him in front of the supermarket. Without even thinking she finds herself crossing the road and making her way inside the store.

"Where have you been?" Fusco's a little mad at Valentina. He's still wet, just out of the shower, and she just walked in, wearing her jeans. She must have gone out. "Women get kidnapped here!" he shouts.

She bursts out laughing—no empathy for his worry.

"Men, too, can get kidnapped." She never misses a chance to take a feminist stand, he notices. "In any case, Italy is as safe as any other place, if you don't lead a dangerous life."

She's also intolerant of clichés and prejudice against her country. He knows that and respects it. After all, he's from Italian origin, too, and in Italy he feels both out of place and totally at home—hard to explain. It's just that he woke up and she was nowhere in sight and he didn't know where to look for her.

"You left your cell phone here and the police called from Rome— they woke me up," he explains. "They want us to relocate. We'd better go get our stuff this afternoon."

"Relocate? Why?"

"It makes total sense to me. They're going to seal the whole apartment, not only Caterina's room."

"Oh, all right. I hope the agency can find me another place to stay."

She looks perplexed now, standing and watching him, as he gets dressed.

"So where have you been, Sweetie?" He now asks with a cheerful tone of voice. *God forbid, who wants to start a fight!*

"I need to talk to you." She sits down on their bed.

I knew it. She must have found out something. *She's such a sleuth!*

She tells him about the two men at the lake shore—the odd couple —and their conversation. *Who the hell is this Belgian? And what about the Russian? Are we talking Russian Mafia, now?* Then she tells him how she followed the small man into the supermarket, hiding behind shelves, and pretending to be interested in the large display of local cheese.

"You won't believe what a display of cheese!" she croons. "The, he went to the bakery shop inside the supermarket—breads, cookies, pastries, you name it! And he bought a huge amount of freshly baked pizza. At that point, I was sure he was buying food for Caterina."

"How so?"

"Nobody can put away as much pizza as Caterina does! And she doesn't even gain weight—the bitch!"

Laurent Labauche hasn't seen her for twelve years—when she'd turned eighteen and left for college. He had his financial secretary deposit funds for college and graduate school in her account and for two more years after she'd finished her Ph.D., so that she would have enough to start her career as an academic. Catherine—or Caterina, as he's told she now calls herself—is a stranger to him—the offspring of an unhappy marriage, which ended with death twenty years ago. She took her mother's name, Pedersoli, and disappeared from his life. Just as well. Their relationship as father and daughter was even more doomed than the one he'd had with her Italian mother—a great Etruscan beauty he'd married more than thirty years ago and had hoped to keep as an art object. The woman had turned into a great disappointment.

Twelve years is a long time, especially if you have no contact. And you hope to have no contact for the rest of your life. With his other children from a previous marriage, he has kept a civilized and aloof rapport. With Caterina that hasn't been possible. He remembers her as a whimsical, capricious child and an argumentative, rebellious teenager.

Twelve years. It's a long time. An email message two weeks ago and one phone call this morning erased it all. The email from a yahoo account sounded like a joke.

Laurent Labauche, we kidnapped your daughter. Send us $10 million and we will release her.

He'd just ignored it. He knew Catherine was a drug user. That was one reason why he'd cut her out. She must have got herself entangled with some low life characters, he'd reasoned.

"Laurent Labauche," a muffled voice had said on the phone. "We have your daughter, Caterina Pedersoli. If you want to see her alive, you need to pay fifty million dollars. In our next communication, we will tell you where to leave the money. If you alert the police, we'll kill her."

Fifty million dollars to see a daughter he'd never planned to see again in the first place—what a joke! It must not be a coincidence that fifty million dollars is the exact sum that thirty pieces of his Etruscan collection cost him. Jacqueline Spear, his curator and latest life partner, assured him that it was a good deal—and that her source, an Italian tomb raider, was reliable. And now, with all this mess at the collection—Jacqueline resigning, the Italian Art Ministry uncovering an illicit deal between art looters and his collection among others—it can't be a coincidence. The art looters and the kidnappers might be connected. No way, he can tell the police about that. He also suspects they might have tapped his phone.

And what is he supposed to make of the email two weeks ago? Maybe it was not a joke after all. Why the steep increase in the ransom price? Did she change hands?

A few days before, the police had alerted him. The Italian police suspected a kidnapping, but had no idea who it could be. Then a lead had failed to materialize. A day later, the kidnappers' phone call.

One thing is for sure, Catherine—or Caterina — has chosen the worst way to break twelve years of silence. As usual, and just like her mother, she's a tremendous pain in the ass!

CHAPTER FIVE

AN ADVENTURE IN THE FOREST

"You do what we tell you!" the big man screams. Caterina recognizes him by his thick lips, even though he wears a ski mask like the rest of them. He's the one who kidnapped her at the airport. "*Capito?*"

He must be the boss, the mind behind this whole operation. She's been giving them a hard time. The small man with the local accent must have complained. She refused to eat. She spit on his face. *Never show weakness*, she tells herself. She stares the big man in his dark eyes, the only visible part of his face, other than his lips.

Never show weakness. It's second nature to her. Never show weakness or else they'll find you out. When did she learn that? It must have been a long time ago, because she doesn't remember ever reacting in any other way. She doesn't remember ever having been vulnerable. Maybe, at the time of the farmhouse in Tuscany, she might have been different—a child, an innocent child. That must have been the last time. After that, it has always been do it to them before they do it to you.

The big man now grabs her by her shoulders and shakes her with his hard hands. He's too strong for her to fight back—not with her hands and feet tied down. She keeps on staring him in his eyes—a spiteful stare. Then he spits on her face, and lets her drop on her mattress. And it all comes back.

He beat her every week, maybe even every day. Caterina can't remember how often. She only knows that her mother's face had become permanently discolored, her eyes always lowered in unbearable humiliation. The abuse had started when they'd moved to the States. Her mother didn't speak any English and was too beaten down to react, to look for help. At some point, she must have convinced herself that for some unfathomable reason she deserved it all. He beat her until there was nothing left of the beautiful lively girl he had met during a summer vacation in Italy, the girl he had married and brought with him to Belgium and then to the States. He beat her until she was diagnosed with cancer and she let herself die. That's when Caterina decided to take her mother's last name.

I hate you Father, I hate you so much! As she cleans her face with her shirt sleeve, curled up on the mattress, Caterina hears the big man's voice in the next room.

"That will do! Let's move her as soon as possible."

I hate you, Father, and I hate all men like you. Those unlike you, I despise.

"What about women?" a therapist had asked her--the only therapist she had seen.

Women. She couldn't stand women. She spotted the vulnerability right away. It disgusted her. If they were strong and assertive, that triggered her too. Her anger, disguised as spite and competitiveness, knew no limits.

Why did her mother ever allow him to destroy her like that? Why did she leave her behind in the hands of that cruel, sick man? Who would have ever thought that the son of a wealthy banker, a shrewd investor himself, a rich, good looking, well-groomed man was a brutal wife beater? He hid everything behind a slick appearance. That much she'd learned from him. To hide it all. Or else she might end up like her mother.

"We need to reason about this," Fusco mumbles, opening his eyes and yawning. A change in the car speed at the Cassia intersection with the road to Trevignano wakes him up.

"What about, *Tesoro*?" Valentina pats his knee and chuckles. "Were you dreaming about Caterina?"

"Was I snoring?" *This jet lag is a bitch.* He must have fallen asleep as soon as they left downtown Rome, because he doesn't even remember crossing the city's outskirts. It's still light, he notices.

"Oh, just a bit. Actually, your snoring kept me company, while I was driving. Awful traffic at this hour!"

Then he remembers. The car was parked in a little square with a garden and a statue at the center—quite usual in Italy—right across from the apartment building. They had just loaded the car with Valentina's luggage—*how did she manage to accumulate so much junk in four weeks?*—-and his luggage. The agency would find them another apartment in a few days. In the meanwhile, they might as well travel. They would start with a few days at the Bracciano lake. The Enchanted Villa was quite comfortable.

As she'd started the car heading toward Viale dei Fori—the archeological section from the Roman Empire—Valentina had started telling him about a phone conversation with Franca she had had that afternoon, while he was checking his email.

"I had texted her yesterday requesting information about Caterina," Valentina had said.

"Yeah? What would Franca know about Caterina?" he'd remarked. "Last time I talked to her, she seemed quite disconnected from the department."

"True, but she can get some information through former colleagues who have worked with Caterina this past year. Even Jason Graves might know a lot. After all he was the one who insisted on hiring her."

"And let's not forget Rupert Dukakis who's got such a big crush on her." Fusco had felt the effect of Valentina's enthusiasm overpowering his skepticism.

"That's right. The only problem is that both Dukakis and Graves are on vacation, presumably in Italy, but I don't know where."

"So did you manage to get some information from Franca?"

"Well, on such short notice she was only able to have a brief conversation with Gloria, her former colleague. Remember Gloria?"

Of course, Fusco remembered Gloria—an elegant Italian woman in her fifties—Franca's colleague, who had accused Franca of stating her intention of killing the dean for academic affairs during a phone chat with no less than Valentina herself. *Who could forget her?*

"So what did Gloria have to say this time? Did she overhear some juicy phone conversation?"

Valentina had chuckled. They had just crossed the river Tevere on a bridge decorated with the most ominous looking statues of eagles—a relic from the Fascist thirties. They then headed for a neighborhood with streets bordered with tall trees. The traffic was rather heavy, but that didn't seem to overwhelm Valentina, a Sicilian quite used to traffic jams in the cities of her own island.

52

"Apparently, Caterina is the daughter of a wealthy Belgian banker. That might be the reason why they kidnapped her."

That makes sense, Fusco had thought—the ransom, of course. He'd leaned his weary head back against the headrest and closed his eyes intending to doze off for a few minutes, and drifted off into a heavy sleep.

"I wasn't dreaming about Caterina," he now explains, "but the moment I woke up I thought that things don't add up in this darn case."

"That's right, they don't. You know this is the first time you can openly discuss a case with me."

"Well, it's not my case. I'm an outsider, and I'm happy to be an outsider. We need a vacation."

Tall thin trees border the road descending toward the lake. The sunset is coloring the sky with purple hues.

"Starving?" Valentina's head turns slightly toward him. "Should we go to the same *trattoria* as last night? *La Casina Azzurra?*"

"You bet! Great food!"

"And reasonable prices, even with the dollar down the drain."

"It doesn't make sense," Fusco continues at the restaurant, after they've finished their dishes of lasagna. "Why did the pizza boy tell you that he had seen Caterina two days before, when you hadn't seen her for more than a week? And what was the director of the Italian center trying to hide...what's her name?"

"Novak, Laura Novak. Did I tell you that she used to be the provost in Santa Corona when I used to teach there?"

"Yeah, you did. What was she like? I mean other than keeping down the lecturers and things like that, which I understand are the rules in the system."

"The only thing I can remember is that she had a way of manipulating situations in her favor. She built her husband's career from nothing. He suddenly became associate professor without ever having been assistant professor, and with no major publications to his credit."

"Nice person! But really, why did she act so strange when you went to talk to her? What did she know about Caterina that she didn't want you to know?"

Valentina shrugs her shoulders and grimaces, expressing uncertainty, as the waiter takes away her plate and replaces it with a dish of grilled eggplant. A moment later, he brings Fusco his grilled lake fish. It's dark now and the lights from the other lake communities sparkle across the water.

"Are you sure you don't want some fish?" She's always eating so little, Fusco notices.

"No thanks, I'm fine." Valentina shakes her head. "I think Novak might have known of Caterina's drug habit and was covering it up. She might have known where Caterina was hiding, and why. The person who called at home, when she didn't show up was just a secretary who was concerned about the class schedule." Valentina chews on a bite of her eggplant. "Novak might have reprimanded her and told her to mind her business. The secretary looked embarrassed when I visited the office."

"And what were they looking for in Caterina's room? What..." before he can continue a kick reaches him right on the left shin. *Jeez, before this is over our legs are going to be black and blue.* He stares at Valentina, his expression asking for a clue. Why did she kick him?

Her eyes move to the left. Two men—one tall and large with a wide head and the other one small and thin—have just parked outside the garden of the Casina Azzurra and are making their ways toward a table right behind theirs.

The tail light appears and then disappears as the Fiat speeds up the hillside in the darkness of the night. It is a country road—narrow and sinewy—recently paved in a fast and sloppy way, with holes covered by thin layers of asphalt. The driver knows the road well because he speeds up without hesitation. Fusco and Valentina follow him, against their better judgment. Yet, they know what they're doing. They can't miss this opportunity. Fusco turns around for a second and is struck by the reflection of the moon on the lake waters. *Weren't we supposed to be on vacation?*

"We need to be extremely cautious," he tells Valentina, who is driving, keeping up with the kidnapper's car with great mastery. "I don't carry a weapon and chances are that he does."

She nods and she keeps on driving, up the hill at full speed. From a distance—and they have to keep some distance—it looks like the Fiat is slowing down now. Is it going to stop? Valentina slows down too, but after a minute they realize that the pavement has ended. The Fiat had to slow down because now they are on a dirt road, with a very irregular ground full of stones and no asphalt. Then, the asphalt resumes and the Fiat speeds up again leaving them behind. Once they reach the paved road, the Fiat, way ahead of them, turns to the left.

"It must be some country lane," Fusco remarks. "Slow down! Let him go ahead for a minute or two."

Once they reach the turn, they see the Fiat approach a fork and take another road to the left.

"Once you get there, take the right fork," Fusco wants to play it safe. "This way he won't realize he's being followed."

He can hear Valentina breathe heavily. She sits up, close to the steering wheel—much closer than her usual way, which is the way a short woman sits at the wheel—tense and watchful. She must be scared. *Why am I dragging her into this dangerous situation?* Even though she's the one driving, he feels responsible.

"Are you sure you want to do this?" They can still turn around and head toward the lake and end the night in their comfortable room at the Enchanted Villa.

"Yes," she doesn't hesitate. "It's a great break."

At the fork she turns right—the pavement getting more and more uneven. To their left, a very large open meadow stretches uphill. Fusco turns around and spots the tail light of the Fiat as it proceeds on an uphill path bordering the meadow. They continue slowly, at the boundary of another property only to find themselves a few minutes later in the midst of a thick forest. *Weren't we supposed to be on vacation?*

"You need to find her another place," the big man with the Calabrian accent had said while he chomped down his pasta at the "Casina Azzurra." Valentina was sitting right across from him. She'd kept her eyes on the man while she was trying to be inconspicuous.

"When are we going to contact the Belgian?" the other guy, the small nervous chap asked. "Does he even know that we took her?"

"We? Not our business...Certainly, not your business."

Too bad that Nick's Italian is too limited, Valentina thought. He's not getting it all. She noticed Fusco's eye movements. He was trying desperately to listen to the exchange right behind his back.

The waiter walked toward Valentina and Fusco. He collected their plates.

"Anything else? Some dessert? Gelato? Coffee?"

Should they have ordered something else while waiting for the kidnappers to finish their meals? Or would it have been better to leave now and wait for them hiding somewhere?

"How are our friends doing?" Fusco had asked her, catching her eye, while motioning with one hand to the waiter to hold on.

"First course," she'd whispered in English.

"Coffee for me," Fusco had turned to the waiter and then to Valentina. "Would you like some dessert?" Of course he knew she suffered from severe sweet tooth syndrome.

She'd ordered some gelato.

As they'd waited for their orders, they'd struck a nonsensical conversation in English.

"Should we follow our bliss?" she'd asked, putting a strong emphasis on the word "follow."

"You bet!" he'd answered. "It's such a rare opportunity!"

As they'd walked by the kidnappers' on their way out, Valentina had noticed that they were on their second course—a huge second course. Kidnapping must help develop an appetite.

Once inside their car Fusco and Valentina had caught up and drawn up a plan. Then they'd sat hugging and kissing, like the couple in love they were.

"Why don't we just go to our *pensione*?" Fusco had whispered in her neck.

"And forget about all this?" Valentina had felt it was a tempting option.

Right at that moment, the two men got into their car ready to leave. She'd started her car and the chase had begun. They'd followed them to the main square where the small guy had dropped off the big man at the parking lot, and had continued on the road along the lake, across town, and through the outskirts, all the way up the hills surrounding the lake.

"We can park now," Fusco says as soon as they reach the forest. "Leave the car hiding here in the woods."

We have to use extreme caution, Fusco repeats to himself, feeling horrendously guilty in dragging Valentina into this mess. We're too close to a major discovery to let it go. Sure, we could alert the police, but what if it is the wrong lead? What if the police take their time to get here? The kidnappers might move Caterina. That's their plan anyway, or is it?

They walk back to the meadow, the moonlight helping them find their way. A country lane, with an uneven ground full of rocks and holes, borders the lower part of the field. A rather high hedge covers their bodies as they walk. Valentina's gait is a bit uncertain in her summer sandals. Fusco reaches for her hand and holds it. She's quivering, he notices.

They approach a gate. Beyond it, a long graveled path ascends toward what appears like another stretch of the forest. *Is there a house, inside this forest?* Despite the apparent wilderness of the place, there must be a house, because there is a name on one of the pillars supporting the gate.

"Let's see if we can read the name on the gate," Fusco suggests, knowing that despite the full moon it won't be easy to read in the darkness.

Valentina pulls out her cell phone and turns on the flashlight. They decipher a name: Pietro Nicoletti.

They squeeze their bodies through a narrow opening between the gate pillar and a stake at the end of the fence stretching throughout the lower part of the meadow.

"We can't walk on the gravel," Fusco whispers into Valentina's ear, pulling her toward the dirt rain canal at the side of the road. Luckily, now it's dry. It must not have rained for a few weeks. "We would be too visible and too noisy. We might wake up some dog."

They climb the hill, crouching—the ground hard under their feet. Their apparent destination seems to be the border of the forest. No house in sight. No lights. No human presence.

The house appears suddenly after a single row of very tall trees and takes them by surprise. It is a wooden house—unusual in this part of Italy, where most houses are built in *tufo*, the local stone, and covered with plaster. The Fiat is parked in front of the wooden house. They look up searching for human presence, but the lights are off. Kidnappers sleep, too. Fusco feels reassured. Where do they keep Caterina?

They notice that the upper part of the house—the part designed for dwelling—is built above a basement with narrow windows at the top. There is no way for them to peek through the windows because they are placed too high. Fusco gestures to Valentina to follow him as he makes his way to the side of the house. Because of the hill, the basement windows on the side are close to the ground. They crouch on

59

the dirt. Valentina pulls out her cell phone and flashes the light inside the basement.

"There she is," she whispers in his ear, after a short moment. He notices Valentina's excitement even before he can detect a human form on the ground of the basement, a disheveled head of hair, a woman stretched on a mattress, her feet chained.

A moment later, as they exchange a glance mixed with triumph and horror, they hear a dog bark—a long frantic bark, alerting its master of a foreign presence on the property.

CHAPTER SIX

A SHOT IN THE DARK

"That stupid woman ratted on me." Laura Novak is on Skype with her husband. "The police came to the center today and asked lots of questions."

"Who is this woman anyway?" her husband, Alistair Funkelfinkel sounds mildly curious. He is in Prague where he's the director of the University of California program abroad, just as Laura directs the Rome program. They're the golden couple of the California university system—always on the move throughout Europe. They haven't been back in Santa Corona at their teaching jobs for quite a while.

"Oh, I doubt you would remember her. She used to teach film at Santa Corona and now teaches at the Santa Abelina campus. She's Italian, or rather, should I say, Sicilian. Her name is Valentina Snupia."

"The name sounds familiar somehow. Who the hell is she? I can't put together the name and the person."

"Just slightly taller than me." Laura is extremely short and very conscious of it. "Brunette. I'm not aware of her research. I was told she works on film noir."

"Was she the one who wanted to give a talk and you refused to let her do it because she was a lecturer?"

Alistair remembers people, Laura notices. He notices pretty women especially. And that annoys her because she's several years older than he is and at that critical age when a woman is no longer young and yet nor really old—neither this nor that. Snupia is pretty, even though in a very conventional way—long dark luxuriant hair, classical features, large eyes and a small but curvaceous body.

"And she went around you," he continues, unaware of how annoyed Laura is. "She gained support from the director of the college and managed to give her talk anyway. Well, then it makes sense. She's getting back at you."

"Is that it?" Laura had suspected it. "That makes sense. She's Sicilian. Vendetta—you know." Laura is very discriminating when it comes to Italians—bordering on prejudiced. Even though her degree is in Italian literature, she's not at ease dealing with Italians. Italy is not a pleasant place to live, as far as she's concerned. And yet running the abroad program in Italy is so highly regarded. It bears such a stamp of elegance and refinement. That's why she fought so much to get the job.

"Too late to stop her," she hears Alistair say.

"I should have told her something when she came to talk to me. Now, it's too late."

"Why didn't you?" He sounds reproachful.

She's hurt by his comment and by the condescending tone of his voice. *Doesn't he know how hard it was for me to keep everybody happy—everybody who matters?*

"It's because of the Graves," she tries to explain, sounding a bit defensive. "Caterina comes from the same school, Princeton, and had the same dissertation advisor. Jason Graves is the one who got her the job at Santa Abelina. With him gone at the Florence center all the time, she was the right person to place at the Santa Abelina department to teach his courses."

"Isn't she a lecturer?"

"Yes, for now."

"What did Snupia want to know from you?"

"That I don't know. She just said that Caterina had disappeared. I didn't want her to suspect that I knew anything. It's such a delicate matter, such a thin line between privacy and disclosure."

"It's a delicate matter," he agrees with her. "You were saddled with a difficult situation. It wasn't your job to tell her anything. What did you tell the police?"

"Nothing! I told them I didn't know Caterina well. What else could I say? The drugs?"

"You did the right thing," he reassures her. "You never know what the press would do with that."

"Contrada Terme, the first left and then left again," Valentina hears Fusco speak in his halting Italian to the police using her cell phone.

She hears it as if it were happening to someone else—not her, not him. They have tried to use the phone for the last fifteen minutes, but couldn't get any reception. Only now that they have almost reached Trevignano, they have been able to connect.

"A woman in chains," Fusco explains, answering a question the policeman must have asked. "We suspect she's Caterina Pedersoli." And after another pause, he resumes: "The owner's name is Pietro

Nicoletti."

Valentina keeps on driving following the country road—fields on each side, a mountain in the background, the moon shedding light on an unfamiliar landscape. The city lights appear at a distance and seem to restore normality in a situation where nothing is normal any more. Even the driving seems absurd to her, yet reassuring. *If I keep on driving we might be safe.*

When they finally reach the first houses of the town and the lake appears at a distance— only a few minutes of real time, but an eternity in her perception—something in her starts to melt. She notices that her hands are shaking. They might have been shaking all along, except that she hadn't noticed it.

"I will call back in a few minutes, as soon as we reach our hotel," Nick is just saying. "The connection isn't good on the cell phone."

He disconnects and turns to her. "How are you?" He looks concerned and almost guilty, as if he were the one who'd dreamed up that nightmare.

She tries to smile, to reassure him that she's all right. But her face doesn't seem to respond to her intention. Her smile comes out as a strange grimace. Nick places his hand on her knee and even his touch feels alien. As they hit the road along the lake, she notices her whole body for the first time in an hour. Her shoulders are clamped, her neck contracted, her pelvis and thighs hard as rocks.

As she parks her car in front of the Villa Incantata, her rigidity suddenly melts and she bursts into hysterical laughter, losing control of her bladder.

"It's ok, darling," she hears Nick say while he caresses her back. "Let it all out."

She keeps on laughing, hunched over the steering wheel, unable to speak. Peals of uncontrollable laughter shake her entire body and never seem to end.

"I'm letting it all out, Nick," she finally mumbles in-between sobs. "I peed on myself."

Now, it's his turn to laugh.

The flowery print on the chintz curtains matches that of the cover of the overstuffed chairs and the bedspread. They are old fashioned and just like the dark oak furniture of the room they speak of a by-gone era. As he looks around the room, Fusco feels a soothing sensation. Each object of their bedroom at the Villa Incantata reassures him and makes him know that they are safe inside these walls. Even the wooden shutters with the green paint peeling seem familiar, as if he had lived there a long time.

The house, they were told, belonged to a patrician family that had lived for at least two centuries here on the lake shore. The tall majestic pines surrounding the house must have been planted eons ago. Their branches touch the walls of the building, almost trying to enter the rooms through the balconies.

Unable to fall asleep, Fusco looks at Valentina, who has finally collapsed on her side of their bed. It had taken her a lot of convulsive laughing and crying, while she brushed her teeth and she showered away urine and tears, to reach a point of exhaustion.

"I never knew I had this much fear inside of me," she'd admitted.

While she was falling asleep in his arms, he'd kept repeating to her: "I'm so sorry. I should have known better."

"I would do it again," she'd whispered.

His mind wanders now and he can still hear the barking of the dog, just as they'd spotted Caterina chained on a pad. The entire adventure of the night comes back to him. He's there again in that dark forest, holding Valentina's hand and looking around for a way-out.

Should they have gone back the same way they'd come—down the gravelly path, all the way back to the gate and from there to the uneven country road which would lead them to their car parked in the forest? This would have been the most direct escape. The advantage would have been that they would not have gotten lost. Yet, it would have been the potentially most dangerous route. They would have had to cross the lane in front of the house and make themselves visible from the house.

Fusco had grabbed Valentina's hand and pulled her toward the forest in the back of the house. A gut feeling had told him that it was the safest escape, even though the most difficult one to pursue—no country lanes, no trails.

He'd heard a door open on the side of the house. A man must have been alerted by the barking dog. Luckily, Fusco had noticed, the dog didn't belong to the kidnappers' house. It was the neighbor's dog, held back by a tall iron fence. There was no way that the dog could hunt them down.

Fusco and Valentina had proceeded swiftly into a forest with low thick trees, their jeans and shirts torn by branches and thorns, their feet, hands and arms scratched. The gunshot had caught them by surprise.

"Down," he'd muttered, pushing Valentina on the dirt floor of the forest. For a moment, their anguished breathing and the thumping of their hearts were the only sounds they could hear. Then, the forest sounds resumed—leaves rustling and birds chirping. They felt soothing. He'd looked back and had not been able to see anybody following them. The man must have used that single shot to scare away possible vagrants.

When they'd finally reached their car—a longer walk through the forest than he'd expected—they'd looked at each other's torn clothes and scratched arms, hands and feet, and the full awareness of the danger they had just escaped had hit him as hard as a blow to his gut.

"Let's not go back the same way," he'd suggested. "It's safer to drive through the forest. They might see our car from the house and try to follow us."

Valentina had hesitated. "The ground is very uneven. There is no asphalt and the lane looks rather narrow."

"Even so, let's try. Would you like me to drive?"

Shaking her head she'd started the car. Driving seemed to make her feel better. She'd silently handed him her cell phone. He'd immediately tried to reach the police in Rome.

"The traffic in Rome is always congested, no matter what time," signor Albertini, the owner of the Villa Incantata warns them, as he pours hot caffe latte in their cups. He's a tall and fat man in his fifties with a wide friendly face and gentle manners. He's serving them breakfast himself, because it's a bit too late for breakfast and the waitress has just left for the morning. The bread is warm, the caffe latte hot and aromatic, and the fig preserve is delicious. "It's from our fig trees, just in the back of the house," signor Albertini explains in response to Fusco's delighted remarks.

"You're better off with the train from Anguillara," he suggests. "The station is fifteen minutes from here and the train takes less than an hour. And then you're downtown and don't have the hassle of having to park your car."

It makes total sense to Fusco. Valentina hesitates. She always prefers the car, he notices. However, she gives in to his insistence.

"Yes, I'm quite exhausted," she concedes. "After last night, I feel like I could sleep forever."

By the time they reach downtown Rome, it's almost twelve and the traffic is congested as usual. They hurry to the police station, to report last night's events, as they have been requested to do. Fusco hopes to receive some information from the policemen, but he knows that this might not be the case. Police have to keep the secrecy. That's true everywhere, he tells himself, reminding himself of how secretive he is when he's working on a case.

"*Caro collega!*" The young policeman, the *commissario* from the police station at the airport greets Fusco, shaking his and Valentina's hands. "You haven't started your vacation yet!"

What is he doing here at the downtown station? Fusco wonders, rather pleased to see him.

"Oh, my vacation, our vacation..." Fusco smiles, raising his eyebrows. "I wish they would let us go on vacation!"

The *commissario* ushers them inside an office and invites them to sit down. "Because I was the one to receive the information that you reported about Caterina Pedersoli's kidnapping, I've been officially assigned the case."

That explains his presence here. Fusco is now ready to give their piece of information.

"As I reported on the phone at about ten o'clock P.M., we might have stumbled on Caterina, chained in a basement in the countryside. I gave the policeman in charge all the directions on how to get there. My fiancée also talked to the policeman in charge during the night and gave him all the details."

The *commissario* shakes his head and sighs. *Not a good sign.* When he raises his head, he stares Fusco in the eyes.

"All I can tell you, dear colleague, is that by the time our men got there, later this morning, there was no Caterina Pedersoli, only her mattress and an empty plate. The house upstairs had been vacated as well."

Oh, shit! Fusco can't hide his disappointment and he notices that the bad news has had some impact on Valentina as well.

"As I reported, we'd heard a rather suspicious couple discuss the possibility of moving a woman, who might have been Caterina," Fusco explains. "We had no idea that would happen so soon."

"They might have noticed that you followed them. That might have made them speed up the operation. From that point of view, I wish you'd called the police before you embarked on that adventure."

"In retrospect, I wish so too," Fusco feels humiliated and furious at himself. "On the other hand, we had no way of knowing for sure that the odd men at the restaurant were involved in the kidnapping. The only way we could test that was by following them."

The *commissario* nods. "I also wish that we'd got out there sooner. Unfortunately, bureaucracy and the law didn't allow us to perform the operation in a speedy manner."

That's right! Why didn't they send a bunch of policemen right away?

"Let me ask," Fusco changes pace. "And I know you may not be able to answer me. Who is the villa's owner, the Pietro Nicoletti whose name was on the gate of the property?"

The *commissario* lowers his gaze and hesitates. When he eventually lifts his eyes, he smiles at them with unexpected complicity.

"Pietro Nicoletti is an art dealer. That's his front. In reality, he's a well-known art looter of Etruscan tombs. He's been a main furnisher for famous American museums and in particular for a private collection, owned and funded by Caterina's father."

Interesting, very interesting!

"I read about a major scandal in the American art world," Valentina interjects at this point. Fusco knows that she's always well informed about such matters.

"That's right," the *commissario* nods. "The Italian Art Ministry has been pushing for some clarity over this point for some time now. An operation led by the *carabinieri* discovered about a year ago that some major pieces of Etruscan art, which had been missing, had been looted and sold to American museums and private collections."

"Can you tell us the name of Caterina's father?" Valentina seems very curious now. She's her usual lively self again.

"You will read it in the papers anyhow," the *commissario* concedes. "Laurent Labauche, a billionaire and art collector, who specializes in Etruscan art. He's Belgian but lives in New York. His collection is recent, but very good, I'm told."

"I remember reading his name," Valentina exclaims. "But I had no idea that he was Caterina's father."

"She must have changed her name," Fusco interjects. "That makes me think that she's not close to her father. That might create further complications in the kidnapping."

"That's right," the *commissario* nods again. "She took her dead mother's last name when she turned eighteen, twelve years ago."

"You said Pietro Nicoletti is an art looter and dealer. Where is he now?" Fusco wants to know, so that he can then let it all go and move on with their vacation.

"He's under house arrests here in Rome. What you saw last night is his vacation home," the *commissario* explains.

Lucky him! He must have had a vacation at some point in his life. And Fusco looks at Valentina, hoping that now they can start their own vacation.

As they cross Piazza di Torre Argentina, directed to Valentina's favorite little trattoria, Fusco holds her hand and asks her:

"Wouldn't it better to leave the area north of Rome?"

"Why? Don't you like it?"

"Of course, I do. It's just that it's so close to the Etruscan area."

The trattoria is in Piazza Farnese— a beautiful large square with no traffic, several restaurants with outside tables and a grand palace designed by Michelangelo, which is now the site of the French Embassy.

"Where would you like to go?" Valentina asks as they sit down facing the palace.

"I've always been interested in Naples. What do you think?"

"I haven't been there in years," Valentina tells him. "Naples it will be."

"Great!" he lifts a glass of white wine to her. "Let's leave this whole adventure behind."

"Let's start our vacation!" And Valentina drinks it up.

However, once they're through with their bucatini alla carbonara, Fusco notices that she's vacillating.

"It wouldn't be so bad to go see some Etruscan tombs," she says with an almost imploring tone. "They're so close and Etruscan artifacts are hard to come by."

"So tell me about the Etruscans." He's now genuinely curious. He doesn't remember much about this ancient civilization and college seems such a long time ago.

"They're more ancient than the Romans," Valentina starts to explain. "They settled in the area north of Rome and in Tuscany—a very evolved civilization. Unfortunately, their language is not known to us. They left behind beautiful frescoes, urns, vases and plates."

By the end of the meal, Fusco is sold on the Etruscans and they've agreed they're going to visit the Etruscan tombs and museum in nearby Tarquinia. No danger of running into Caterina's kidnappers any more. Let the Italian police take care of that problem.

CHAPTER SEVEN

A FACE ON THE PLATE

The new location must be closer to the ocean. Even though she couldn't see it—her head covered by a hood—she smelled it and heard the roar of the waves, when they pulled her out of the trunk of the car. *Why have they moved me again?* Even though her mind is a bit dulled and confused—the shot they gave her must be some heavy sedative, no doubt—Caterina remembers the commotion of the night.

A dog barking woke her up. Then she heard the rustling of leaves outside the basement window. A door opened and a few minutes later the sound of a gunshot resonated. She overheard her jailer talk on the phone in an agitated tone of voice.

"They found us out!" he screamed. "We need to move her right away!"

After a minute's silence he resumed: "No! We can't wait! They must have followed us! They know where she is! If you don't come here right away, I'm going to leave. I'm not gonna go back to jail! Not me!"

After a while, before dawn, they came to pick her up to take her away. *But where? Where am I?* She hears a few cars driving on a nearby road. Her hood off now, she looks around in the semi-darkness of the space surrounding her. It might be a garage turned into a basement. The floor is cemented and the only source of light comes from a faint bulb hanging from the ceiling. And then there is the usual mattress on the floor and the bowl of food and one of water. *My life as a dog!* The absurdity of her situation makes her laugh and then cry. She, who never cries, actually has tears coursing down her cheeks. She may be cracking up and, much to her surprise, it doesn't feel bad.

A man with a ski mask on his face walks down from a side door, just a few steps up. It is not the same wiry guy, her jailer at the house in the forest. He's more robust and taller. He carries a tape recorder.

"Now, we want you to record a message for your Dad," he says in a heavy Neapolitan accent. He places the tape recorder a few inches away from her face. "When he hears your desperate appeal, he'll fork over the money. And we'll let you go immediately. See, it's a win-win situation. You do some damage to your beloved Dad and we get the dough."

Win-win situation? Oh, no! This is a situation that has slipped through her fingers——a situation that has backfired. *Damn Mickey Mouse!*

"There is a connection between the kidnapping and Mickey Mouse," Fusco blurts out as they drive back to the lake.

"Excuse me!" Valentina looks amused. "Didn't you say that we're starting our vacation now?"

"Of course! But there is a connection." He'd better shut up and never mention the blasted case again.

Now they've reached the fork on the road from the Cassia highway.

The lake communities to the left and Calcata to the right. As they leave the highway, Valentina, at the wheel as usual, makes an unexpected turn to the right.

"What are you doing?" Fusco asks but already knows the answer.

"Tonight, we're going to have dinner at the vegetarian restaurant."

"You miss a nicely licked spoon, don't you?" Fusco teases her. "Unlikely, he's going to say anything interesting. He seemed pretty guarded last time."

"True!" she agrees. "But don't forget that it was noon. He was only mildly stoned. By this time at night, he might have had quite a few joints."

Tonight there is no trace of Mickey Mouse. The young man who greets them appears to be quite professional. He escorts them in an upper room with rustic benches and the view of the forest below.

"Who organizes the tours to the old quarry?" Fusco asks in his slow Italian.

"There is a guy in charge of that," the waiter answers without batting an eye. "He often comes here for dinner. Are you interested?"

"Mildly," Valentina answers hurriedly. "It sounds like a long walk. It's getting too hot for that."

She's being cautious, Fusco notices. *Last night's adventure has left a mark.*

The man nods in agreement and hands them the menu. A few minutes later, he comes back with a basket of rustic bread, a carafe of white wine and a bottle of mineral water. They order risotto with wild mushrooms.

"Why did you ask about the tours?" Valentina whispers.

"The quarry was mentioned in her notebook, together with Mickey

Mouse and the restaurant."

Fusco has a feeling this isn't a productive lead. In any case, it's a hard one to follow. As they leave the restaurant, he glances over the poster advertising the guided walks through the forest to the quarry. He shakes his head.

"I would like a gelato," Valentina's sweet tooth strikes again.

"O.K., Sweetie," he follows her toward a coffee house with outdoor seating. Nothing like an evening under the stars on an Italian summer night!

"The operation is compromised," they overhear a man say, as they cross the square on their way to the ice cream parlor. "They had to move her."

They exchange a knowing glance and immediately slow down.

"Where is he, now?" another voice interjects.

"He had to leave. It was getting too dangerous."

What are they talking about? Is it mere coincidence, or is it connected with the kidnapping?

"What a mess! Too many interests involved…"

They sit down at a small table and turn around toward the square and have a good look at the two men whom they overheard talking. In the semi-darkness of the square, they don't seem familiar. Could it be that the kidnapping is having a huge resonance in the area and everybody talks about it?

"Chocolate and hazelnut," Valentina orders.

She always looks so cheerful when she's around dessert, Fusco notices. *Almost better than sex.*

She turns to Fusco. "What are you going to have?"

"A small limoncello," he doesn't share the same enthusiasm for gelato, but he's developing an interest in Italian liqueurs.

"Do you think there might be a lead in the quarry?" Valentina asks as soon as the waiter leaves.

Fusco shakes his head. "Too late for that, I'm afraid. Still it would be interesting to visit. There is a guided walk in two days…"

"O.K., and after that Naples."

A dinner out with the Graves is always a treat for Laura Novak. Even though they are equal on the administrative ladder—both couples having achieved the much coveted status of education abroad directors—the Graves are much better connected than Laura and her husband Alistair Funklenickel with the higher echelons of the American educational system. They've also managed to establish some rapport with highly-placed Italian academics.

"What's new in Florence?" Laura asks. She doesn't want to bring up Caterina—not at first—even though it will be inevitable at some point in the conversation.

"You mean in Milan?" Eleanor Eastmar, Jason Graves' wife, promptly corrects her. She's the new director of the program in Milan, while Jason has been in Florence, now for several years. "And how is Alistair doing in Prague?"

"Right, Milan…Alistair loves Prague." Laura is always a bit intimidated by Eleanor—a fast talker who takes over the conversation and directs it whichever way she wants it. Laura can only do that if she's in the presence of people of lower academic ranking—the teachers at the language center here in Rome, or lecturers back home in Santa Corona.

"I was in Prague two years ago," Jason interjects. He's much easier going. "I loved it. Such an old world charm! Beautiful architecture. So much better than these Italian cities, plagued with heavy traffic."

"Other than the food, I don't see much advantage in being in Rome," Eleanor continues. "Milan is possibly a different thing—a more elegant city."

"Oh, come on! It's not a particularly attractive city," Jason is the only one who dares contradict Eleanor. "Horrendous climate, fog, smog!"

"At least, you don't get kidnapped!" Now it's Eleanor's turn. Laura feels relieved that she's the one to bring it up.

"What do you think of that?" Laura hopes the Graves might have an opinion about it.

"What's there to think?" Eleanor's response is prompt as usual. "Rich father, daughter going around without a bodyguard, country with incompetent police, kidnappers galore. There you have it!"

"Actually, the situation might be more complicated than that," Jason always offers a more balanced view, Laura notices. "Labauche is an art collector in trouble, as many art collectors are these days."

"What does that mean?"

"It means buying from looters opens you up to the world of crime," Jason pours Laura some wine. "And Caterina is a daring soul."

Daring soul? Is this as far as they're going to go? No mention of the drugs? If this is all they want to say, Laura is all right with it. She sips her wine.

"Daring soul, you say," she finally musters her courage. "Have you ever noticed some strange behaviors?"

Jason nods. "At times," he admits. "See, Labauche is also in trouble because the Italian authorities found out that his curator was involved with some looters. So now they're demanding some pieces back and they're pressing criminal charges against the curator."

It is clear they're not going to go back to discuss Caterina. Laura is not going to compromise her good relationship with the Graves. They're useful. She still has some climbing to do.

Not all the tombs are open to the public. What a shame that Italy doesn't have the money to keep all of its incredible art patrimony open and preserved as it should. Fusco finds the frescoes in the tombs fascinating. They're having a wonderful day, after all—*their first day of real vacation.* Even the heat, quite extreme in the middle of the day, doesn't seem to bother them. The tombs are cool, below ground level, and most of them with marvelous fragments of frescoes.

"The art objects, which were found inside the tombs are kept in a museum in Tarquinia," Valentina tells him as they exit their last tomb for the day. "Of course, many urns and vases and jewelry were stolen and sold to private collectors."

"Let's go see the museum."

A short drive through the countryside—a rather flat landscape, quite different from the hilly and verdant terrain around Bracciano lake—takes them to Tarquinia, a small Medieval town. The museum is inside an aristocratic palace, but it is temporarily closed for the lunch break.

"Let's have something to eat," Fusco heads toward a trattoria on the main square with outside tables and an arbor covered with fragrant vines.

A discarded newspaper is lying on a table. Valentina picks it up. They haven't had the time to buy a daily paper this morning. As they sit down, she glances over the titles of a number of articles. One grabs her attention and she starts reading.

"The kidnappers have asked for fifty million dollars," she lifts her head after a minute. "They've contacted her father in New York."

"At least, we're heading toward the solution," Fusco remarks. *At least, I hope so.*

"I don't know if that's the case," Valentina shakes her head. "Labauche declared that he won't give in to their requests. I'm really starting to feel sorry for Caterina. With a father like him, I can see why she's so disturbed."

"This may be part of a strategy," Fusco tries to rationalize. "I'm sure his phone is tapped."

They eat their lunch in silence. The kidnapping looms large and casts a shadow over their enjoyment of art, food and culture. Later in the afternoon, not even the beautiful artifacts inside the museum seem to lift the heaviness. One urn after another, vases after vases, plates, jewelry—all the testimonials of a lost and enigmatic civilization—are on display, separate and disconnected from the place where they originated.

"For Labauche, objects like these are more important than his daughter," Fusco observes. "And they are not even part of his heritage."

Even though he understands the love of beauty, the consciousness of the collector strikes him as something cold and greedy. Suddenly, an empty spot inside a large glass case catches his eye. He motions to Valentina to approach.

"Read the inscription," he points to a label and a photograph. It shows the photograph of a plate —a missing piece—decorated with a female head with wide dark eyes.

"The plate has been missing since June, 2010, when it was stolen," Valentina reads. "Known as the Etruscan Princess among scholars of the Etruscan civilization, because of the aristocratic female painted on it." She stares at the photo of the missing piece and moves back a few steps, turning toward him, deeply struck. "My God, the head looks like Caterina!"

He opens the door and closes it before he turns on the light. Laurent Labauche has never allowed anybody in this part of his residence—not even Jacqueline Spear, his lover/curator with whom he shares the same appreciation for art. It is a small square room—not bigger than many Etruscan tombs—with the walls decorated with fragments from tombs—the same tombs from which the jewel of the crown comes. At the very center of the room, a plate of incredible beauty stands, protected only by a glass case. No one has seen it. *No one will ever see it, as long as he's alive.*

He's turned seventy this year. Mortality has begun to stare him in the face. His heart has given him some problems. He lives alone; the life he's chosen for himself. His business ventures hold less and less interest for him. His collection—recent, yet rich and very specialized —has become the centerpiece of his activities. And at the very center of all, there is this object of incredible beauty, this secret pleasure he indulges in every evening, with an almost sacrilegious act of total devotion. Every night, he opens the door and closes it before he turns on the light. He spends only a few minutes in the room. The light may discolor and ruin the painting. For no reason in the world would he share this beauty, which is only his own, with any other human being. *Why should he?* The Etruscan princess is his only true love.

CHAPTER EIGHT

SEE NAPLES AND THEN DIE

"So what are you saying, Honey?" Fusco asks as soon as they are back in the car, leaving Tarquinia and heading for Trevignano. Valentina as usual is at the wheel. "Does Caterina resemble the Etruscan princess portrayed in that stolen plate?"

Valentina nods "yes," her mind lost in thought and her gaze fixed on the road ahead.

"But wait a minute," Fusco presses on. "I pictured Caterina as a blonde. I only got a glance of the woman on that mattress, but her hair looked fair to me."

"That's right!" Valentina concedes. "Her hair is blonde. Actually, it looks blonder than it really is. I'm sure she bleaches it to make it look almost whitish, as is the fashion now. But her eyes are dark and elongated—almost oriental."

"I noticed the eyes of most figures portrayed in the pottery and also in the fragments in the tombs looked somewhat oriental. Why is that?"

"According to some Etruscan scholars, the Etruscans came initially from Asia Minor and settled in various regions of Italy—northern

Lazio, Tuscany, Romagna. They were culturally more evolved than the tribes populating Italy at the time. So they had a civilizing impact on the locals. It seems like they also interacted with the Greeks who lived in Southern Italy. That's visible in their art objects."

"Interesting! But what has this to do with Caterina and her appearance?"

"I don't know, Nick!"

"Well, it's a series of interesting coincidences, to say the least." Fusco now reasons aloud. "Caterina looks like a woman on a plate, which was stolen and her father appears to be involved in Etruscan art. What do you make of that?"

"Life imitates art, maybe?"

By the time they reach their hotel on the lake, they are ready to switch the subject.

"What about going to Naples?" Fusco suggests as they stretch on their bed, cuddling together.

"Don't you want to go to the quarry tomorrow?" Valentina asks in-between yawns. She's quite tired from all that driving.

Why is she always trying to stay in the area? Fusco wonders.

"No way!" he answers quickly, before she has the time to continue and maybe try to convince him. "It's too hot. And I don't want to keep on investigating a case which isn't even mine."

"Right!" she agrees. "Let's officially start our vacation. They say: See Naples and then die."

"No shit! That doesn't bode well, does it?"

The sound of traffic never stops—not even at night. It's a noisy city, because it must be a city, Caterina decides, a busy southern city.

Maybe Naples, or one of those smaller towns close to Naples. Human voices seem Neapolitan. She's no expert on Italian dialects, but she tries to guess. And the bread is salted and very tasty. Didn't someone say that Neapolitan bread is particularly good? Have they delivered her to the Neapolitan Camorra—the Neapolitan brand of mafia? The thought terrifies her. Why has she got herself into this mess?

"*Tuo padre ha detto che non paga!*" one of her jailers told her yesterday. *Your father said he won't pay.*

She's not surprised. Not now that the effect of her drugs has worn out and memories of their relationship have come back to haunt her. He never showed her any love. Why should that change? *The question is: what are they going to do to her now?* Don't kidnappers cut pieces of their victim's body to intimidate the relatives and bend them into submission? She remembers hearing of a story many years ago. It happened before she was even born. Getty's grandson got his ear cut off.

"The situation in Italy has become progressively more dangerous," her apartment mate, Valentina, had pointed out to her one evening. It must have been during the first week, when Valentina was still trying to befriend her. After that, like everybody else, she'd given up. "The old crime world— the various kinds of Mafia— enrolls their young workers from poor areas, where enormous numbers of immigrants from Eastern Europe and Africa have joined the ranks of the local poor. The drug trade promises easy money."

Why had they discussed that? Maybe Valentina had noticed some of her unusual behaviors and tried to warn her. *None of her business,* she had thought then, finding her annoying. Caterina had let her finish her little spiel and had responded with one of her sarcastic remarks.

"Did your cop boyfriend provide you with all this information before he put you on the plane for Italy?"

That's how she always put an end to other women's attempts to befriend her. Needless to say, she had no female friends, with the exception of a few with whom she did drugs. She'd been able to keep her habits separate from her academic profession. She actually had a theory that drugs had sustained her success, making her hyper and somewhat indifferent.

It is hard for her to reason, now, when what sustained her for years has been taken away and replaced with its opposite—sleeping pills and sedatives to keep her down. Her mind is now fuzzy, with long repressed memories emerging and troubling her night and day. She tries to chase them away—too painful to deal with.

The reality of her dependence hits her in the face—a ten-year addiction to cocaine and methamphetamines. Yet, the plan seemed to make a lot of sense. It seemed the only way to sustain her habits, get her out of debt, and take revenge on her father. Things had instead gone awry from the very beginning. The entire operation had spiraled down from the start. She'd trusted a group of minor low life types living at the margins of serious crime: tomb raiders, minor drug dealers, people she'd had fun and had casual sex with. She felt adventurous and outrageous while she kept testing the extremes she had always been drawn to. They'd sold her down the river of organized crime, ready to exploit her potential wealth.

Am I going to get out of this alive?

"Careful when you're trying to cross the street," Clelia Palombelli warns them, holding on to both of them as if Fusco and Valentina were two five-year old children. "Two weeks ago, right where we're standing now, a jerk on a motorbike lost control and pushed me down to the ground. I'm still doing physical therapy. My butt is black and blue."

Even though he feels a little embarrassed from being treated like a preschool kid at age forty-seven, Fusco must admit that Naples' traffic can be terrifying. He looks at Valentina for comfort. She's pursing her lips, trying not to laugh, gazing at Clelia, her former high-school teacher, with a mixture of amusement, tenderness and admiration.

A Neapolitan by birth and upbringing, Clelia had come back to Naples after retirement. She's a spry and youngish looking seventy-five-year old—wavy grayish short hair, a tanned face and a springing pace. She speaks with a Neapolitan accent, pronouncing her words in a clear, resounding voice. It's much easier for Fusco to understand her than the Romans with their nasal tones.

Yesterday, Valentina gave her a call to announce their visit to Naples and Clelia insisted that they should stay with her. She'd come to pick them up at the train station, where they'd arrived after a short train ride from Rome. As they'd stepped out of the station, they found themselves in a different world of narrow winding streets and ascending levels. In Naples the presence of the sea is felt everywhere. A city sprawling out on hills facing the ocean, with its rising neighborhoods connected to each other through funiculars and stairways.

Clelia uses the car only to go out of town, she explains to them. When she's in Naples, she hates to drive, and managed to convince Valentina to leave their car in Rome. Driving in Naples would be a bad idea. She's led them to the funicular—the most peculiar train going uphill and cutting through various areas of the town. After a short ride, they'd found themselves in the Vomero, a middle class neighborhood of the city a few blocks away from Clelia's apartment. During the short stroll, an unpleasant reality emerges and attacks the senses of sight and the smell. Giant piles of black garbage bags—six feet high— are placed at every corner.

"Isn't this terrible?" Clelia makes distressed gestures toward the piles. "I don't know how much longer we can take it. Garbage hasn't been collected for ten days. People are going crazy and in some poor neighborhoods, they've started to burn it."

"Doesn't that release dioxin?" Fusco feels alarmed.

"Of course," Clelia nods in agreement and points toward a cluster of buildings, enclosed inside a small gated community. "That's my place."

The only problem now seems to be crossing the street in front of the building. The traffic has no rules and just as the imploring pedestrians manage to negotiate a truce with the vehicles, making them stop for a second, a rogue motorbike appears threatening to run them over, showing no pity.

"It looks like drivers take the light as a suggestion," Fusco points to the red light signal. "And then they do pretty much as they please."

"This beautiful city has an unruly and violent soul," Clelia explains as they cross the courtyard and approach the main door of her building. "My poor butt can testify to that."

As they enter the fourth floor apartment, after a ride in an old fashioned elevator, yet another world is revealed. Clelia's place exudes elegance and good taste—modern and antique furniture, family portraits, luxuriant plants and shining marble floors. *What an oasis!*

Fusco thinks, suddenly relaxing. *This is how people survive in a chaotic city.*

Shortly, after they settle down in the airy dining room, in front of a delicious lunch prepared by Carmela, Clelia's smiling housekeeper, Valentina tells her former teacher of all their misadventures with Caterina.

"They probably brought her here," Clelia comments. "This is a city where it's easy to hide a kidnapped person. Do you want to bet?"

Oh, no! Fusco silently implores. *Not again!*

"Don't let this enchanting view fool you," Clelia says as they stroll down from the peak of Posillipo. The panorama of the bay—the islands, the coastline, the picturesque city sprawling from the hills to the ocean—is dazzling.

"The son of a close friend of mine has recently disappeared," Clelia continues, leaving Fusco and Valentina no respite.

"What do you mean disappeared?" Valentina asks.

Fusco glares at her and sighs. *Oh, no,* he silently implores, *not again!* He's been imploring that for two days now. To no avail, because Clelia is extremely fascinated by Caterina's kidnapping and tries to feed them all sorts of information about Naples' infinite criminal possibilities.

"Well, his mother hasn't seen him for a while and doesn't know where he is," Clelia explains. "It's not the first time this has happened. Rumor has it that he's infiltrated the Camorra."

"Infiltrated the Camorra?" Fusco repeats. He's not sure he understood Clelia correctly.

"The Camorra, as you may know, is our own brand of organized crime," Clelia makes it sound like it is some local product like the delightful *provola affumicata* she has served them for lunch. Then she sighs and shakes her head. "Giuliano is a journalist and he's determined to expose Camorra. He has found no better way to do that than pretend to be one of them."

"Is he a police informant?" Fusco asks. *Why am I getting sucked into this?*

"No, not really. Actually, I don't know much about it and I doubt even his mother knows much. She confided in me. She's very concerned."

"He might not visit her to protect her," Valentina reassures Clelia.

They are now in front of the former monastery of San Martino. It is a majestic building containing a museum of the Neapolitan baroque.

"Let's go in." Clelia decides. "You will like this."

As they stroll from one cloister to a gallery and another cloister and a church and an exhibit of Neapolitan Nativity scenes, Fusco falls in love with Naples and its glorious past. *If only the Camorra and the traffic did not exist,* he finds himself thinking.

"Let's make a little DVD message for your father," the Intellectual says and helps her sit up.

Despite the ski mask, Caterina always recognizes him. His rather small hands feel almost gentle on her arms, when he touches her—no calluses, clean fingernails. His voice and his eyes give him away. His Neapolitan accent has a softness and sing-song quality, which is totally absent in the harsh tones of the other jailers. They shout at her. He speaks almost in a whisper. His eyes are the most peculiar trait. The other jailers never even look at her. For the most part, they avoid any eye contact. He stares at her, his glances full of compassion.

He doesn't come in often, but his visits make life more bearable for Caterina. At times, she feels, however, that his behavior confuses and weakens her. She always thought that in order to survive she was supposed to act and feel tough. What would happen if she became gentle? *What would they do to her?*

He turns on the lights. He doesn't tell her what to say. She stares at his small digital camera and starts to talk to her father, after twelve years of silence. She speaks with her usual bullying frankness. Emotions come up. She can feel them in her chest, even though she tries to keep them down. She doesn't cry—no, she doesn't do that. Maybe, her feelings don't show up in her voice or her eyes. In any case, her father wouldn't notice them. They had told her he's refused to pay so far. She would have been surprised if he had.

Once she's through talking, the Intellectual turns off his camera, pours her some water. He doesn't look at her in the eyes, now. He turns off the lights and leaves.

"So how do we go from here to there?" Fusco asks as they walk out of San Martino monastery into the dusk of a warm evening.

Children are playing in the square in front of the monastery. A bus is stationed at the other end of it ready to take them down the hill to the main hub of the Vomero neighborhood. A terrace borders the side opposite the monastery and sits overlooking the city and the bay.

Fusco doesn't want to be disrespectful, but he's genuinely curious. He's been presented during the last two days with evidence of a very refined civilization—palaces, churches, monasteries, art galleries. At the same time, in every neighborhood (even the upper middle class neighborhoods of San Martino and Posillipo) he's noticed piles of uncollected garbage, unruly traffic and the evidence of an overpowering criminal presence. Often, when she's accompanied them in some of their excursions through the city, Clelia has pointed out the Camorra links inside the commercial life of Naples.

"That store is connected with the Camorra," she's said more than once, walking in front of a commercial venue. "I never shop there. I don't want to support crime with the little money I have."

Now, Clelia listens to his question and sighs. She doesn't respond. Maybe she feels his being a foreigner would make it too difficult for him to understand the complex reality of the Italian South.

"Lack of social justice," Valentina responds. "To put it simply, poverty fuels crime. Overpopulation and unemployment on one side and the illusion of wealth presented by the Camorra and the drug traffic on the other side—these are the main players of today's reality."

"Actually, the Camorra controls almost every aspect of work and commerce in this city," Clelia interjects as they board the bus.

"Do you mean to say that there is no choice, that every aspect of life is dominated by organized crime?" Fusco feels a chill too hard to bear after having spent four hours contemplating the beauty and art of this magnificent city presented in the collections of the San Martino monastery. And hasn't he noticed the humor, warmth and friendliness Neapolitans exude?

The bus advances in the evening's heavy traffic and now stops at piazza Vanvitelli, the main square in the Vomero. It's an exuberant place with restaurants, stores and *gelaterie* in every side of its octagonal shape. It's swarming with people and cars.

"No," Clelia concedes. "Maybe that is too bleak, too final. There is a lot that is vital in the social structure of this city. There is a lot of social work, volunteer work everywhere. There is a great artistic life—theatre, music, art and design, not to mention cuisine."

"Speaking of cuisine," Valentina interjects as they get off the bus. "Nick and I would like to take you out for dinner. Do you know of a place where you would like to eat?"

"Oh, thank you. You're so kind. There is a great pizzeria in the next block. It has been there for many decades. Just to give you an idea of how old it is. My parents used to take me there when I was a child. The pizza is fantastic."

It bodes well, Fusco cheers up. If a true Neapolitan says that the pizza is fantastic, then so it is!

Just a block down from the square, they find a very authentic pizzeria with walls covered with white tiles, family portraits, photos of early twentieth-century Naples, and ancient logos of the restaurant when it first opened.

A little later, when their order comes in—a pizza, which smells delicious and tastes divine—Fusco surprises himself by asking Clelia something that he'd never thought he would ask.

"When we come back from Capri, would it be possible for me to talk to your friend, the mother of the journalist who has supposedly infiltrated the Camorra?"

CHAPTER NINE

A POT PLAN

At first, he refuses to watch it. When Steven, his personal assistant, brings him the envelope containing the DVD, Labauche shakes his head in denial. Even before opening the envelope, he knows its content.

"Who brought it?"

"I don't know, sir," Steven answers in his always ceremonious way. "Philip, our new concierge, brought it up a few minutes ago. I asked him who had delivered it. I noticed it had your name on it, but it didn't appear to have been mailed. Philip said it was delivered by a courier. He didn't know who it was. "

Steven places the silver plate with the envelope on the coffee table.

Labauche walks to his inner sanctuary, his temple, the room with the plate of the Etruscan Princess. He walks fast, with determination, down the corridor, but then lingers in front of the door. He hesitates. He turns around and traces his steps back to the living room.

For a whole day, he refuses to watch it. He goes about his business —his financial ventures, his board meetings, business lunch, his art

93

foundation and dinner with his curator. He stays out late. He doesn't talk about the DVD with anybody. He doesn't consciously think about it. He notices that people tiptoe around him even more than they usually do. *Why is that?* He wonders.

When he eventually comes back to his condominium facing Central Park, he's unable to sleep. He feels the presence of the intruder inside his home. The DVD has a life of its own. He can't ignore it. At 3 am, Labauche capitulates.

When she first appears on the screen, he doesn't even recognize her. *That is not Catherine!* She's not the child he used to know—his biological offspring. Not only has she changed in twelve years, she's become someone else, someone uncannily familiar. *Who does she remind him of?* Not her mother, for sure. Laura had an olive complexion and dark thick hair, a strong jaw and very regular features. Her body was exuberant and curvaceous. At least, that was the Laura he'd met during a summer vacation in Florence more than thirty years ago. A cheerful, smiling, spunky twenty-something girl, with those incredible dark elongated eyes—that's how he remembers her now. He pushes away all the other memories. *No! I won't go there*, he tells himself, trying hard to concentrate on the image on the screen.

The eyes, yes, the eyes—that's it! That's what they have in common, mother and daughter. The woman on the screen has none of her mother's healthy exuberance, though. Catherine—or Caterina—has his puny, thin, tall body and his fair complexion. He remembers her blonde hair, when she was young. Her eyes, though, are nothing like his pale blue eyes. Her eyes are Etruscan. They stare at him from the screen.

He's so totally taken in by her appearance that he can't concentrate on what she's saying. Her hair is cut to the skull. The kidnappers must have done that—or maybe not. Dark circles border her black eyes and make them stand out even more in her thin pale face. The expression of those eyes is what mesmerizes him.

She's not imploring him to do something for her. She talks to him with the spite he's familiar with from their past relationship. The grief, which transpires as she talks addressing him, "Father, we don't love each other," with her aggressive honesty, the grief is new to her, but so familiar to him. The grief comes from an ocean of suffering, someone else's suffering—someone he doesn't want to remember. As Caterina's voice continues her plea for her young life, Labauche rushes down the hallway and into the bathroom as vomit dashes out of his tight jaws.

This is not the first time Valentina has been to Capri, but it's definitely the best. Three wonderful days in the most enchanting place, climbing up with Nick all the hills of this island named after the goats —its first inhabitants—and then descending down to the ocean, swimming in unbelievably blue waters, roasting in the sun, cooling off in the caves off the coast.

"This is what I call a vacation!" Nick tells her as they walk along the lane that leads them to "San Michele," Axel Munthe's house. "We deserve it!"

"Are we finally on vacation?" she shouts mimicking a coach before a basketball game.

"Yes, we are!" Nick shouts back. "And we're going to stay that way."

"San Michele" is a white fortress—partly the house of writer, philanthropist and art collector Axel Munthe and a museum of ancient objects that testify to the glorious past of the island and to the Swedish doctor's passion for all things beautiful. Strolling through the rooms and the luxuriant and well- kept gardens, Valentina and Fusco take in the peaceful and refined atmosphere.

"A wonderful view of the ocean and the coast from every side," Valentina observes. "What an interesting life, Axel Munthe must have had!"

"And to choose to end it, here, in this wonderful island…"

As happy as they have been since they've left Naples, with its voluptuous beauty, challenging traffic and obsessively dominant Camorra, something has been left unsaid between them—an ever present subtext that neither one of them wants to mention. Valentina knows that they both feel the weight of their silent thoughts.

What are we going to do when we return to Naples? Not that there is a lack of places to visit in Naples and its vicinity. That's not the problem. The uncertainty she feels is in part created by Nick's wish to meet with Clelia's friend, the mother of the disappeared journalist who might have infiltrated the Camorra. *What am I going to do?* Valentina wonders. *Should I accompany him, or should I stay out of it?* Not only has Nick not asked her to join him in this new inquiry, he hasn't even mentioned it to her, after making the sudden and unexpected request to Clelia.

I don't think he wants me involved in this. She knows how bad he felt after their night adventure in the forest near Trevignano. The horrific sound of the gunshot still reverberates in her memory at times. Since that night, she has woken up in cold sweats and with her heart pounding, only to find herself in a comfortable bed with Nick asleep and happily snoring next to her.

I'm afraid he wants to go alone this time, she concludes, as they walk away from the "San Michele" villa and stroll along the Anacapri village. She doesn't know how she feels about it. It is not a particularly dangerous thing to go and talk to an older lady about her son. On the surface it seems quite innocent. Yes, on the surface… The problem is that Nick doesn't want her involved in anything which might be even vaguely dangerous. Maybe her reaction to the night adventure has made her look fragile to him. The thought is disturbing to Valentina.

There is more left unsaid and unsettled between them. Her uncertainty about the future of their relationship stems from her refusal of traditional roles. She now understands what happened in her previous marriage and wants to avoid the same mistakes. She'd gradually accepted being a successful doctor's wife. A once passionate and spontaneous rapport had become conventional and lifeless. She'd lost herself in the marriage. Her inability to conceive had made things worse. While she'd obsessed about her infertility, her husband had moved on, started an affair and had a child with his lover. The grief of that failure is gone, but what she's learned about herself from that experience is very present. She can be easily sucked into traditional roles. She won't let that happen again. She won't let the vitality and joy of their love be dispersed by the drudgery of everyday life. It is not easy to refuse Nick's marriage proposal though. Valentina knows that it comes from a genuine desire of his. It comes from love. She knows he's more traditional than she is and his concern about her safety stems from that. She feels that she needs to be his equal to preserve the integrity of their relationship.

She distracts herself by rummaging among the coral jewelry on display on a stand at the side of the road.

"I like those," Nick breaks the silence pointing to a pair of pink coral earrings. "Why don't you try them on?"

She puts them on and looks at herself at the mirror hanging on the side of the stall. Then she turns to face Nick, smiling.

"You look very cute! Do you like them?" She nods yes. He turns to the vendor. "Quanto?" and he buys them for her.

Should he talk to her about it or just let it go? Fusco wonders. Valentina hasn't said a word about it—not a word. And that's unusual. She's very open, always ready to discuss everything—even too much so. But this time, not a word. *What is he supposed to do?* If he talks to her about it, she might feel like he wants her to go along with him. If he doesn't she might feel like he wants to exclude her, that he's on some kind of macho trip. *God forbid! No macho trip! Not the macho trip, not with Valentina!*

The truth is that as much as he would like to have her share everything with him, he really doesn't want to expose her to danger—not after that terrible night in the forest. A week has gone by, but it feels like time is suspended when he thinks of that awful adventure. He should have known better. He should have put his foot down and kept her out of danger. Trying to find Caterina is not her job—that's the police's job, the Italian police. He reminds himself—the Italian police, that's right! It's not the job of an American cop on vacation in Italy either.

As they walk to the funicular which is going to take them down to the main village and to a restaurant for their lunch, Fusco realizes that keeping Valentina out of this meeting with Clelia's friend is not as simple as it sounds. He's noticed that at times there is a feeling of something unsaid between them—even when they're having a lot of fun, even when they're making love… He should broach the subject. He should choose the words, so that she doesn't feel he wants her to do anything. She can choose. That's it. Valentina needs to know that no matter what she chooses to do, it will be okay. And the memory of his marriage proposal emerges and makes him feel uncomfortable.

"What's the point?" Valentina had said. "It's not that we can start a family…" Her eyes had clouded.

He'd reached for her hand and squeezed it. "We're still a couple."

"And we're committed to each other," she'd agreed.

"Look at Franca and Bill," he'd tried to argue. "They don't have kids and they're so happy together."

"And we're happy, too" she'd looked into his eyes. "It's just that I don't see the point of getting a document to prove it. Not right now, anyway."

That's where they'd left it—in limbo.

On the surface, he reasons, a talk with an older lady doesn't sound dangerous, does it? On the surface…

The problem is that the older lady is the mother of a journalist who's trying to infiltrate Camorra, a journalist who has at least temporarily disappeared. Clelia's words keep on playing in his mind: "This city has a violent and unruly soul." And also: "They must have hidden her here."

As they find a table with ocean views, the fragrant aroma of freshly fried eggplant and roasted peppers welcomes them inside the *trattoria*. *We'll talk about it after lunch,* Fusco decides and pulls out a chair for Valentina. For now, let's just enjoy the moment!

Today, the Intellectual brought her some good pizza with eggplant and mozzarella. Now, she knows for sure that she's in Naples or nearby. The pizza has a rather thick, very soft and oily crust. As much as she enjoys the pizza, the thought of being in Naples scares her. *I'm in the hands of the Camorra. Now, I know it for sure.* The realization terrifies her. It blocks her stomach. It takes her appetite away.

"You didn't finish your pizza," the Intellectual points out, when he steps down into the basement a few minutes later. "Didn't you like it?"

She's so taken back by his question that she hesitates. Why on earth does he talk to her like that? He sounds like a normal human being trying to establish a rapport with another human being. What is he trying to do? Doesn't he know that there is no such a thing as a normal rapport between a prisoner and a jailer?

"Actually, it's quite good," she hears herself answer. "I'm just not that hungry right now."

"Maybe later?" and he leaves.

What did just happen? She wonders. In just a few weeks, she's lost a sense of what a normal exchange sounds like. When this man, whom she's nicknamed the Intellectual, walks into the basement and starts acting like he's her waiter and she's a customer, her sense of reality is challenged. She responds to him as if she's ready to buy into the version of facts that he's presenting to her. What is he going to ask her next? "Coffee or tea?"

Not that she's ever been very capable of keeping fiction and reality apart—often being sucked either into the literary fiction of her books or into drug induced illusion.

Memories of recent *trips* have been haunting her. Whatever

happened to Mickey Mouse and his group of friends? She wonders more out of curiosity than real care. She ran into this group at the Vegetarian Restaurant in Calcata. They had formed a co-op and had been running it for several years. It was a large and diverse group of people—some drug users, like herself, and some not. They were all involved in the guided tours to the old quarry and in a number of ecological projects, such as protecting the vast forest surrounding Calcata and promoting a slow and a sustainable lifestyle. She found them interesting, totally different from the stuffy academics she had been hanging out with during the last eight years. Most of them were artists, art dealers, cooks and organic vegetable gardeners. Although their ages spanned thirty years, most of them shared a sense of vitality and purpose. At times, among them she felt out of place, but for the most part she found they exuded an uplifting energy.

During a guided tour to the old quarry, she'd hooked up with the restaurant cook, Mickey Mouse. His nickname came from a number of T-shirts with a Mickey Mouse logo that he used to wear. He was constantly stoned, very funny and entertaining. He'd invited her to his apartment overlooking the forest. He'd cooked a tasty meal for her and they'd smoked a few joints together. Even though her preference went to methamphetamines and cocaine, and had rarely smoked marijuana, she'd enjoyed sharing joints with him. It was good for sex. It was during one of these *trips* that the plan got dreamed up.

"Wouldn't it be fun to pretend to kidnap you?" Mickey Mouse had come up with the idea. "If your father is as rich as you say, he wouldn't mind coughing up some money." He'd passed her a joint. "Wouldn't it be great to distribute wealth around?"

They had laughed hard. *Sure, why not?* Her father had cut her off a few years ago and academic jobs at the starting level don't pay well. Life in Santa Abelina was expensive and her habit was costing her a pretty penny. Her credit cards were maxed out. That was why she'd applied to teach summer courses at the Foreign Exchange Institute in Rome—a job well below her qualifications. And she was also sharing an apartment to keep her expenses down.

The next time she went up to Calcata, Cosimo—that was his real name—had come up with a few more details.

"Marijuana seems to give you bright ideas," she teased him. "I always thought that it would slow you down."

"You don't know what you've missed, you speed girl!" he passed her a joint.

"I guess I don't," she inhaled. "I never had the opportunity to take it easy and lay back like you do."

"Oh, come on!" he laughed. "I simply chose a different lifestyle... You can, too. You're sitting on a goldmine and you're not exploiting it."

That's how they cooked up the plan—one joint at a time.

She finishes up her pizza and then she stretches out on her mattress. She doesn't want to talk to the Intellectual when and if he comes back. She doesn't want to buy into his version of reality, whatever that is. She's the prisoner and he's the jailer. Period!

The apartment is in the old part of town—in what they call *i quartieri spagnoli*—the Spanish quarters. The main door opens into a wide hall and, beyond that, into a courtyard resembling a cloister. The stairway to Pina Materassi's first floor apartment is wide, with steps in white stone. The bronze plaque on her door bears her late husband's name: Dr. Francesco Materassi—Magistrato.

"Her late husband must have been a judge," Valentina explains to Fusco. Clelia had told them that Pina Materassi is a widow.

Pina opens the door just a few seconds after they've sounded the bell. She's a neatly dressed lady in her late sixties—a white and black printed silk dress, black sandals with moderate heels, a short haircut and a light make-up on a face that shows all her anxiety in the lines marking her forehead. She invites them to come in.

As they walk in, Fusco is struck by the darkness of the place in the warm and sunny mid-afternoon. The heavy wooden shutters are ajar and the dark curtains are pulled. This keeps the place somewhat cool, but it also accentuates the rather formal décor of the living room with its dark walnut antique furniture. They're invited to sit on a sofa upholstered with dark red velvet.

"Clelia told us about your son," Valentina tells her. "You can trust us. My fiancé is a detective for the police in California."

Pina relaxes a little as she sits down on an armchair opposite to them.

"I haven't seen Giuliano for more than three weeks," she sighs. "Usually, if he can't come and visit, at least he calls me on his cell phone. But I haven't heard from him for more than a week—just a short phone call. The last time he came here he told me that he was infiltrating the Camorra. He'd been doing it for a while. That's why he wasn't able to come and visit any more. He didn't want to raise suspicion."

"I imagine he wanted to protect you as well," Fusco interjects.

Pina nods. "That's right." Then, raising her eyes to meet theirs, she asks them, "Would you like some ice tea?"

"Thank you," Valentina smiles.

The ice tea lightens up the mood, Fusco notices as he sips it and finds it a bit too sweet.

"Clelia told me about your friend," Pina Materassi says.

"The reason I wanted to meet you is that Caterina seems to have disappeared into thin air," Fusco explains. "I don't think we can exclude the possibility of her having been sold to the Camorra."

"Do you think my son would know that?"

"It's a possibility." Fusco puts down his glass on the coffee table. "Did he tell you what kind of tasks he has to perform to pretend to be working for the Camorra?"

"He was working for a while in the garment industry with some Chinese workers. He told me that the Camorra owns most of the garment industry in this area and that it provides garments for high fashion, too. When he called, he only said that he was being moved somewhere else. He didn't tell me where."

Pina pauses. Maybe, she's trying to be cautious, Fusco notices.

"We don't want to know where he works," he tells her using a very calm tone. "The only thing I would like you to do for us is to ask him when he calls you if he's heard of the kidnapping of a young American young woman."

"I'll ask him," Pina agrees. "He may not tell me."

"He may not tell you." As he says that, the sadness of her expression strikes him deeply.

CHAPTER TEN

THE DIG

As they walk along a road of the excavated Roman city of Pompei, Fusco finds that his mind wanders. He turns toward Valentina who follows him—wearing shorts, a tank top, a baseball cap and sunglasses —while reading a map of the site.

"It seems like this entire trip to Naples and surrounding areas is an excavation," he tells her.

"What do you mean?" Valentina looks a little puzzled by his observation.

He moves into the shade and pulls her away from the scorching sun.

"It's just a thought," he tries to clarify it to her and to himself. "There is a reality on the surface, and then another one underneath."

She nods in agreement. "I think I know what you mean. The problem is how deep do we want to dig?"

As usual, Valentina goes to the root of the problem. *How deep do they want to dig?*

Not only does this question apply to what they now call the

"Caterina problem," but also to their personal lives. Memories of his first marriage have been surfacing during the last few days. Was he really happy? Was Melissa, his first wife, happy living with him? They'd met in high school, gone to college together and got married immediately after graduation. They'd had a child, Sofia, who's now a college graduate and living with her boy-friend in New York City. Does he really remember being happy during those twenty-two years of marriage? Certainly, during the first few years, when they both were so young and enthusiastic, there was a joyful feeling in their relationship, but afterwards everything had settled down into a routine, comfort, cherished habits, mutual fondness and respect—all good stuff, sure—but happiness, where had the happiness gone? Maybe, Fusco wonders, this is what Valentina fears—the routine, the loss of enthusiasm and communication. And who can blame her?

Some memories stand out of those twenty-two years. The birth of their daughter—that brought a lot of joy but also such a huge responsibility. They were both young and poor, but so hard working. They'd made it, but in all that work they'd lost the lightness. Their sense of purpose had dampened everything else. And his work—oh, his work that he was so good at—had come first, always first. The better, the more competent he had become the less present he had been in his marriage. When Melissa's cancer had invaded their lives he had realized how poorly engaged in their relationship he had been in the last few years. Her struggle and then her dying had brought a new dimension to his life—loss and depression.

He'd struggled with deep depression for two years after losing Melissa. That's why he'd moved to Santa Abelina. He could no longer concentrate on his very demanding job in New York City. He'd felt he needed a change. With Sofia away in college, his house in Brooklyn felt too empty. Yet, the move had not been easy. The depression had not lifted in the small and beautiful California town. He'd felt even more alienated, unable to deal with his inner demons. The slow pace, the lack of interesting cases, even the lack of serious crime to investigate had unnerved him, until the Vessely case had come along, and with it Valentina.

His main issue now is his whole relationship with his work. His identity as a cop has become a challenge. During the last decade, too many cases of police brutality have emerged. He can't say anymore that they are a few rotten apples. His pride in his job—serving a community, keeping it safe—it's all gone. And what about the traffic cops at Santa Abelina? He has seen them inflict huge fines to drivers for the slightest infractions. The excuse? The City needs money. What a way to create income for the city! The whole reputation of the force, down the drain!

Maybe, Valentina is right. *How deep do we want to dig?*

They have been walking since early morning inside the excavation sites, trotting along roads paved with stones, visiting one patrician Roman villa after another. All built around a central courtyard, with rooms decorated with astoundingly beautiful wall murals, the villas also differ in some details of style. One of the murals in one villa bears the depiction of some explicit sexual practices.

"You know," Valentina giggles as they leave that villa. "When I visited here last time during a school trip, I was not allowed inside that room. This is the first time I ever saw those murals."

"You're an adult, Sweetie!" Fusco chuckles, "Now you're allowed to enjoy ancient pornography."

"Yeah, I was maybe ten year old."

They now reach the main square, where the inhabitants of Pompei used to conduct their public affairs. Columns mark the place where the temples and civic buildings once stood.

"It's unbelievable," Fusco holds Valentina's hand as they stroll through the square, "such a prosperous and civilized city was wiped out in just a few hours by the eruption of the volcano, Vesuvius. It gives you pause to think about that."

"Our modern equivalents are the typhoons and earthquakes." Valentina points out. "Everything is transient."

They walk inside the museum, close to the exit of the archeological site. More information about life in the city awaits them. More striking for Fusco are the objects, which were found in the houses—jewelry, combs, household items. Then in the last room, the people froze in terror or were caught in their sleep by the lava, which, at the same time killed them and preserved the exterior shape of their bodies forever.

"Look!" Valentina pulls him toward two entangled figures. "They were caught by the lava while they were making love."

How deep do we want to dig?

Driving away from Pompei, Valentina heads towards the coast. They're starting to get very hungry. It's past their usual lunch hour, but they didn't feel like eating in Pompei.

"I'm sure we can find some pleasant little *trattoria* facing the ocean," she reassures Nick. who's getting hungrier by the minute. "And the food will be better than in Pompei."

"You were afraid the food in Pompei would be ancient," he teases her, "maybe found in one of the excavated houses, well preserved and everything, but still with some lava here and there…"

He hasn't lost his sense of humor, she notices. That's good*! Still, we need to talk. We need to see if we can decide what to do. As soon as we get to the trattoria and we sit in front of a nice lunch, I will bring it up,* she tells herself. He'd asked her if she wanted to join him in the visit to Pina Materassi.

"Of course," she'd said. "Of course, I will go with you. No problem."

They'd gone, they'd talked to Pina and they'd left Naples the following day for a trip to the excavation sites in Pompei and then the Amalfi coast. If Pina's son showed up at his mother's house, or even if he called and was willing to reveal something about Caterina, then they would go back to Naples. That's what they'd told Clelia when they'd left for their trip.

But then what? If we obtain some information about Caterina, what do we do with it? And how likely is it that the Camorra has kidnapped her?

That Clelia said so isn't enough to guarantee anything. Clelia is bright and spry, but what does she really know?

Half an hour later they're finally sitting down on a little terrace facing the azure waters of the Tyrrhenian Sea, sparkling in the sun. A cool breeze makes the early afternoon heat more bearable.

"Pasta with clams" they both order.

I'm too famished to worry about gaining weight with pasta, Valentina reasons. If I gain weight, I will worry about it later. She puts off discussing future plans until after they've filled themselves up. Much to her surprise, Nick is the one to bring it up.

"You know, Honey, I really appreciated you coming with me to talk to signora Materassi. My Italian is still too shaky for me to have done that alone."

"Oh, *Amore*, no problem," Valentina is taken back. That's good he's bringing it up. "Actually, I meant to ask you. What are we going to do with the information we might get?"

Nick smiles. He looks a bit amused, she notices.

"Do you think we could take on the Neapolitan Camorra?"

They both laugh. The waiter brings them their pasta and that keeps them quiet for a few minutes as they ravenously attack their food.

"This is nice," Nick breaks the silence after a few minutes, just as they're starting to feel less hungry. "I mean, even what we did in the forest near Trevignano was quite daring…"

"And I know I wasn't quite up to it." *There! She said it.*

"What are you talking about?" Nick grabs her hand across the table and squeezes it. "You were absolutely great. I'm so proud of you for the way you handled that nightmare."

"Oh, no!" She tries to set the record straight. "I laughed, I cried, I even peed on myself."

"So what?" he looks very earnest as he looks in her eyes. "That's a normal physical and emotional discharge. It's healthy to react that way. But on the scene of the crime, so to speak, you were totally in charge. You let it go afterwards, and that's good."

Valentina feels relieved. "I'm so glad you see it that way. Because we hadn't talked about it, I was afraid you thought I let you down with my reaction."

He shakes his head. "No way! You've never let me down."

He resumes eating and a few minutes later, he searches her eyes again. "As for your question about what we're going to do next, I've no idea. So far we don't know anything, except that Pina has an interesting son."

"That's right!" Valentina hears her cell phone tone playing an aria inside her purse. She picks up with an incredulous expression on her face. *Who's calling me now?* "Pronto! Oh Clelia!"

Valentina gets up and walks toward the railing looking for better reception.

"Oh, no! Really?" Clelia is telling her that Giuliano Materassi, Pina's son has called his mother and has agreed to talk with them some time soon. She hangs up and turns toward Nick.

"You won't believe this!" she says sitting across from him.

Today, the Intellectual touches her lightly around her elbows and helps her get up.

"I'm going to take you to the bathroom upstairs so that you can have a shower," he tells Caterina, speaking softly with his slight singsong, the Neapolitan accent of the upper and middle classes. "I have to put a hood on your head," he almost apologizes.

He helps her on the short flight of stairs, and then opens a door and pushes her inside ever so lightly. After he's closed the door, he tells her speaking from outside: "You can take your hood off. When you're done, knock on the door and put the hood back on."

The shower is clean and the water is refreshing. There is even a towel for her and new clothes—a pair of jeans, a tee-shirt, underwear and a bra, which are just a bit too large for her. She knocks on the door, puts the hood on and he takes her down to her dungeon.

A few minutes later, he comes back with some tasty food—a *pizza di scarola*. Why is he going through all this trouble for her? More importantly, why is he working for organized crime? He has the manners of an upper middle class young man. His softness reminds her of a short story by Neapolitan writer, Fabrizia Ramondino who describes Neapolitan men as soft as dough.

"Today, we need to make another DVD for your father," he tells her when he comes back to pick up her plate.

"I've told my father all I had to tell him," she says looking straight into his dark eyes, the only thing she can see of his face hidden under the ski mask.

"I'm sure there is more you want to tell him," he goes toward the door "if you think about it."

She has a feeling he will be back soon.

He has heard her talk to her father. He's heard her plea for her life. He may understand English, Caterina ponders. Not that it makes any difference. It would have made a difference just a few weeks ago. She never opened up to anybody. *Never show vulnerability.* It makes no difference now.

"I shouldn't pay with my life just because we don't love each other," Caterina remembers her spiel. "I know the power of your indifference. Twenty years have gone by, but I haven't forgotten her. I haven't forgotten how you let her die, how she let herself die. I've escaped your implacable indifference just to find myself caught again into the trap of your financial power. It is because of your money—the money which I refused—that I find myself in this fix. I'm not appealing to your compassion. You don't have any. I know that. I'm asking you to look at the situation with cold logic. We both have that."

If the Intellectual knows English, he may have understood her little spiel. He may even have understood what remained unsaid, and the little melodramatic lies—*the money which I refused.* Caterina knows she never refused anything. She never was offered any financial support except for what was strictly necessary when she was going through her studies. It is true that if she'd been acquiescent, if she had looked the other way, if she'd made it easy for her father, money would have flown her way. That would have meant betraying the other one, the one who'd died twenty years ago—not her dead mother, but the ten-year old Caterina.

She closes her eyes now and stretches down on her mattress on the basement floor. She sees herself at age ten—long skinny legs, blond ponytail and dark eyes—and she recognizes her core—what's left after everything has been stripped away—pretense, cultural embellishments, cosmetic beautification and even alcohol and drugs. Nothing's left but that core—the motherless ten-year old. She couldn't betray her, could she?

As for the other shameful lie—*it's because of your money that I find myself in this fix*—the Intellectual may see through it. He may know her pathetic story. He may have been told details which she ignores and would love to learn. He may have the answers to her questions: When did Mickey Mouse sell her to the big players of organized crime? How much was she worth?

"You don't have to do a thing," Mickey Mouse had told her. They were in bed in his room in Calcata. It was a lazy Sunday morning. The entire town was closed down until one in the afternoon when the tourists might show up for lunch. Cosimo didn't have to be at the Vegetarian Restaurant until noon. Nothing to do but smoke a joint and day-dream about her wealth to be.

"What do you mean, I don't have to do a thing?" she'd inhaled. "You make it sound too easy." Those were her last words spoken in wisdom. After that, it had been sheer madness. They'd made a plan. She had to disappear, hide where nobody would find her.

"Where would that be?" she'd wondered.

"Look around!" Mickey Mouse had pointed to the thick forest below. "Do you think anybody would be able to find you down there?"

She'd been on the guided tour to the old quarry and had had a glimpse of the surrounding forest—*la selva*, as they called it, using an ancient word. Nobody could possibly find her there. Mickey Mouse was right. Despite his hazy expression and slow speech, he had some brain after all, she thought. He'd never had it easy. "I'm from the land, generations of poor farmers. I had to learn how to survive, unlike you, Princess." She'd felt at a disadvantage with her privileged background. She'd never had to learn how to survive and she never did. Better let him plan.

Maybe, the Intellectual knows all the details of the kidnapping, which I ignore. Maybe, he knows how gullible she can be. She doesn't care anymore.

He's back with his small video camera. She sits up and looks straight toward him.

"Father," she starts. "I need your help. I'm in big trouble."

No more lies, she tells herself. *I'm going to tell it as it is.*

Several decades ago the soil started to rise on its own, Fusco is told. Here, they call this natural phenomenon, *bratisisma*. He's not sure of the English name describing it and his small dictionary is no help. The consequences were a terrifying disaster for many people who had to leave Pozzuoli and be relocated in the towns on the other side of the Bay of Naples. Then twenty some years ago the metal industry collapsed and Naples lost its plant in Pozzuoli.

"Twenty thousand jobs were lost then," Clelia explained to him while having lunch in her dining room today. "Twenty thousand jobs went to crime."

Clelia volunteers once a week as a librarian at Pozzuoli's public library and she's arranged for Fusco to meet Signora Materassi's journalist son, Giuliano, in the main hall of the library.

"Books are donated. As they come in, they go out," Clelia spoke about it with enthusiasm. "There is such hunger for culture!"

The public library was once part of the plant. Now, the building, which once housed the plant's offices, is used for this social service almost entirely run by volunteers.

A few minutes before three in the afternoon, the crowded bus lets Fusco off, right in front of an odd looking squat building.

As he walks into the library, Fusco gets a glimpse of himself reflected by the glass door. He's in his disguise attire—an Indian yellow shirt, which he bought in one of the many street markets downtown, and a blond wig with long hair, which makes him sweat. He has to refrain from laughing. At home, Valentina had been unable to.

"You're so funny!" she'd burst out laughing, tears coursing down her cheeks. "I wouldn't be able to recognize you!"

"That's good!" he'd joined her in her amusement. "That's the purpose of the whole thing. You know, Sweetie, I used to go *under cover* a lot in my young days. And I often used even more outlandish disguises than this one."

He now spots Clelia seated at one of the tables at the center of the main hall. They have come separately, just to be cautious. She's driven her car and has arrived earlier. Clelia motions him to join her in a side room.

"This is where we teach some of our free classes," she explains. And then looking at her watch, she turns toward Fusco and whispers: "We'd better go out in the main hall. Giuliano might be early."

The main hall is deserted on this hot summer afternoon. Only a few visitors are seated at the tables. Clelia and Fusco borrow books and sit down right across from each other at one of the empty tables. They open their books and pretend to be totally immersed in their reading.

Five minutes later, Fusco raises his eyes and looks outside through the glass doors. He notices a scooter circling the square in front of the library. A young man in white clothes parks it close to the entrance and then pushes the glass door open. He's reasonably tall, olive skin, a short beard, hair cut down to zero and very dark intense black eyes. He borrows a book and sits next to Clelia and right across from Fusco.

"It's him," Clelia whispers to the young man without raising her eyes from her book.

"The answer to your question is yes," Giuliano whispers, his eyes intently fixed on his book. "She's okay for now. I will contact you soon."

"Where is she?" Fusco asks. He knows he won't get an answer, but he tries nonetheless.

"I can't tell you now," Giuliano answers with a resolute tone.

A few minutes later, the young man talks again. "Why do you want to know?"

"I'm a detective. That's what I do." That's the first thing that comes to Fusco's mind.

"You will have to wait. It's not safe for me to tell you now."

"Is she in the hands of the Camorra?"

"Yes, but it's a minor spinoff. That's all I can tell you now."

He closes his book with a hurried gesture. He gets up and returns the book to the librarian. He leaves the library. A few minutes later, Fusco hears the roar of the starting and then crossing the square.

Clelia and Fusco sit still with their books in their hands, pretending to be immersed in their readings. They wait a little longer and then they walk out of the library toward Clelia's parked car.

"It's the first contact," Fusco comments as he keeps on walking toward the bus stop, leaving Clelia behind.

CHAPTER ELEVEN

A RECKLESS LIFE

"I wonder when Giuliano will contact us again," Fusco remarks as they climb hand in hand the very high bridge of the Accademia in Venice. "I hope he does within two weeks."

They have reached the top and they turn to face the Punta della Salute, the imposing white Renaissance church on one side of the Grand Canal, marking the opening of the intricate maze of canals to the lagoon and the islands. It is sunset and the waters are tinged with the purple color of the sky. After a whole day of trotting around narrow lanes, canals and bridges, getting lost and finding their ways through waves of tourists and quiet neighborhoods, the sunset on the lagoon provides a much needed respite.

"You hope he does within two weeks," Valentina repeats. "If he contacts us later, you won't be in Italy any more. But I will be here."

"Well, in that case, please don't go to the appointment." Fusco feels very worried. "Just let the police know."

"Giuliano has made it clear that he doesn't want police intervention just yet," she points out.

That's right, he doesn't.

"Then just drop it. Nothing you can do," he feels this Caterina problem is way over their heads. "It would be too dangerous for you to even go and meet him."

"You did it," Valentina remarks with her usual spunkiness. "If it wasn't too dangerous for you why would it be for me?"

"Well…" *How do I get out of this?* Fusco hesitates.

"Because you're a cop and I'm not, right?" she suggests with a vaguely irritated tone.

"That's right," *It's better to admit it*, he decides. Then changing the tone he jokes, "And I wear a blonde wig."

They burst out laughing while they walk down to the other side of the bridge, headed toward the Art Academy.

"Tomorrow morning, I would like us to visit the art gallery here at the Art Academy," Valentina suggests. "I remember seeing some amazing paintings of the Venetian school."

The last two days in Venice have been a much needed diversion from what they've come to call 'the Caterina problem.' With no cars, a slow pace and one enchanting view after another, Venice is the ideal place to forget about the issue, which has been haunting them since the beginning of their Italian vacation.

After last week's encounter with Giuliano Materassi, they've found themselves in a quandary. They know for sure what they only guessed before. Caterina is hidden in Naples or nearby, firmly in the hands of the Camorra, and Giuliano is taking a big risk even letting them know that much. Out of loyalty to him and admiration for his heroic effort to battle Camorra, they haven't talked to the police.

"What good would it do to talk to the police anyway?" Valentina had argued after Fusco's secret meeting with Giuliano. "We don't know where they keep her."

"That's true," Fusco had admitted. "It's hard for me not to tell the police, because of my job and my background. This really goes against my grain, but I guess, we need to wait. Anything else might compromise Giuliano's work and survival."

"And it wouldn't help Caterina either."

They'd settled and they would wait. However, they needed to take time off. Waiting in Naples would have been nerve racking and even dangerous.

"Venice is far enough, "Valentina had suggested. "And it's an absolute must-see."

Now, inside an old *baccaro*—a restructured local tavern—they look for the first available table and contemplate which Venetian specialty they're going to order.

"*Sarde in saor* and *risi e bisi*," Valentina proclaims after a cursory look at the menu.

"Whatever, you say, Sweetie," Fusco sits down with an expectant look on his face. "Italy is such a diverse culinary and cultural experience."

If only they didn't have the Caterina problem!

The Intellectual hasn't been here for two days, Caterina notices. The other jailers are coarse and loud and not interested in making her life more bearable. Even though their faces are always covered with ski masks, she can't help noticing their energies. They must be on drugs, she observes, heavy stuff, mind altering. They don't talk to her, except to give orders. They throw the food in her direction, almost begrudgingly. They must come from abject poverty, she speculates, from childhood privations. They don't offer respect because they never received it. Having money is their only aspiration--lots of it and whatever the cost.

Fear invades her whole being. Her bowels contract and her breathing speeds up. She imagines them in the streets of Naples, on their scooters snapping handbags from older women, trigger happy with powerful weapons. They're all very young, some barely teenagers, recruited in the most desperately poor sections of town. *I'm in the hands of the most dangerous people.* The thought takes her breath away.

She's out of water, but she doesn't make requests. She'd rather be thirsty than talk to them.

"What are you doing, ha?" One of the jailers had yelled at her a few days ago. "Always drinking! The more you drink, the more you've got to pee. Don't you know that?"

"She thinks she's at the grand hotel," another one had interjected. "The princess, here! If it were for me..." and he'd made the gesture of a knife cutting her throat.

"If your father doesn't pay, that's how you're going to end up," and he laughed making a loud and vulgar sound.

She hadn't responded. She'd stretched on her mattress, facing the wall. A sense of despair had taken hold of her. Why had she allowed herself to end up like this? Mickey Mouse had said it would be easy. *A reckless life.* That's right! The thought had crossed her mind that some aspect of these Camorra kids' lives mirrored her own. The same 'do it to them before they do it to me' attitude, the world stinks—that's how she'd lived, making herself harder and more callous every day. The

Mickey Mouse plan was the result of that attitude, but it also had a component of improvisation and naiveté

She'd spent a couple of days camping out near the old quarry while Cosimo had contacted her father--to no avail. Her father must have seen through it. He hadn't responded. He hadn't even called the police. At least, that's what Cosimo had told her. Other characters got involved in the scheme. She'd started to get worried.

One day at the end of that first week of her disappearance, she'd even gone back to Rome. To make herself visible, she'd stopped at the *Pizza al taglio* place where she would usually have lunch. Then, following a sudden impulse, she'd showed up at Novak's office, walking in unannounced.

Olga, Novak's secretary, also known among her Italian colleagues as the "*cane da guardia*" (the watchdog), had screamed after her: "The director is busy now!"

She'd ignored her. She'd walked in, closed the door behind her and settled down on the chair opposite to Novak's desk before the amazed director had had the time to invite her to sit down.

"What's up?" Novak had asked, showing a slight alarm in her face.

"I may need your help," Caterina had begun, speaking fast and breathlessly. "I have good reasons to believe that some people might be planning to kidnap me. I thought they were my friends, but now I suspect their motives."

From the change in Novak's expression, Caterina had immediately sensed that she'd made a mistake in coming to see her boss. Novak had begun fidgeting with some pens and papers on her desk, taking her time to respond. When she'd finally raised her eyes to meet Caterina's gaze, the director's expression was glacial.

"I don't see how I can help you," she'd told her, talking with a very distant tone. "You may want to consider hiring a bodyguard. After all, an heiress like you should not be walking around without some protection. The one thing I wouldn't do is to go to the police."

"Why not?" Caterina had considered that possibility and the only thing that had prevented her from doing it was her fear that the authorities might find out about her own part in the shady deal.

An enraged Novak had confronted her. "Are you out of your mind? Do you have any idea what that would mean for the Center??" She'd glared at her. "The gossip from the media might engulf us. Think about your protector, professor Graves. He would not appreciate the negative publicity."

Caterina had sensed that Novak was suspecting her of some wrongdoing. That evening she'd gone back to Calcata and decided to wait and see. She'd felt the need to be on top of things.

"Who are these people?" she'd asked Mickey Mouse. "I just got a glimpse of them and didn't like them."

"Don't worry about it," he'd tried to reassure her. "They look worse than they are. They're okay. We need them to get things going." He'd passed her a joint, but she hadn't inhaled this time. *I'd better keep lucid,* she'd thought.

The following week, at night in his apartment, she'd woken up and heard them talk in the other room. Mickey Mouse and one of his rough looking friends, but also other men whose voices she'd never heard before, were discussing her kidnapping. She'd approached the closed door, not daring to open it.

"We need to keep her for a while," a gruff voice was saying. "We need to do things seriously."

"She's worth a lot," she'd heard another voice interjecting. "I did my research."

"That's not the deal I have with her," Mickey Mouse had protested weakly, very weakly.

"Well, then" the gruff voice had responded angrily. "You can always give her your share."

"Or, maybe, you shouldn't be part of this," the other voice had rejoined. "You should leave it to professionals."

At dawn, she'd sneaked out of the apartment. Mickey Mouse was asleep. He smelled like marijuana. She'd driven to the airport and tried to find a flight back to the States.

Stretched on her mattress, she now wonders. *How did I ever get myself into this? Will I come out of it alive?* The throat-cutting gesture floats through her mind and never leaves.

The light filters through the cracks and the sound of cars driving on the highway resumes. Then the Intellectual walks in. Totally unexpectedly, he steps down into the basement with his calm pace. He sets a bottle of water and some appetizing food in front of her.

Talking in his whispering sing song he asks her, "How did it go during the last two days?"

She looks at him, at his face hidden behind the mask, at the intense and gentle eyes, she hesitates, even more disoriented by his kindness than she is by the other jailers' brutality.

Then, before she can check her own words, "It's hard without you," she says while tears coursed down her cheeks.

She didn't expect that. Where did these emotions come from? A glacier inside of her is melting. *Oh, shit! Global warming is hitting. Who's going to save the polar bears?*

Never moving his gaze from her, the Intellectual fishes out a white clean handkerchief from his jeans back pocket and offers it to her.

"How about a shower?" he suggests.

Stockholm syndrome, Caterina thinks, as she wipes her tears in his handkerchief and sobs some more. *Stockholm syndrome,* she watches herself enjoying the Intellectual's gentle touch as he guides her up the stairs leading her into the bathroom.

Under the stream of lukewarm water, more sobs come. *This is so uncomfortable.* It was easier to be hard, she tells herself, even though she knows that something has shifted and she can't prevent the glacier from melting.

The islands in Venice's lagoon are a world apart. They are small communities which subsist on their own. After a brief stop at San Michele, the cemetery island, where Venetians spend their afterlife existence, the next stop of the *vaporetto* to the islands is Murano. This is the island where the blown glass objects—chandeliers, lamps, vases — are made.

For Valentina this is the second time she's been to this island. The first time was during a vacation with her parents. To her, the island looks unchanged.

"If there have been any changes, they must be minor," she tells Fusco. "Maybe, people talking on cell phones. That's the only noticeable difference."

Fusco and Valentina walk holding hands around the island, which looks like a miniature Venice, except for the glass factories. Then they settle down for an hour in front of a factory oven to watch a demonstration of blown glass art.

"This is so fascinating!" Fusco whispers to her, as they observe the various phases of this ancient art.

Valentina points to the glass maker, who has just completed an elaborate glass flower, the ornamental piece of a lamp.

"As he blows into the pipe, you would never believe that an object of such perfection would come out."

They eventually buy a small vase—the only piece they can afford.

The next stop is Burano, the island famous for the hand-made lace. As they disembark, a completely different world awaits them. This is a fisherman island, where houses are painted in bright colors, each different from the other. Fishing boats are docked in the canals and embroidered cloth—linen, garments and even lace umbrellas—are displayed throughout the alleys. Even though, just as in Murano, tourists swarm Burano, the island seems one more step removed from the modern world. It's for the most part a quiet and bucolic place, suspended in a distant time and space.

"What amazes me most about Italy is how all these different cultural realities coexist within the same country," Fusco remarks as they fish through layers of lace and embroidered garments on a stand.

"It's because Italy was this assemblage of different countries before it became unified into a nation state, not that long ago," Valentina explains while pulling out an embroidered blouse from a pile.

They eventually buy a blouse for Valentina, a table cloth and an embroidered umbrella for their house in Santa Abelina, before they move to Torcello, their last stop for the day.

Now, they find themselves in the midst of a green Eden—fields on both sides of a dirt lane leading to the Cathedral. The sign pointing in the direction of the church promises an early Medieval building.

Valentina, who has never visited Torcello before, expects a small town from the Middle Ages, only to find out that the Cathedral and its cloister are in the midst of meadows.

"What an idyllic place," she observes.

For the first time today, she's tempted to mention the 'Caterina problem.' She checks herself just in time. They agreed not to talk about that issue before they've embarked on their excursion to the islands.

"Yes, this place is idyllic," Fusco concurs as he sits on Attila's s throne—a stone chair in the middle of the meadow in front of the church—and poses for Valentina as she takes his photo. "We needed this complete relaxation."

After the visit to the Cathedral, and a tasty meal of polenta and calamari in a country tavern, they head back for the boat which is going to take them back directly to Fondamenta Vecchie in Venice. They both take in the tranquility of the lagoon, as they sit, enjoying the breeze on the open deck. The mild pastel colors of sky and water are in sharp contrast with the vibrant tones of the Neapolitan coast, which they've left behind just a few days ago. *This is what we need now,* Valentina feels, *this tranquility.*

"When I relax so deeply, I'm reminded of the stress involved in my work," Valentina says. "I've been so dissatisfied with the academic power games for so long now."

"I know how you feel. We're in the same boat," Fusco points to the physical boat they are in. "I find my work harder and harder. It's not only that in Santa Abelina there are fewer interesting cases, it's also that the team work I was used to has disappeared... I don't feel I belong anymore."

Valentina knows. She sighs. "I wonder what we could do to improve our situations. Over this past year, you have told me stories of your life as a detective in New York. I'm always fascinated when you tell me those stories. I wonder if we could write together, using pseudonyms. It would give us something interesting to do together."

"Hm…I'll think about that. You're a great writer."

"You're a wonderful storyteller."

As they reach Venice, Valentina checks the messages on her cell phone. Two have arrived while they were on their island excursion. The first is from the Roman agency that is trying to find her an accommodation. The other one is from Clelia.

"We've found you a small place in Trastevere. We need you to contact us right away," an impersonal voice announces in the first message. "Valentina, Nick! Call me back. Giuliano can see you Thursday," Clelia shouts all excited.

"Thursday is in three days," Valentina turns toward Fusco. "We'd better drive south tomorrow."

She turns around facing toward the azure Paradise of the lagoon, before heading back into the intricate maze of narrow alleys. They join the crowd of tourists following the signs that point toward San Marco square.

Going to Italy is impossible. The thought flows through his mind as Labauche listens to the new DVD, which was delivered, by UPS this time, just a few hours ago, The kidnappers didn't take a chance with a private courier as they did with the previous DVD. *Never mind,* he tells himself, as he tries to concentrate. He looks for details that might give away the location, but there aren't any. His focus is all on

Caterina's gaunt and pale face. The hair cropped to the skull makes her large elongated eyes stand out even more. This time the tone of her message is different.

The previous message, which he's watched many times, was filled with the anger and manipulation he's familiar with. She was still nagging him for the love he denied her, for the love he hadn't given her mother. She was still accusing him of neglect, coldness and cruelty. *A strange way to ask for help,* Labauche ponders. *It sounds like: Fuck you and help me!* The apparent frankness of the message didn't fool him though. The accusations were a way of saying to him: This is your chance to make up for all your past misdemeanors. *But is it?* Will there ever be a chance to make up for past mistakes? Not in Caterina's world! He knows that much. No matter how many times he listens to the first DVD, the message is always the same. No matter what you will do, I will still hate you. No matter how much money, you spend on me, I won't forgive you. *I cannot be bought.* He has to admire her for that, in spite of her outrageousness.

Only at the end of the first DVD did Caterina mention her endangered life. Only then did she hint at her young age. Every time he hears her voice turning from rage to regret and sadness, he feels sick at the center of his whole being. He hasn't been able to go to his inner sanctuary any more, to his beloved Etruscan princess. Pleasure, real pure pleasure, has been taken away from his life, never to be returned. That's how Caterina has punished him.

Quite surprisingly, the second DVD—only a few days later— doesn't contain any accusations, any scores to be settled, any fuck you messages. She doesn't even begrudge him his money. Caterina goes immediately to the core of the issue. "Father, I'm in serious trouble," she says. "My life is in danger." She also adds: "If you want to get me out of here, you will need to come to Italy."

That's what I cannot do. Labauche turns off the DVD. He feels caught in a dilemma that has no solution. Going to Italy puts him in danger. His curator, Jacqueline Speers is under investigation in Italy for buying stolen Etruscan art for his private collection. Everybody knows that the centerpiece is the plate of the Etruscan princess. Pietro Nicoletti, the liaison between Jacqueline and the tomb raiders, is under house arrest in Rome. It has cost Labauche money to keep Nicoletti quiet. The Italian authorities have been pressuring Nicoletti, offering him the equivalent of parole in exchange for names, which he has so far declined to reveal. The balance can be tipped any time and it can land Jacqueline in jail and Labauche indicted by the Italian justice system. Through the grapevine, an offer has come to him from some officers in the Italian Art Ministry. Relinquish the Etruscan princess, and we will drop our charges against your curator.

Labauche is only moderately worried about Jacqueline. The Italian justice system is notoriously slow. It will take years for the legal process and the investigation to be completed. Organized crime acts fast, though. Caterina might be right. If he went to Italy that might help in setting her free. The Italian investigators who are taking care of Caterina's case informed him that her kidnappers are presumably involved with the Etruscan tomb raiders.

For him, going to Italy would mean returning the Etruscan princess. *I cannot do that,* he decides as he walks down the hallway and opens the locked door to his inner sanctuary. *Life without her is meaningless,* he repeats to himself, pushing down on the door handle.

Trastevere is bursting with life, night and day. Even after the many buses and trams running through Viale Trastevere have stopped for the night, the noise of people, cars, and scooters continues for awhile. The maze of narrow alleys on both sides of the main avenue host a mixed group of inhabitants—the working class, that has lived for centuries in this oldest neighborhood of Rome, and artists, who have settled here in more recent decades. It's a hot summer night. The breeze is late in coming from the river.

After several hours of driving on the busy *Autostrada del Sole*, heading south, Fusco and Valentina have settled in the apartment the agency found for them—a tiny place with a nice balcony overlooking a private garden and a back alley.

When the agent had first showed it to them, Valentina seemed perplexed, but Fusco felt it was okay. He didn't care to scout around in the summer heat.

"It's really small, but it's central," Fusco had tried to convince her.

"Do you think so?" Valentina had still looked uncertain. Fusco knew that for her the heat was not a problem. She was accustomed to the extreme summer climate of her island. "Isn't it too noisy?"

"If you want to be downtown," he'd argued. "You need to put up with the noise. It's a convenient location."

They took it, and the moment the agent left, Fusco felt at home. *At last, the two of them, alone.* No more sleeping in people's homes as guests or at bed and breakfasts, no more hotels. The need for privacy, repressed for so long, emerged suddenly.

During the night, they make love slowly and passionately. They don't care that the windows are open on both sides of the apartment and the neighbors can hear their moans and grunts. At dawn, they walk down and buy freshly baked *cornetti* from a bakery, which has its own oven.

"Aren't they heavenly?" Valentina's sweet tooth hits again, Fusco notices and smiles nodding yes.

They spend most of Wednesday resting and trying to keep cool—the wooden shutters ajar all day. Only until darkness falls do they go out in the crowded streets, looking for a restaurant for a late supper.

"Trastevere is supposedly famous for its good restaurants," Valentina tells him. "For some reason, I've only tried the restaurants on the other side of the river, where the Jewish ghetto neighborhood is."

This is their last evening by themselves. Tomorrow morning, they're taking the early train for the short ride to Naples. The appointment with Giuliano is set for the afternoon. They haven't decided yet whether they're going to come back to Rome the same evening or spend the night in Naples at Clelia's

They choose a restaurant on Viale Trastevere. The menu appeals to them and the tables on the sidewalk promise a pleasant coolness. The waiter escorts them to a small table for two. As they sit down, Fusco notices that Valentina's expression changes from cheerful and relaxed to tense and angry. She's staring at someone seated behind his back. *Not, the kidnappers again, I hope.* He immediately turns around. It's a couple of Americans. The man is very tall, in his early forties, somewhat preppy looking. The woman is at least ten years older, extremely short, and wearing thick glasses.

"Who are they?" He wants to know why their presence is making Valentina so upset.

"I'll tell you later." She gets up and approaches the couple.

"Hello!" and she keeps on talking pretending to ignore their bewildered expressions. "Don't you think it would have been better to cooperate when I came to talk to you? That might have prevented Caterina's kidnapping."

CHAPTER TWELVE

THE ETRUSCAN PRINCESS

"Giuliano called early this morning," Clelia tells them as they walk into her apartment. "He decided the best way to do this is for him to come over for dinner tonight."

"Okay," Fusco says. "Is this the least dangerous way for him and everybody else?"

He almost misses the adventure of dressing up as someone he's not —some low life character. The dinner party sounds so tame, so bourgeois.

"Oh, I don't get to dress up," Valentina jokes. She, too, seems a little disappointed. "I was planning on wearing your blond wig, Nick."

"I wouldn't have let you wear it. That wig is mine!"

They spend the day resting and getting ready for the evening meeting. It is another hot day, but a cool breeze blows from the ocean toward Clelia's flowery balcony. Fusco spends a good part of the day sitting under the shade of the verdant plants on the small terrace, reading several newspapers they've purchased at the nearby paper kiosk and other news clips Clelia has put aside for them. He looks for articles about Caterina. There are many, both in the dailies and the weekly magazines. However, none provide any new and relevant information. Most articles seem to gloss over the important issues involved in the kidnapping—the criminal organization behind it, the request for ransom—and spend a lot of ink gossiping about the glamorous sides of the story—the heiress and the billionaire father.

After a nap in the early afternoon, Valentina moves to the kitchen to help Clelia and her housekeeper cook the meal and set the table. A feeling of normality settles inside the cool and elegant dwelling, Fusco notices. It almost feels as if the unpleasantness of the previous evening had never happened.

The images of the previous night at the restaurant in Trastevere flash through his mind as he listens to the women's cheerful chatter in the kitchen.

Valentina was standing tense and enraged as she addressed the two strangers, while the woman had pretended she didn't recognize her.

"Who are you?" she'd asked scornfully. "If you don't leave us alone, I'm going to call the police."

"You know very well who I am," an even more enraged Valentina had answered. "I came to talk to you almost a month ago, when Caterina Pedersoli first disappeared, and you refused to give me any information."

At this point the man had turned to Valentina. He stood up and pulled a chair for her, politely inviting her to join them.

"I'm Alistair Funkelfinkel," he'd introduced himself, even though Valentina had briefly met him a few years ago in Santa Corona. He was speaking with the tone of a person who wants to diffuse anger. "Would you like to join us for dinner?"

Fusco, who was observing the scene from a short distance, couldn't help being amazed at the couple's disparate behavior. The man was diplomacy personified, while his companion appeared to prefer the bully approach. Responding to his politeness, Valentina had changed her tone.

"Thank you," she'd said resisting his invitation to join them. "I'm having dinner with my fiancé. I just couldn't help remarking about Caterina's problem. She was my housemate and she's now in serious trouble."

"I'm aware of it," the man had answered, still standing, while Professor Novak, with her lips pursed stared at her wine glass. "We're so sorry. The reality is that we don't know and didn't know anything about Caterina. That's why my wife wasn't able to give you any information."

"You know, I doubt it." Valentina had said, still standing and now stepping back. "I have a feeling that professor Novak had some information, but wasn't willing to share it. Anyway, it's too late now…" She'd nodded to him and moved back to the table where Fusco was sitting.

"Just an impulse," she'd commented as if she wanted him to understand her sudden outburst.

"Those two are hiding something." She'd picked up the menu.

"I think you're right," Fusco had poured her some wine. "He's too polite and she's too rude. Who are they, anyway?"

Valentina had reminded him that Laura Novak used to be a Dean at Santa Corona, the UC campus where she had taught before moving to Santa Abelina. Novak subsequently acquired a much coveted appointment as director of the exchange program in Rome. He'd remembered then that Valentina had contacted her when Caterina first disappeared, and Novak refused to give her any information that might have helped her in finding her housemate. The polite man was Novak's husband.

What exactly were they hiding, though? He asks himself now, taking a shower and getting ready for the meeting that may bring them closer to finding Caterina. *The question is: Can we resume our vacation if we find her?*

Today, Caterina discovers the Intellectual's name.

"Hey, Franco," she hears one of the other jailers yell at him in the upstairs apartment. "Why are you getting her this good food?"

She doesn't hear his entire answer because, as usual, he talks softly. She gets the gist of it, though. Something like, "why not?" And then she hears his steps as he walks down into the basement. So, his name is Franco.

Today, besides the good food and a big bottle of mineral water, he brings her a book of short stories by Francesca Ramondino.

"I thought you might like it," he says fishing it out of the paper bag in which he carried her *mozzarella in carrozza*. "I heard you teach Italian literature."

For the first time in several weeks, she smiles. Someone has recognized her as a person with a job and professional interests—not just the heiress who can be bartered for a pile of money.

'Thank you. I like that writer."

"I thought you might."

"Has my father responded to the DVD?" she asks even though she knows Franco can't answer that question.

"I wouldn't know," he shakes his head. "And if I knew, I couldn't tell you."

He sits down in front of her. "How about making another DVD? It might help."

"No! Not today."

Not today. I've become too vulnerable. I can't talk to my father feeling the way I feel. Vulnerability is not something my father would understand. She would like to tell Franco all this, but instead, she shakes her head.

"Okay, some other time," he says and gets up to leave.

When she hears the door close after him, Caterina feels like she's been abandoned. *Stockholm syndrome,* she whispers to herself. I never knew what's like to depend on others so completely. I couldn't even imagine such a situation where every aspect of my life is dominated by others, where their cruelty can affect me so deeply, and even the slightest gesture of kindness can bring tears to my eyes. I've become a total puppet in their hands.

She eats tasty food and drinks the mineral water. Why does he go out of his way for her? Even the book now! She opens it and finds that he's marked some passages in pencil and scribbled some notes on the sides. More and more intrigued, she starts to read, trying to decipher his handwriting. It is clear this is a book which belongs to him. The notes are not for him though. They're written in English. "Be patient," Caterina reads. "Quite soon things are going to change. You've not been abandoned."

Not abandoned. That's what she needs to hear. Franco's trying to let her know that someone is trying to free her. *Why is he doing that?*

Last night, she woke up before dawn and couldn't go back to sleep. The memory of her kidnapping never abandons her. She will never stop blaming herself for not screaming when she felt the gun pointed against her back.

She was at the ticket counter at the Leonardo da Vinci International Airport. She was pleading with an employee.

"Anything, please!" She'd implored. "I need to get back to the States immediately. It's a family emergency," she'd lied.

"I'm sorry." The employee, a pretty brunette with bright red lipstick, had kept on staring at her computer. "I don't see any openings for today in coach."

"Then try in business or in first," Caterina had insisted even though she knew she couldn't afford to pay for either one.

"I've something in first class," the brunette had announced, relieved that she could finally accommodate her.

Caterina had handed her a credit card and it had bounced—insufficient funds!

"Try again tomorrow," the employee had tried to comfort her. "I checked every airline. Everything is booked today. Maybe, tomorrow, there might be a cancellation. Who knows!"

I don't have until tomorrow, Caterina had felt the urgency, as she'd started to move away from the counter.

"Come back later," the employee had suggested. "One never knows. There might be a cancellation, you know."

She'd walked toward the escalator, headed toward the upper floor where most of the restaurants were located. A cappuccino and something to eat seemed like modest goals for the moment. Then she might rethink her strategy. Maybe, she should go back to her apartment in Rome. Maybe, she should talk to someone. Valentina might be willing to help her. Maybe, she should talk to the police and tell them she felt threatened. She didn't need to tell them everything. She certainly wouldn't tell them her part in the scheme.

She'd ordered at the counter and then she sipped her cappuccino while still standing. *The passport!* Oh, shit! She'd left her passport in her room in Rome. She needed to go get it in any case. A cancellation might materialize later on. It wasn't even noon.

She'd looked around as she'd finished her cappuccino. The place was quite full. She'd walked toward the exit, headed toward the parking garage where she'd left her rented car. That's where they got her. Three men—two at her sides and one behind her with a gun pressing against her back. They'd pushed her inside a car. And that had marked the beginning of her new life.

Every night now she wakes up and, with her heart pounding, she lets the images of her kidnapping play in her mind's eye. How did she ever let this happen? Is she really not abandoned? With the eraser at the other tip of the pencil that he's left behind, she erases his words and hides the book under her mattress.

"I don't know what you're talking about." Jacqueline Speers looks puzzled.

"Some heads have to fall," Laurent Labauche, her lover and employer, repeats the same sentence over and over.

They are in his apartment, in his living room, waiting to go out for dinner, but they are standing, neither going out nor staying in.

To Labauche it seems clear that there has been some mismanagement in their operation. Someone has to pay for the mistakes. If it is true, as the Italian police contend, that some tomb raiders are involved in Caterina's kidnapping, then whoever is in charge of establishing contacts with the Etruscan raiders must have made some big mistakes.

"We're stuck, Laurent," she tries to make him reason. "We've paid Nicoletti and he's stopped talking with the police. More than that, I don't see what else we can do."

"Nicoletti, that bastard, has let the kidnappers use his house in Trevignano. He's sent us a signal."

"Didn't you tell me that they moved her?"

"Yes, they did. And that made things even worse. Instead of being held by petty criminals she's ended up in the hands of organized crime. At least, that's what it looks like."

Jacqueline sits down. There is no way they can discuss this in a restaurant.

"It seems like the tomb raiders are unhappy with us. They always complain that we don't pay them enough for their risks. Maybe the kidnapping was a way to let us know--to threaten us."

"But then why did they sell her down the river of organized crime?' Labauche feels frustrated by his inability to control a situation that is slipping out of his hands. Jacqueline seems unable to help him. Her sharp mind seems dull tonight. It is as if she's avoiding the issue.

"Organized crime must have offered them the money that we didn't give them," she suddenly blurts out.

He wishes she hadn't said that. She was the one in charge of dealing with the tomb raiders. She's the one who didn't pay them. He faces her with all his anger.

"Why didn't you pay them when they made their first request?"

"Look Laurent, you were the one who said your daughter could not be trusted. You suspected she might be involved in some scheme, a way to squeeze money out of you, a way to finance her drug habit."

He sits down too. He's feeling defeated. "When the first request came, it seemed something very unprofessionally put together. We didn't suspect the tomb raiders were involved in it."

Jacqueline puts her hand on his knee. "Maybe at first they weren't involved in it. They might have joined the kidnapping later."

"I may have to go to Italy in the next few weeks and face the music."

He feels he may have to give up the one who sustains him with her exultant beauty. Jacqueline doesn't even suspect the depth of his impending loss. Her interest in art is solely cerebral. His is an affair of the body, the emotions and the mind—an unrequited love, a true obsession.

Jacqueline stands. "Let's go out Laurent," she extends her hand toward him. "You need to eat."

The sound of the intercom marks the beginning of a new phase. At last, the much awaited guest has arrived. Fusco hears Clelia's quick steps resound on the marble floors.

"Yes, Carmine, let him park in my spot," Fusco hears her impart instructions to the attendant at the entrance of the gated community. "I've moved my car to Mrs. Cerciello's spot. She's being so kind to let me use it."

All these elaborate maneuvers had been arranged in the afternoon. The gated community, to which Clelia's condo belongs provides a parking spot for each condo owner. It's important for Giuliano not to have to park outside on the street, so Clelia traded parking spaces with a neighbor who doesn't own a car.. Less exposure meant less danger.

When the elevator stops at the fourth floor and the door opens, the young man who walks into the apartment is quite different from the totally circumspect thirty-something whom Fusco had met a week ago at the public library in Pozzuoli.

"How are you zia Clelia?" Giuliano greets his mother's friend with kisses on both cheeks and a bouquet of flowers. Fusco notices the *zia* (aunt) Giuliano uses to address a close family friend. Clelia is equally effusive toward him.

"I haven't seen you in so long, Giuliano! Your Mamma and I were so worried about you!" Then, turning toward Fusco and Valentina, she introduces them. "I want you to meet my dearest student and her fiancé. They live in California, and she teaches at the university and he's a captain with the police--a very good detective!"

The cordial tone is set and continues throughout dinner. At first, it doesn't look like they're ever going to talk about Caterina, but rather about the respective families, Naples, and the wonderful food. Giuliano is cheerful and relaxed. *Has he really infiltrated the Camorra?* Fusco wonders.

"So how did you meet Caterina?" Giuliano's question comes unexpectedly.

"We're colleagues in the same university," Valentina starts to explain.

She then continues by giving in concise terms all the background story of their acquaintance and Caterina's subsequent disappearance. Giuliano follows her tale with his sharp dark eyes, as if he didn't want to miss any details. He nods silently.

"We saw her being kidnapped at gunpoint at the Rome airport," Fusco interjects. "It was the day I arrived from the States."

"At that point, she'd already been missing for over two weeks," Valentina adds. "When we came back home from the airport, we found out that her room had been searched."

"Two days later we followed two odd guys that we had every reason to believe might be her kidnappers," Fusco volunteers more information. "As it turned out, she was kept captive in the basement of a house out in the sticks, near Bracciano lake."

"By the time the police arrived there, they had moved her," Valentina continues. "We don't know where she was moved. Nick told me that you know where they are keeping her and that she's in the hands of the Camorra."

Giuliano nods again and then sighs. He must be weighing how much he can share with us, Fusco reasons, observing him closely. Behind his appearance of a good Neapolitan young man from the upper middle class, Giuliano hides the depth of a man who has a big plan in mind.

"Yes," he nods again, staring at both of them with great seriousness. "Caterina is in the hands of the Camorra. I've seen her often. She's all right, considering her situation. I imagine the Camorra, at some point, must have taken over the operation. They've contacted her father in New York for a ransom. So far, no resolution is in sight."

There is something chilling in Giuliano's calm. *Should we trust him?* Fusco wonders. Why is he playing hard ball with the Camorra?

"Excuse my nosy question," Fusco says very politely. "Since you know all that, why aren't you calling in the Police?"

For the first time, since they've started talking about Caterina, Giuliano smiles. He has an almost shy and reserved smile.

"That's my problem," he acknowledges. "I infiltrated the Camorra just about a year ago. I've collected enough material to put together a large dossier. I know enough to really make a difference in the battle against organized crime."

"So you're afraid that, if you come out now, you may compromise all your work. Is that it?"

"That's one thing," Giuliano nods again. "The Camorra will also target me, my mother and my whole family. I'm working on getting police protection before I do anything."

"I understand." Fusco wants Giuliano to know that he appreciates his efforts and his dilemma. "But we're still very concerned about Caterina's life"

"I am, too. Believe me." Giuliano expresses his own deep and personal feelings. "That's why I'm here. We need to find a way out."

CHAPTER THIRTEEN

AN ACADEMIC GAME

"You want stuff, *principessa*?" The young punk Rosario, who's in charge today, pushes a bunch of pills toward her. "Don't be bashful! We've plenty of those here."

Caterina hesitates. She doesn't want them. She's done with them, but she doesn't want to hurt Rosario's feelings. She's afraid of his reaction. If she refuses he might feel slighted and his behavior might become out of control.

"Thank you," she says and grabs one. "I'll have it later."

"Please yourself!" he says.

He appears to be very young—no more than fourteen or fifteen. He speaks with a loud voice in the Neapolitan dialect of the poorest of the poor. He moves around with the jumping and nervous movements of a meth addict. He looks vulnerable and ready to explode. The gun, showing through his pants pockets, looks ominous. When he leaves, Caterina sighs with relief.

Drugs—she's over. The kidnapping has forced her into rehab. Not that she couldn't have obtained some drugs from her jailers—drugs are the only things not scarce in their circles. Somehow, having been concerned about her survival has distracted her from her obsession with drugs.

Suddenly, the little scandal she provoked at the Italian Exchange Center more than a month ago comes to her mind. She'd traded in weed, which Mickey Mouse provided her with in great abundance, for cocaine, which one of her male students peddled. Another student—a girl with red hair, freckles and a sanctimonious attitude—had reported her and her classmate to the director, Laura Novak.

Novak had called her into her office. The director had looked extremely embarrassed, as if she were the one responsible for the whole mess. She'd cleared her throat a few times and fidgeted with the papers on her desk, avoiding Caterina's eyes. It was clear that Novak didn't know how to broach the subject.

Caterina remembers that, at first, she'd no idea why she'd been called into the office.

"I need to talk to you about something a bit troubling," Novak had finally started, while gesturing with her hand for Caterina to sit down. "A student made some wild accusations against you."

"Me?" Caterina, who'd started to suspect why she'd been called in, decided to act very surprised as the best line of defense.

"Of course," Novak had hurried to reassure her. "I don't believe a word of it."

"What's the accusation?" Caterina had asked just to play on the safe side.

"Oh, you won't believe this!" Novak had giggled. "She says you peddled drugs."

"What an imagination!" Caterina had giggled too, even though she didn't think it was funny. "Who's this student?"

Novak had told her. "The solution is for you to stay away from the center for two weeks, while I change your courses with another teacher. When you come back, it will be forgotten."

The temporary suspension had turned out to be quite helpful. The first week she'd planned her first failed disappearance with Mickey Mouse.

How easy, she now thinks. *I got off the hook so easily.* Of course, Novak didn't have much of a choice. She didn't want to displease Jason Graves, who'd recommended Caterina to her. She knew how these things worked. She herself had been very accommodating with Dukakis, her supervisor in Santa Abelina. The poor schlemiel had a crush on her and had got himself busy trying to create a ladder job for her. She'd let him believe all year long that he might stand a chance with her. She'd even gone out with him when he'd stopped in Rome for a short visit. What a farce! The entire world of academia now appears to her so small and petty. That's another part of her life that appears so remote from the Caterina who's now captive in a basement in or near some part of Naples.

Isn't it amazing how situations and social circles can appear small, even though I'm viewing them from the tiniest and most constricted place I've ever been? Caterina wonders.

Life in Trastevere is almost like the vacation they'd dreamed of. Since they came back from Naples, Fusco's been telling himself that this is as good as it gets. A centrally located place in Rome, good food, visits to the Forums, cathedrals and the museums, strolls through enchanting verdant parks, picturesque neighborhoods—what else can we expect? I'm here with my love in this beautiful city. *If I could only chase away all worry about Caterina!*

"You know," he tells Valentina as they stroll through an idyllic park next to an ancient church on the Aventino hill, facing a breathtaking view of Rome below. "You know, my dilemma here is not a minor one."

"You mean Caterina's situation." She understands right away with her usual sharp perception.

They sit down on a marble bench.

"I've been a cop for too long to accept Giuliano's request without questions." Fusco pushes the pebbles nervously with his feet. "What if something happens to her? She's in the hands of dangerous people."

"He seemed to be aware of that," Valentina sighs. "The question is: what would happen to Giuliano and his mother if he reported the kidnapping without securing some police protection for himself?"

"More than anything he will have to make sure that he can stay anonymous once all he has discovered about the Camorra becomes public. He cannot keep on running all his life—not to mention the danger to his mother."

"So you're saying staying anonymous, maybe changing his name—that's more important than anything."

They get up and walk toward the railing of the view point. The river Tiber and the other side of town open up in front of them. From up high, Rome displays a timeless quality—the eternal city, as it is sometimes called. The sound of traffic rises up to the top of the hill muffled and distant, leaving the peace and tranquility of the Aventino hill untouched.

The memory of the evening with Giuliano surfaces in Fusco's

mind. *Who would have ever thought that I would meet such an unusual character during my Italian vacation?*

"Is there any way for the police to come and liberate her without creating a major slaughter?" Fusco had asked Giuliano, after they'd settled in Clelia's living room with their after dinner coffee.

"That's possible," Giuliano had nodded with an expression of deep concentration in his dark eyes. "There are times when I'm the only one in charge."

"Of course, you would have to disappear, immediately after freeing Caterina," Fusco had suggested.

"That's right, I would have to or else be eliminated shortly afterwards." Giuliano had smiled nervously. "As you can imagine, I do have a different identity for the Camorra—different name, profession and residence."

Even though he'd felt somewhat curious, Fusco hadn't asked him what his name, profession and residence were for the Camorra. The less you know the better, he'd thought then.

"When the police come to free her, my different identity won't help much," Giuliano had continued. "It won't take very long for the Camorra to trace me back to Giuliano Materassi, the journalist."

"Can't you create another identity—a third identity—to protect you and your mother from retaliation?" Fusco had felt the tension rise in the room. He'd looked at Valentina seated on the couch next to Clelia, across the room. Her usual liveliness had faded away. She was seated with her legs crouched underneath her, while she fidgeted with the hem of her red silk blouse.

"A third identity is what I'm expecting from the D.A.'s office," Giuliano had answered. "Luckily, I'd been working on that for a while, well before the kidnapping occurred."

"What about her father?" Valentina had interjected, bringing the discussion back to Caterina's survival. "Is he willing to pay the ransom?"

"That's somewhat complex," Giuliano had explained. "My English is certainly not perfect, so I may be wrong. What I gathered from the DVDs, which I recorded for the ransom request, the father/daughter relationship is troublesome to say the least. There has been major trauma in the past—stuff they haven't dealt with at all."

"I'm aware of that," Valentina had stretched her legs and sat up straight. "I already suspected problems when we were sharing the apartment a month ago. Then we found out that she'd even changed her last name, like she didn't want to be identified as his daughter. She didn't want to have anything to do with him."

"That's right! She feels her father neglected her and her mother, who must have died when Caterina was very young, from what I gathered from her communications with her father."

"The police in Rome told us the father is a major collector of Etruscan art." Fusco had contributed another piece of information. "Unfortunately, some of his best pieces come from tomb raiders. I wonder if that complicates the situation even more."

"It may," Giuliano had leaned forward, placing his elbows on his knees. "I'm not familiar with the petty crime connected with art smuggling, but I know that her first kidnappers were Etruscan tomb raiders."

"Why would they be involved in kidnapping her?" Fusco had wondered. "Were they unhappy with her father, maybe? He might have short changed them."

"Maybe," Giuliano had nodded. "From what I understand, Caterina walked into the trap quite recklessly. She made friends with small time criminals, minor drug dealers, tomb raiders and so on. They ended up selling her down the river."

"I was afraid for her from the beginning," Valentina had volunteered. "I noticed she was a drug user and she went out with odd people, some more so than others. Despite her apparent self-assurance, she was quite naïve."

The conversation had ended late at night with Giuliano promising that he would direct all his efforts toward a fast resolution of Caterina's kidnapping.

"I don't think there is imminent danger," he'd reassured them. "Even though the father hasn't responded to the ransom requests, there is a feeling this might still happen. Caterina asked him to travel to Italy. If that happens, things will evolve."

He'd promised them he would keep them posted.

"Look," Valentina brings him back to the present, pointing toward a large building right across the river. "That's Regina Coeli, the men's prison."

"Really?" Fusco glances at the map, which Valentina has spread open. "That's why the windows have iron bars."

"It's actually quite a model prison," Valentina informs him. "But still it's a prison."

"Would you like to see the inside of the church?" Fusco suggests, touching her elbow and moving away. *Enough with crime!*

It's amazing how differently we remember things, Labauche tells himself as he listens to Caterina's first DVD. "You're responsible for her death. Your cruelty and indifference caused it!" Caterina proclaims with relentless wrath. *Responsible, cruelty, indifference*—these three words reverberate in his mind day after day. He doesn't even need to listen to the DVD, but he does it over and over again. He's not surprised by Caterina's anger. Even though they haven't seen each other for twelve years, he knows that Caterina resents him and he's steeled himself against her feelings—whatever they might be. He's against any sentimentalism. For him life is hard, a tasteless hoax that we need to endure. Art is the only respite, as far as he's concerned.

But cruel, he's not. When Laura was diagnosed with cancer—quite a shock, given her young age—he offered to pay for all possible treatments. By then their relationship had gone down the drain. There was barely any love left. If she hadn't died, the marriage would have ended in divorce. Despite his insistence, she'd refused any treatment. Depression had taken over. Was he responsible for that? How so? He respected her decision. After all, the treatments might have been too painful to endure.

It takes two to keep a marriage afloat and two to sink it. The move to the States had been his attempt to save that marriage. He wanted to give her the opportunity to live up to his expectations. The practical side—a big promotion at the family bank—had been a further incentive to relocate to New York. Actually, it was Laura who had been the first one to call him indifferent. Not the most accurate word to describe his personality because indifference implies a lack of feelings. His was more the impossibility to access feelings, which reside in a sphere of their own in the remotest recesses of the mind. And she misunderstood his apparent coolness toward her.

Cruel he was not. Yet she had the power to make him violent. It only happened once, or maybe twice. It's hard for him to remember that and recognize that part of his personality as his own. She had the power to dig deep inside him and unleash parts of his being that he himself didn't know existed. Only then, in some perverse way, was she satisfied. Only then would she let it go.

What did she really want from him? "Feelings," she had shouted at him. "That's what I want from you!" Just as he had not been jealous of her flirting and infatuations, he'd expected her to let him have his affairs—just sexual stuff, of course. Her intensity, her jealousy and possessiveness had created a wall between them. He'd ended up drinking and womanizing too much, working too late, and displaying a behavior that matched her intensity if only on the surface. During the last few years of their marriage, they'd been on a course for disaster.

It had all started with a basic misunderstanding—art for life. He'd fallen for an Etruscan beauty, the human replica of an image on a vase or a plate. He'd endowed her in his imagination with all the qualities that one would imagine an Etruscan queen would have. Weren't Etruscan women famous for their permissive sexual behavior? Hadn't he noticed traces of this liberal attitude in the Florentine parks where lovers freely expressed their lust for each other? At first there had been lust in their relationship—lots of it.

The mistake had been the marriage after they'd conceived a daughter. That's when lust had not been enough for her. She had none of the regal and permissive behavior of her Etruscan distant ancestors. She was caught in a sentimental love dream. He realized it too late. Taking her away from Europe might have helped her in growing up— she was much younger than he was. That's what he had thought at the time, and had been so wrong. Sentimentalism was deeply ingrained in her. She'd expected feelings from him, just as he'd expected her to live up to her artistic equivalent—the Etruscan princess on the plate.

And now, twenty years later, his daughter shouts at him, with the intensity that echoes back to her mother. "Your lack of feelings," she accuses him, "that's what killed her! Your lack of feelings might deprive me of my life at my young age!"

Labauche turns off the DVD player and walks down the hall to the secret room where his only true love awaits him. She has no demands for him, no expectations—except a lifelong devotion and unyielding adoration.

"What could I have done?" Laura Novak feels frustrated. "Given the situation, what was there to do?"

"You should have been more diplomatic, Laura."

Her husband, Alistair Funklefinkel, feels equally frustrated and a bit concerned. The situation might explode any minute now and involve them in a shady affair, which they'd never asked to have anything to do with. And partly, this is due to Laura's inflexible behavior.

Fearing unpleasant encounters, they've been cooped up in their apartment in Trastevere and haven't been out to eat in their favorite restaurant for almost a week.

"Easy for you to say!" Laura complains. She gets up and paces back and forth like a caged tiger. "Here comes this low level academic woman demanding explanations, which I had no duty to give her. And what difference would it have made to talk to her? Tell me that!"

"It might have avoided a police investigation, for one thing."

"The police came and went," she rebuts. "I didn't tell them a thing and they didn't find a thing."

"That's all very well. I just wonder whether telling them what you knew would have been helpful in finding Caterina. Why all the damn secrecy?"

Laura now goes from frustration to wrath. How on earth can he be so naïve? Why doesn't he see all the work she's done on his behalf.

"The secrecy, you say? Do you know who Caterina is? Do you know who stands behind her?"

Alistair nods and sighs. Yes, he knows.

"Okay, I agree. You were in a delicate situation. To tell the police about the drugs Caterina had brought into the Italian Exchange Center…

"Not to mention the drugs she bought from the students," she hastily interrupts him.

"Right!" Alistair agrees. "To tell the police all that might have opened a box full of worms and it might have been embarrassing for Jason Graves…"

"Who's the one who recommended her to me and basically made me hire her for the summer job," she can't restrain from reminding him how things really stand.

"I know how obliged you are to Graves. He is after all the one who's behind this entire Italian program abroad."

"Not to mention all the help he's given us in your career," she interrupts him again.

How can he forget that? She'd better remind him.

"What I'm trying to say is that talking to Snupia when she came to ask you about her apartment mate might have been helpful."

"How could I tell her that, after finding out her roommate was trafficking in drugs, I had asked her to stay away for a couple of weeks, until I decided what to do with the students involved? That was none of her business. I didn't feel I could trust her, given our past history."

Alistair looks puzzled for a moment.

"Past history?" he repeats. "You mean the lecture that you didn't want her to give many years ago back in Santa Corona, right? See, that's the problem. You should have been more diplomatic with her back then and let your differences slide later on. You could have said that there had been some problems and Caterina was not teaching that week and your secretary had got confused and called her. That's all you needed to say."

"Maybe so," she agrees, too tired to continue arguing. "I guess I panicked because of the drug episode. I didn't know her. She was not part of our circle. I couldn't trust her. I tend to cling to hierarchy, as it should be and I forget that that's not a very practical thing to do sometimes."

"And the other night, there was no need to threaten her with calling the police," Alistair continues. "In retrospect, it might not have been such an outlandish idea to let Snupia know that you knew that her apartment mate was in danger."

The memory of the unpleasant scene when Caterina had come to appeal for help is still troubling for Laura.

"Oh, no! How could I have told Snupia that Caterina had shared with me her fear of a possible kidnapping? That's like an admission of guilt."

"You're right! That would have made you too vulnerable," Alistair now strikes a more conciliatory tone. "After all, there was nothing you could have done. When Caterina came to ask for help you were caught between a rock and a hard place."

"As an administrator I had to choose to protect the Center and the entire Foreign Exchange program from a scandal," she proclaims vehemently. "I have my allegiances."

Alistair nods approvingly. "Yes, I agree. The only thing I ask is that next time you run into Snupia, please be polite and diplomatic."

"Luckily, you handled it well the other night," she acknowledges, sitting down. No point in arguing after all. "Let's go out anyway."

"Yeah, there are many restaurants in Rome."

They get up, still hesitant, and with an air of complicity, they open the front door.

CHAPTER FOURTEEN
A DARING PLAN

So much time to think, sleep and dream—memories take over, night and day. Caterina's energy is gradually fading. Lack of air, light and movement are starting to take their toll on her body. Her mind, though, is hyperactive in a quite different way than it used to be. Emotions she had always managed to keep at bay are now running the show. Dreams are vivid and haunting. Memories of long passed moments of her childhood take hold of her throughout the eventless days.

What ever happened to those girls I used to play with at the farm in Tuscany? Caterina wonders. The sunny days of those long gone summers find their way in her mind's eye. Oh, to be so happy, playing for hours with total abandonment! Running up and down the hills, through the fields, calling each other, laughing out with wholehearted joy—*that was the last time I was happy and innocent.*

Nonna Tina has been dead for at least fifteen years. Caterina had lost touch with her after that last summer in Tuscany. Once they'd moved to the States, her family had never gone back to Italy. Grandma hadn't come to Mamma's funeral in the States. When Caterina had started to study Italian in college and to travel to Italy every summer, she'd never gone back to the farm. By then, Nonna had passed away. Caterina was told that Nonna had never recovered from her daughter's premature death. *Who told me that?* As she searches her memory, a slip of paper emerges—a letter sent by an aunt. But what had happened to all those little girls, her cousins, her playmates, and the rest of the family? She'd erased them, locked them out and refused to have anything to do with them. *What do I need them for?* That's how she'd felt then. It was as if opening that door—her mother's family door—would invite in a flood of emotions she didn't want to deal with. Much easier to pretend there was no family, no ties to them and deny the very existence of her own feelings.

Suddenly, the most awful memory, which haunts her to this day: her parents fighting in the room next door, her mother crying, her father hitting her. *Where were we then?* It must have been after we moved to the States. She sees herself as a nine year old, running outside in the backyard of their house in Connecticut, her hands covering her ears.

I never adjusted. Now the truth of her deep isolation stares her in the face. What about all the success—the private schools, the Ivy League colleges, the high grades, the connections, the promise of a career—what about all that? For the first time, she recognizes the split at the center of her being. *I'm not that one, the one who lived that life of success in the States.* I'm this one, the victim, the prisoner, the loner —her present condition seems more authentic despite all its horror. Who was that arrogant bitch who navigated academia? Who was that blonde woman who spouted presumptuous sentences and who put out such an effort in creating the void around herself? Caterina doesn't recognize her any more.

The realization of her total maladjustment comes with deep pain. She feels heartbroken, as if she were participating at the memorial service of someone so close that her departure from the earthly plane cannot be without dire consequences for those left behind.

She's so absorbed in her inner process that she doesn't even hear Franco's steps. Caterina is almost startled by his presence when she spots him walking down into the basement.

"What's going on?" he notices her somber mood.

She doesn't know what to answer. She can't stop her tears from coursing down her cheeks.

Now the situation is clear. It couldn't be more so. Laurent Labauche walks through Central Park. His place has become unbearable—the walls closing in on him. Even the inner sanctum, the room of the Etruscan princess, has turned against him. There is no pleasure left for him, no respite. The park is not much better. The open air used to distract him and relax him. That's why he'd bought his residence right across from the meadows. Today he can't even focus on the natural setting—the lanes with runners huffing and puffing, the verdant slopes declining toward the waters of the lake and the high-rise buildings bordering one side of the public property. He sees it all but nothing registers with him.

After the phone call, everything is clear. What he suspected, what the police suspected is now clear. The kidnappers are connected with the tomb raiders—Pietro Nicoletti, in particular, that son of a bitch, whom he has paid to keep his mouth shut. He now wants more. He wants it all back. It makes total sense that the amount the kidnappers initially requested is exactly the same as the price he paid for his pieces, including the plate of the princess. And that's what they want back, the plate, the centerpiece. Nicoletti— Labauche is now sure he's behind all this—must need the plate to exchange for his freedom. Emissaries from the Italian Justice Department had contacted Labauche a few months ago.

"Charges against Speers, your curator, may be dropped, should the plate, widely known as the Etruscan princess, be promptly returned to its location."

He'd decided against it. He'd paid for the plate a more than fair amount. If there were issues of justice, it was the duty of the Italian Justice system to take care of. Why didn't the Italians crack down on the tomb raiders? Unable to handle their criminals, they turned against collectors like him. The Etruscan princess was his and his alone. He wasn't going to give up what gave him so much delight. He'd paid for it. But money wasn't the real problem. It was so much more.

Returning the plate would have set him and his curator free to travel to Italy. But that's another issue. Did he really want to go back to Italy? Leaving aside Caterina's kidnapping, he has no desire to go back there. The country he used to love no longer exists. Destroyed by dishonest politicians, organized crime and a humongous influx of immigrants, the Italy of his youth has disappeared.

Now, because of his refusal to deal with the Italian Justice department, the police must have turned to Nicoletti and offered him a deal. *Put pressure on the American*, they must have said *and we will release you*. And Nicoletti, cooped up in his tiny downtown Rome apartment for two years now, must have come up with a plan. Now, Labauche knows what that's all about. He's paid Nicoletti to keep his mouth shut—to no avail. The *schmuck* requests more because he wants it all.

Labauche has been told the Neapolitan Camorra is holding Caterina captive. But the Camorra wouldn't trade an Etruscan plate against his daughter, would they? Or maybe they would. He ignores how deep the link between the tomb raiders and organized crime is. There is a lot he doesn't know.

The phone call last night has set in motion a train of thought that he's unable to stop—a true obsession. Everything has shifted. It's no longer the plate against his freedom to go back to Italy. No, now it's the plate against his daughter—an impossible trade in. *How can I give up the object of my delight for a daughter I haven't seen for twelve years?* He keeps asking himself. *And how can I not?* It all comes to that.

"You give us the plate," a muffled voice had said on the phone, "and we give you back your daughter."

Even common criminals assume that a daughter is well worth a plate. The thought keeps surfacing in his mind, no matter how much he tries to reason it out and chase it away. *It's a false choice,* he tells himself. Just a few weeks ago, another muffled voice had requested a large sum of money for ransom. Why have they changed their demands? Are we dealing with the same group of kidnappers? A little over a month ago the initial ransom had been much more modest. The clumsy way in which that first request had been delivered—an email from an Italian yahoo address—had seemed more like a hoax than the beginning of a nightmare.

Labauche has been told that Caterina has changed hands. She's gone from petty thieves to hardened kidnappers and to organized crime—the danger for her life gradually increasing. That might explain the changing demands and the steeper and steeper ransoms. It also makes sense regarding what he suspects to be Nicoletti's involvement in the dirty deal. How he feels, though, is beyond understanding. His body feels heavy and his legs seem unable to sustain him. He collapses on a park bench and hides his face in his hands. For the first time since his childhood, he bursts into irrepressible sobs.

The distant sound of the waterfall feels refreshing and extremely appealing after a hot day. Fusco and Valentina had hit the excavation site of the Villa di Adriano in Tivoli very early in the morning, trying to avoid large crowds and intense heat. The remains of the Roman emperor's magnificent villa extend over a wide terrain in the midst of a very bucolic countryside.

"You can only imagine what it must have been," Valentina commented, pointing to the floor mosaics.

"It's amazing how well kept the floors are," Fusco rejoined, "even though the walls have for the most part collapsed."

Valentina had read about the history of the place from the guide book. *What a belated education I'm getting.* Fusco had felt grateful for Valentina's higher level of education.

Despite their best intentions to stay longer, by ten o'clock, they surrendered. The first tourist bus had just poured its human content at the entrance of the site as the morning breeze had died out.

"Let's go to town," Fusco suggested. "Let's go cool off with a cold drink."

Even Valentina, a relentless excavation fan, had given up as the first wave of noisy tourists had washed in.

"A cold drink doesn't do much for me," she'd objected, "but a *granita di caffe* would hit the spot."

"I'll go for that." *Of course, Valentina's sweet tooth never fails,* Fusco had observed.

After a pause in a ventilated caffe in downtown Tivoli, they'd moved to the Renaissance palace where thick walls provided natural air conditioning. They'd taken their time exploring room after room of artifacts ,which were a testament to several generations of privilege and refinement.

Now, they descend to the geometrically designed Renaissance gardens surrounding the Palace. The large rectangular pools collecting the waters at the center of the park give off a cool and refreshing feeling.

As they proceed on the path flanking the long rectangular fountains, Fusco and Valentina hold hands. The approaching sound of the waterfall is now a roar.

"Let's go behind it, inside the grotto!" Valentina is excited.

"We're going to get all wet!"

Fusco points to a couple on their way back from the cove. Their hair dripping and moist clothes sticking to their bodies, they walk past them, smiling happily.

"I don't mind getting wet," Valentina strides toward the grotto. "Do you?"

"Well," Fusco agrees. "It's a hot day. We're going to dry out right away."

The cave behind the waterfall is cool and moist, with the slippery ground covered by moss. Trying to keep her balance, Valentina grasps

Fusco's arm. *What an enchantingly uncanny view*. Fusco admires the rectilinear cut plants and the large basin of the fountain, through the thick wall of swiftly descending glistening liquid. The deafening roar of the gushing waters covers their words to each other. Yet, the gypsy music of Valentina's cell phone tones come faintly through.

"Later," Valentina sighs. "I'll check it later."

"Why did you invite him over?" Fusco asks, sweating near the boiling pot of water for the pasta.

Even with all the windows of the apartment open and the ceiling ventilator going at full speed in the tiny living room, it is too hot to cook dinner. *Why on earth didn't she ask Giuliano to meet them at a nearby pizzeria?*

"Well, he said he was in Rome for the day," Valentina stirs the sauce. "It's not that I wanted us to die cooking. After all, we bought most of the food already made at the *rosticceria*. I was concerned about something else."

"What?" Fusco chuckles and salts the water. "Were you afraid of the Camorra following us?"

"Not unlikely," Valentina tastes the sauce and then adds salt. "We should learn from our enemies' mistakes."

"What're you talking about?" He lowers the flame under the boiling water and adds salt.

"Remember how much information we got from those two stupid kidnappers at the lake restaurant?"

Who could forget it! *And what we did with the information! Who could forget that adventure!*

"So you must have decided that you preferred to die of heat rather than be shot by organized crime." They both laugh.

The doorbell rings.

Later, in bed, they're still wide awake despite the late hour. The conversation with Giuliano comes back to haunt them.

"A little breeze is starting right now." Fusco would like to avoid talking about what they've learnt tonight. *Tomorrow, there will be time, tomorrow.*

"Il *ponentino*," Valentina says and Fusco looks at her surprised. "That's what they call it here in Rome this wind that arrives late in the night during summer."

She must not want to discuss what we've heard and what we've been asked to do, Fusco reasons. But as he tries to fall asleep, enjoying the *ponentino*, even more now that he knows its name, Fusco can't chase away Giuliano's words. "The only way is to kidnap her."

At first, everything had been cordial and jovial. Fusco had opened the door and they'd shaken hands.

"So nice to see you both again!" Giuliano had walked in holding a bottle of wine and a carton of ice cream in his hands

"Oh, hazelnut and zabaglione! My two favorite flavors," Valentina had exclaimed smiling radiantly, receiving his gifts. Then showing him inside, she'd added, "I was so surprised to hear your voice this afternoon. We didn't know you worked in Rome."

"Normally, I don't," Giuliano had sat down on the small couch. "I cover the Neapolitan local news. There is a parliamentary law now being discussed that concerns Naples. So my newspaper sent me here to report."

"Does your director know that you've infiltrated the Camorra?" Fusco had asked.

"Of course, I had to tell him. He's letting me work less. Still my name needs to appear regularly, not only because I want to keep my job, but also to diffuse suspicions."

Fusco had gotten up to drain the pasta water in the sink in the kitchen area of the room, while Valentina poured wine and offered Giuliano an appetizer.

"Have you seen Caterina recently?" she'd inquired.

"Yes," Giuliano's appeared concerned. "She's all right, everything considered. But at times she's starting to crack up, to break down emotionally…"

"It must be so hard." Valentina had sipped her wine. "Any end in sight? Has her father responded to the ransom request?"

"Not only has he not responded but the request has changed."

"What?" Fusco had just walked back toward the couch. He was afraid he'd misunderstood.

"Yeah," Giuliano had confirmed. "There has been an unforeseen development. As you may know, Laurent Labauche, Caterina's father, is somehow connected with illegal trafficking of stolen art objects from the Etruscan area. Both the Justice and Art Departments have been putting pressure on Labauche and his curator to return some pieces. All to no avail, so far! One of the main illegal dealers was tried and is now in house arrest, due to health problems. The rumor has it that the judge in charge of his case is offering him a special deal. If he can convince Labauche to return some pieces, the time he has to serve will be greatly reduced."

"How is this connected with Caterina and her ransom?" Valentina had just come back from the kitchen with a bowl of pasta, which she'd placed on the dining table.

They'd all moved to the table, where Valentina had dished out the pasta.

"These are just conjectures, of course," Giuliano had started to explain in-between morsels of pasta.

"Well, you're a journalist," Valentina had joked. "Conjectures are part of your job."

Giuliano had smiled. "That's right! But I hope to back them up with facts. So the other day, one of the punks, who's in charge of Caterina, said that he heard they'd contacted Labauche demanding that he send back a very precious plate, which seems to be the centerpiece of his collection, in exchange for his daughter."

"You mean an art objec?" Fusco had been again afraid of misunderstanding, "an art object instead of the hefty sum of money they'd previously requested?"

"Isn't that strange?" Valentina had observed. "I didn't know the Camorra dealt in art."

"I'm not sure it does," Giuliano had answered. "But the coincidence was striking. Now the issue is, who is behind all this? If the art dealer—his name is Nicoletti—is the one making the request, he will have to return the plate to the Italian authorities. Right?"

"Right!" Fusco had agreed. "In that case, the Camorra would get nothing."

"It doesn't make sense," Valentina had gotten up to bring more food to the table. "Not only would the Camorra get nothing, but Caterina would not be freed."

"She would be in great danger." Giuliano had stared at them with anguish in his dark eyes.

"Have you spoken to the police?" Fusco had asked insistently. "You must do it, at this point!"

Giuliano had nodded. "Yes, I've spoken to the police and told them the location where she's kept. The problem is that the punks in charge are a couple of trigger-happy heavily overdosed types who wouldn't think twice about going on a shooting rampage. That might end up in a massacre."

"Caterina might get killed!" Valentina had exclaimed with emotion, her eyes clouded with tears.

"Do you see a solution?" Fusco had asked. "Are you ever alone with her?"

"Yes, I often am, but not long enough to allow time for a police operation. Also, I never know when I'm going to be alone in the house. The only solution I see is to kidnap her myself. But I would need some help.

That's where things got complicated, Fusco sighs and turns around in bed, determined to fall asleep. *Like hell I'm going to put Valentina in danger!*

"It would only take a moment. You would need to wait for me in the car outside the house," Giuliano had pleaded.

Like hell! Sorry, but I'm here on vacation. He turns around once more to face Valentina.

"We should consider it," an unexpectedly awake Valentina tells him. "It's not a bad plan."

"Let's not talk about it now, Sweetie," he sighs again, snuggling up to her. "Let's try and get some sleep."

CHAPTER FIFTEEN

AN UNUSUAL ROMANCE

He's been gone a week, Caterina notices—a week with punks and teenage addicts, a week of potential violence and explosive tempers. *Maybe, they relocated him and I will never see him again.* The thought darts through her mind and the sense of loss startles her. She never even suspected that she might become so dependent on another person —on drugs, yes, on people, no! Not that she hasn't experienced passion and obsessions for men and occasionally women, but they were always linked to drugs, transient in nature, swiftly burnt out— here today, gone tomorrow!

This one has been platonic so far and it should stay that way. *Just another Stockholm syndrome,* she reassures herself. It's not uncommon for captives to develop feelings for their captors and even accept mistreatments as if they were well deserved punishments. But Franco has never mistreated her—quite the contrary! Unlike the punks, he's provided her with warm showers, clean clothes, tasty and healthy food, and even a book. *I may never see him again.* Fear creeps in, too. What's going to happen to her? She's in the hands of the most dangerous people.

Then, just as an unexpected shower of rain lifts the heaviness of an extremely hot day, he reappears. First, she hears his voice coming from upstairs. It is unmistakably his voice, even though he speaks in a loud Neapolitan dialect to one of the jailers, imitating their rough cadences.

"Yes," he says. "You can go! I'll stay here the rest of the day."

"Okay," the young punk answers. "I'll get to snatch a couple of purses."

"Great!" Franco encourages him. "A little action! Aren't you bored to death staying here all day?"

"Luckily," the punk answers. "I have these."

"Yeah! Who could live without them?"

They must allude to the drugs, Caterina decides. She's become quite good at understanding their conversations in their dialect. At first, she couldn't make out a single word. Valentina—the memory of her roommate in Rome, darts through her mind—, she was so good at all Italian dialects. *Where is she now?* She's probably on vacation with her boyfriend and has completely forgotten about me, her hideous roommate. Their Roman cohabitation seems so remote!

She hears a motorcycle roar away—the punk must have left. A few minutes later, Franco appears on the steps of the cellar. Except that, now he has a face—a dark short beard, curly hair and the deep compassionate eyes she's known for a few weeks.

"Why did you take your mask off?" she shouts, standing up, she doesn't know why.

"Do you want me to put it back on?" he asks jokingly.

And she can see the cheerful person that he must be at times. They burst out laughing.

"It's just that it's so different," she tries to explain.

"It's unexpected," he talks now with his usual calm and low voice —the tone of a person who spends lots of time in his mind.

She nods, but she still doesn't know why he's come back as a person rather than a jailer. She doesn't dare ask because of the role he's played for her for weeks. You don't demand explanations from jailers.

"I'm taking a chance," he says, his eyes becoming very serious. "Not only because now you know my face, but especially because of the things I need to tell you."

"Who are you?" she suddenly knows.

He hesitates, because he must have been hiding a long time. She knows that, too. He hesitates out of habit—the habit of hiding. She walks toward him, her hands outstretched.

"Caterina," he's now determined to talk. "I'm not your jailer. I've infiltrated Camorra."

It makes total sense now. She'd nicknamed him, the Intellectual, before she knew his name. How come they haven't found him out? He's so out of place. Yet, she remembers having heard him speak the coarse language of her jailers. He must have great talent for imitation, for impersonating characters that are not who he is.

"Who are you then?" Now she can ask.

He tells her everything—the long year pretending to be a Camorra worker in the high fashion industry, yes, haute couture. He tells her of the dossier he's prepared and recently delivered to the police. He's waiting to be included in the witness protection program. When that happens, he tells her, he has to leave immediately and start a new life somewhere else. He wants to free her before he's removed from Naples. The police have been alerted as to her whereabouts and they are waiting for the right moment to intervene.

"My father is not going to pay my ransom, is he?" Her voice breaks when she asks.

"No, I don't think so," he holds her hand when he explains it to her. "He wouldn't be able to anyway. His account in Italy is frozen and he has problems of his own with the Italian Justice department."

They hear some noise upstairs. One of the punks must have returned. Franco gets up and walks toward the stairs.

"I need to go to my other life," he smiles, almost amused.

Caterina follows him to the foot of the stairs. He turns around and hugs her. She kisses him on the mouth.

They can't agree on anything, but they both want to spend a few days in Cinque Terre before Fusco flies back to California.

"Then," Valentina suggests impulsively, Why don't we just grab the bare necessities and leave now?"

She feels they need to move. Discussions are useless. After all, neither one of them really knows what's the best decision. She understands why Nick is cautious. One doesn't play hard ball with the Camorra. Yet, she's not ready to call herself out. For now, they need to take time off.

"All right!" Fusco gets up and starts packing.

They throw a few items in their rented car and drive all day to Levanto, arriving just in time to admire the sunset on the waters of the bay. They find a room to rent for the night in a bed and breakfast inside the old *borgo*—the ancient village that developed on a steep hill facing the bay. The castle towers over the hamlet.

"Apparently," Valentina reads now from the guide book while they're waiting for their pizzas in a small restaurant close to the water. "Apparently, this coast was particularly inspiring for the English Romantic poets."

"I can imagine why." Fusco takes in the serenity of the place—the small picturesque town on one side and the low coast on the other.

The following morning they start their exploration. They drive to the first *terra* and then they travel by train, on foot, by bus, on foot again, and by train. They hike along the coast from one *terra* to the next, from one quaint village to another, climbing the steep alleys and stairs that lead to towers looking down to hidden coves and shimmering blue waters. In the evening, they rent a room in one village and spend the night in a quiet and dark community. The following morning they continue their hikes and train rides back to the first *terra*.

"This little vacation," Valentina observes as they walk holding hands toward their car. "This vacation was so needed!"

Yet despite her optimistic evaluation of these three days of vacation, she knows that the heavy weight has not been lifted. They've been by themselves in an absolutely enchanting place. A positive outcome is still possible. *Everything will work out*, she repeats to herself ,but she knows that the quiet between them simply means that they've been thinking, withdrawing into their own separate worlds. A chasm is between them. How did we ever come to this place of separation when we have felt so often like one breathing organism? The night in the forest behind Trevignano comes to her mind, when they discovered Caterina chained and resting on a mattress on the floor of a dark cellar. They'd felt like one heart beating and one mind thinking when they were rushing inside the thick forest seeking a fast escape from the armed thug who might be pursuing them. And now, in front of this overwhelming beauty of bright colors—the sea, the steep coastline, the picturesque villages—in front of all the dazzling splendor of Cinque Terre, they could not be further apart.

The 'Caterina issue,' as Nick calls it, has epitomized all their differences. Valentina feels that her spontaneous and intuitive way of reacting to life and its challenges clashes with Fusco's rational and cautious planning. But how can he be so prudent and hesitant in front of a situation that calls for immediate action? She understands the difference in their backgrounds has influenced who they've become and how they react. However, that difference now weighs heavily on her. It has revealed to her a side of her lover's personality that seems incompatible with her own. How can I commit, she wonders, to someone who's so different from me? And yet, how can I not commit to someone I love so deeply, someone I've felt so closely connected to?

As he drives back toward Rome, at the wheel for a change, Fusco wonders if the short vacation to Cinque Terre has done anything to lift the heaviness and resolve the conflict. Before they left, the only thing they could agree on was that they needed a break to reach a point of clarity.

"How can we refuse to save a life?" Valentina had argued the day after Giuliano's visit to their Rome apartment.

"How can we risk our lives?" He'd argued back. And what he'd really meant was: how can I risk your life?

"Why don't you want to even consider it?" She'd promptly responded, not even guessing the sub-text of his concern. "You've solved so many cases and saved so many lives."

That's right. Why was he so cautious, after more than twenty years spent risking his life and solving case after case? Why was he so hesitant in saving this one life?

"I solved cases and saved lives with the help of a well-trained team," he'd tried to explain to her. "Here, I don't have a team and the case is not mine."

"So unless you're appointed by a chief of police, you don't feel you have a moral responsibility to do anything. Is that it?" Her slightly raised voice showed her anger and frustration.

No, that wasn't it. He's not a maverick, but he can make independent decisions. She knows better than accusing him of subservience to the system. But he's not reckless either. The Italian police can solve the case and save Caterina, using the information that Giuliano can provide them.

"Let's not fight over this." He'd tried to diffuse her anger and avoid being sucked into a useless discussion. "We need some time off."

That's how they'd decided to leave for a few days. Cinque Terre, where neither one of them had ever been before, seemed like the ideal destination. *Has it helped solve our conflict?* Fusco wonders as he drives into the night, approaching the Rome exit. They've avoided discussions, as they'd agreed before leaving for their short vacation, but have they reconciled their differences? *I doubt it,* he concludes.

He's always known that they have differences—personalities, backgrounds and life choices. But aren't Valentina's spontaneity, generosity and intuition the qualities that have enlivened his existence? Aren't they the perfect complement to each other? *Tomorrow, the solution will present itself,* Fusco decides as he parks the car in Trastevere.

Walking in the park early in the morning is becoming a habit. Labauche leaves his place at the crack of dawn. He crosses the street and strides swiftly down the gravelly paths. Only one thought is on his mind. *I have to get used to life without the princess.* He now knows the separation is inevitable. Instead of spending more time with the plate, which was once the object of his delight, he's avoiding it. Lately, he's admitted to himself, the pleasure of sitting in its presence has decreased.

Why is that? He wonders as he speeds up on the path toward the lake. The portrait of the female head is no less beautiful and the art is no less exquisite. It's his response to the princess that, at some point, has shifted. Instead of admiring solely the art and extracting pleasure from the fine execution, he's allowed himself to sink to the lowest denominator. He's let his imagination get the best of him and his emotions sway him. He's found himself trying to conjure up the unimaginable. *Who is she?* He's visualized her jumping from the plate and moving around the room, his residence and even New York City. She seemed to follow him around in his office, in his car, never leaving his mind. He's removed her from her historical and cultural context and placed her in his contemporary reality.

He spots the lake at a distance. The ducks are waking up and waddling on the meadow. He feels the urge to sit close to the water and figure out his feelings. He admits that his attachment to the figure on the plate is tinged with a deeply personal tone. She's no longer an art object. She's a person who runs his life.

He's had many affairs and three failed marriages. Yet women-- lovers, wives and his only daughter--have never exerted much power over him. *Am I losing my mind?* The thought distresses him. He's always prided himself on his ability to keep calm in the face of adversities—the banking debacle, the various financial meltdowns and stock market crashes. Nothing has ever shaken him to the core—even family issues. His ability to detach from hardships and withdraw into his own personal inner sanctuary has kept him sane all these years. His knowledge and appreciation of art has saved him. It has provided him with a place to go during times when other business people could find no respite. He's always been able to detach from all transient things and lose himself in the everlasting world of ancient art. What has attracted him to artifacts coming from excavation sites, as opposed to modern and contemporary art, is that they've already proven their lasting status. They've survived longer than he can possibly survive. Owning them, and creating a daily dialog, with them, are his only claims to transcendence.

Now the issue is that what has always kept him sane has become unbalancing. It is claiming power over him as if his adoration were not enough. A lifetime of devotion appears to be insufficient. Labauche sits on a bench facing the lake. The princess on the Etruscan plate is special. It's the only piece he's ever kept in his own residence rather than his private collection. He even had to create a room that would be adequate for her specific needs of preservation—not to mention the insurance nightmare that he had to go through. *Why her? Why has he personified the figure on the plate?* His head leaning on his hands, his elbows planted on his knees, he asks those questions over and over again. He's sane enough to ask them, but not enough to answer them.

What am I going to do with my daughter? The thought darts through his mind. Not only is the sum of the ransom preposterous, but even if he were to give in, the modality of the payment would be extremely complicated and almost impossible. His bank account in Italy is frozen. His curator would be immediately arrested if she set foot in Italy and even though his legal status is not equally dire, he's facing some major inquiries. Unless he returns the princess he can't really go back to Italy.

But this isn't the real issue. *What's really the ransom? Is it the money or the plate?* He gets up, heading back toward his residence. He hears the noise of traffic in the still distant street. Manhattan is waking up. Some joggers join him on the path, huffing and puffing along. Suddenly, Labauche knows what to do. The outcome is uncertain, but he knows what to do. By the time he reaches Fifth Avenue, the traffic has picked up. As he waits at the light, he decides he'll phone his contact at the Italian Art Ministry. *The princess has to go.* He needs to negotiate her return.

His housekeeper has made coffee. He smells the fragrance as he opens the door of his residence and walks in. It's seven, so he can call his secretary and ask her to book him a flight to Rome for tomorrow—first class, of course.

CHAPTER SIXTEEN

A DIFFICULT CHOICE

She'd intended the kiss to be a sign of friendship and admiration for his heroism. He'd responded to it—full moist lips and male sexual energy—turning it into something else. His hug, which had started as affectionate and friendly, had ended into a tight and passionate embrace. When they'd released each other—the loud music played by the punk upstairs getting louder by the minute—their eyes had locked into an expression of longing and desire. Then he'd rushed upstairs, turning rapidly into the other person, the underdog Neapolitan with a loud voice and coarse dialect. She's heard him shout a vulgar epithet to the young jailer just minutes after he'd emerged from her cellar. It had left her uneasy to hear him rebound so fast, when she was quivering, with her emotions dancing through her body and mind. She had to stretch on her mattress hugging her pillow, pushing back tears.

What have I got myself into? She wonders now, the following morning. She'd always prided herself with her ability to separate sex from deeper emotions. Promiscuous, some might have called her. To her, her ability to enjoy sex with multiple partners without attachments was her defense in her high-risk life. She gambled enough with drugs

—she knew that. She couldn't afford to lose herself in passion. When feelings started to interfere with her casual relationships, she'd always managed to call herself out. *What's happening now? Why is this different?*

She knows the situation is extreme. Her survival hangs by a thread. She's been a prisoner for almost a month, living day by day under the thumb of unbalanced strangers. Her schedule is determined by their whims. They feed her what they want and when they feel like it. They've never cleaned the toilet in the cellar. They've never walked her upstairs to take a shower. They've never washed her clothes or changed the sheet on her mattress. The only person who has treated her with compassion is Franco. Now she knows why. He's not a Camorra criminal. He's a journalist who's infiltrated organized crime. He's stumbled onto her kidnapping by mere chance. She's reacting with gratitude to his kindness. She admires his courage. *Nothing more. And a kiss is just a kiss.*

The sound of steps upstairs announces activity. Whoever was guarding her during the night is now awake. They're flushing toilets. She hears a muffled dialogue. There must be two of them. She smells the aroma of coffee. They're going to bring her some food, if she's lucky. Then, the roar of an approaching motorcycle, followed by the dying out of the engine, announces the arrival of a third person. She hears his voice in his criminal impersonation.

"Franco," the jailer called Nunzio shouts, "are you going to stay here this morning?"

"Yeah, Nunzio," Franco shouts back. "You can go. Snatch a few handbags. Have fun!"

"What about me?" the other punk asks. "I'm out of stuff. I need to get some more."

"Yeah, Carmine," Franco answers again in his loud voice and coarse dialect. "Go get some stuff and bring it back here this afternoon."

"You gonna push it?"

"You bet I am!" Franco's voice reassures him. "In my neighborhood it sells like hot cakes."

He must have invented a whole fictitious existence—dealing drugs, living the petty criminal life.

"Are you going to feed the princess down there?" Nunzio asks him after a short while.

"Yeah, I'll take care of that! You can go."

After she's heard them leave—their motorcycles roaring away— it takes him a few minutes to walk down. *Why is my heart pounding like this?* She feels like a teenager at her first crush.

He steps down with a cup of coffee in one hand and a tray of fragrant Neapolitan pastries in the other.

"Good morning!" he smiles, talking with his usual sing-song. "How are you today?"

He sits down next to her on the floor. He hands her the cup of freshly brewed coffee and places the tray of *sfogliatelle* and *baba`* between them.

The cellar suddenly becomes a park where they're having a summer picnic.

Today it's about communication, Fusco sighs. As soon as they wake up, the day after their return from Cinque Terre, Valentina announces that she wants to call Franca on Zoom.

"We haven't heard from them for ten days," *Them* includes Franca, her husband Bill and of course Pippo—Fusco's and Valentina's rescued dog, the mongrel they adopted earlier this year.

"I hope Pippo is behaving and isn't chasing Nero around," Fusco remarks, knowing well that the intended telephone call is going to be mostly about their pet and his relationship with Franca's cat.

"He was behaving acceptably well last time I called." Valentina gets up and heads for the bathroom.

"One never knows with Pippo." Fusco turns on the flame under the espresso coffee pot. "He always has one up his sleeve."

They both chuckle remembering their pet's escapades.

"I really miss that little scoundrel," Valentina admits, opening the refrigerator and looking inside for something to eat for breakfast.

"You haven't seen him for two months and it will be at least another month before you see him again."

As he says that, the thought of their impending separation hits home for him. Valentina must have come to the same realization because she looks at him with a suddenly melancholic expression.

They sit down in front of their respective computers before the heater turns on its flame on the Roman streets. While Valentina settles down in front of her computer and opens her Zoom account, Fusco checks his emails. After impatiently erasing hundreds of messages, he notices an unknown sender. G.Materassi@lasera.com it reads. Oh, no! Fusco sighs, *not him again!* But it's him, the Giuliano Materassi he's come to dread. He can't be ignored. Fusco and Valentina haven't talked about him or Caterina's ordeal for four days. The vacation is over. He'd better open the email. It's dated today. Giuliano has written it at the crack of dawn.

"*Dear Nick and Valentina,*" the message reads, "*I thought I'd drop you a line to inform you of some recent developments. A colleague of mine, who is in the know in the Justice Department, has just informed me that Caterina's father is on his way to Italy. He's negotiating a deal with the Art and the Justice Departments. In exchange for his immediate return of an Etruscan plate, which his curator bought from an illegal dealer (a tomb raider), he's asking that all charges be dropped against him and his curator. I'm not sure what that means for Caterina's future. Let's keep in touch. Ciao, Giuliano*"

What does that mean for Caterina's future? That's right! That is the question. Fusco turns to Valentina, who's having a pleasant chat via Zoom with her best friend, Franca, in California.

"So is Pippo chasing your cat? … Oh, he stopped doing that… *Meno male!*" She hesitates and turns around to face Fusco, who's observing her. "Just a moment, Franca," she interrupts the conversation, "It looks like Nick just read some interesting message on his email."

Fusco gestures for her to read Giuliano's message. She puts down her head set and trots over to Fusco's computer. Then she goes back to her computer and resumes her conversation with Franca.

"Yes, it is about Caterina. Let me drop you an email so you can read the recent news."

Fusco nods in approval. She's doing the right thing, using caution. They forward Giuliano's message to Franca, with a few comments about the evolving situation. Fusco then listens for a few minutes to Valentina's lively conversation with Franca. She's telling her about their vacation, omitting any details concerning Caterina. She's learning to be prudent, he notices.

Fusco answers Giuliano's email: "*Dear Giuliano, thanks for the information. I have no idea what that means for Caterina's future. I think the situation might evolve very rapidly. Her father may bring the money for her ransom. That may be one possibility. By returning stolen goods he's buying his way into Italy. He doesn't need to use his currently frozen account. It looks like he doesn't want to give his art piece to organized crime. If that's the case, good for him! You also mentioned another piece of information during our conversation a few days ago. The imprisoned art dealer, who's being pressured by the authorities to put the screws on Labauche,—that might be another piece of the puzzle. Labauche may not want to give in to the blackmail, for reasons of his own. I'm just guessing. What I would like to know now is what do you think is going to happen? We're back from our vacation. I'm getting ready to go back to work in California in less than a week. Let's keep in touch, preferably by phone. Ciao, Nick*"

Valentina is now sitting down at the kitchen table and checking the messages on her cell phone. As they'd agreed before leaving for Cinque Terre, she'd turned it off and kept it off during their entire trip. Now, she turns it on and finds one message—it's from Clelia, who left it yesterday. "Valentina," Clelia says in her rather loud telephone voice, "Giuliano's been trying to reach you. Call him. It might be urgent."

Valentina gets up and walks toward the bedroom. *She must have decided something.* Fusco recognizes the meaning of her movements.

"Let's do the wash today and then go back to Naples tomorrow," Valentina announces.

She grabs their soiled clothes from their still undone backpacks and drags them from the bedroom to the bathroom. She fills up the washing machine.

"Newspaper, sir?" The hostess offers Labauche a selection of international newspapers.

Labauche grabs an Italian newspaper, La Republica, and spreads out the page about Italian criminal life. He hopes to find news about his daughter. Nothing that he doesn't know already, he sighs with disappointment. The focus of the news seems to have turned to his trip to Italy and the return of the Etruscan princess—a great victory for the Italian Art Department.

"Something to drink, sir?" the hostess hands him the list of spirits.

"A whiskey, a Chivas, please" he hands her back the list without even glancing over it.

That's what he likes to drink when he has to face a long journey into the night. In seven hours, in the early morning, he'll be in Rome. The princess will follow in a couple of days. The movers are at work in his residence packing the plate with the utmost care and under Jacqueline Spiers' watchful supervision. He's picked the most reliable moving firm in New York, the one he uses for his pieces in the private collection. They're going to work in great secrecy, transporting it to the airport before dawn. It will take at least a day for the red tape to be completed and for the princess to start her return trip. *At least she won't end up in the hands of organized crime. At least, not her!*

It's a good thing he doesn't have to be there and supervise the operation. He couldn't stand it.

"You go to Rome," Jacqueline had told him yesterday. "I'll take care of everything."

"You're sure?" he'd inquired looking at her with a serious expression. "It's a big job."

"I don't mind, believe me," she'd stared back with equal seriousness. "It's the least I can do."

"What do you mean?" he'd asked intuitively knowing what she meant. He'd felt the sudden urge to hear her say it.

"It's my return ticket to Italy," and she'd smiled for the first time in weeks.

He'd felt good that she'd said that much. She'd never admitted it to him, but she must have felt uncomfortable when the Italian Justice Department had indicted her. Not only was it a tremendous humiliation, which had stained her reputation in the New York art world, but it also meant that she could not return to Italy unless she wanted to face a trial and a possible prison term. That must have been hard for her. Unlike him, Jacqueline didn't mind the negative changes in Italian society. She ignored them. For her Italy was the place where she could pursue her lifelong intellectual interest. Nothing else mattered.

"So," he'd remarked, "you think I'm doing the right thing by returning the plate."

"You're doing the right thing," she'd nodded.

Even though they'd been lovers for several years and had shared a common passion for Etruscan art for decades, they'd never talked about their private feelings. They were both very reserved and regarded expressions of emotions as something slightly indecent. He'd never told her what the ordeal he'd faced during the last weeks had meant for him. He hadn't mentioned to her Caterina's DVDs and the inner storm they'd unleashed. She might have guessed something, but she'd never brought it up.

"Flight attendants prepare for takeoff," the captain announces.

The journey is starting. Even though he has to admit that the thought of giving up the princess feels like a major loss, he's satisfied that at least he's not giving in to the request for ransom from organized crime. If Nicoletti is behind the scam, so much the better! If the tomb raider had been pressured by the Justice Department, Labauche had taken away his only chance to buy his freedom.

"You can be assured," his contact at the Italian Art Department had insisted yesterday during their phone conversation, "there won't be any problem for you when you arrive in Italy. The moment the plate reaches Rome, I will ask the judge in charge of the case to drop charges against your curator."

Promising, he'd thought after their chat. Yet, the main problem remains untouched. *Have I done the right thing?* By saving the princess on the plate from the Camorra, he might have compromised his daughter's safety. What if Nicoletti was behind her kidnapping from the very beginning? What if he was connected with the Camorra? Tomb raiders are usually petty thieves, not professional criminals. But in today's changing mores who knows how the geography of crime has evolved. *What if my righteous rage against the dishonest dealer backfires against my daughter? What if I protected the art piece and lost the human subject?*

Thoughts dart through his mind and keep him awake for most of the flight. When he doses off, confusing dreams wake him up again and again. In one dream, the figure on the plate bears Caterina's suffering face—the elongated dark eyes filled with sadness beyond description. In another dream, his daughter's accusing monologue, which he's listened to so many times, becomes an inchoate scream with unclear words and piercing sounds. Right before dawn, in a light dream, his daughter appears to him as a frightened young child. "Why are you afraid?" he asks in a rather irritated tone. "It's because you're yelling at Mamma," the child answers.

The lights are on now and the hostess goes by with the breakfast tray.

"Coffee or tea, sir?"

By the time they land, he's decided to send instructions to hold the shipment of the plate until he has a better grasp of the situation.

At the passport check point, a tall gentleman, who appears to be in his fifties, is waiting for him.

"Mr. Labauche? I'm Pasquale Del Chiaro," he introduces himself. "I'm from the Questura. I need to talk to you about your daughter."

CHAPTER SEVENTEEN

AN UNEXPECTED REVERSAL

The cellar is getting darker and darker. The scant light seeping through the sole tiny window underneath the ceiling is getting faint in the early hours of the evening. The space closes in around Caterina. The gray walls look even gloomier and sadder, while the air feels stale. She misses him already and doesn't even know when and if she will ever see him again. He has a life outside, she doesn't have any. Nobody could call her existence in captivity a real life.

I'm still an adolescent, Caterina tells herself. *I'm acting like one, I'm feeling like one. I even have a crush like a teenager.* She's reached that conclusion after reviewing in her mind the morning hours she's spent with Giuliano—sitting on the floor as if it were grass in a park, holding hands, kissing lightly on the lips, sharing her secret feelings and her life history. And no sex. Yes, no sex! For the first time, she's felt that it would have been too soon. He must have felt that way, too. The place wasn't very conducive. The jailers might come back at any time. And eventually they did, but it was almost afternoon. By then, Giuliano and Caterina had been talking for hours. He'd told her his real name.

Have I ever been an adolescent? She wonders. She has vivid and painful memories of her childhood. After her mother's death, everything is a blur. She'd withdrawn into her room, studying more than was needed to pass her classes with honors. In college she'd started to experiment with drugs and with sex—finding a secret place in which to channel her rage and grief. Maybe, that had been her way to be an adolescent—a lifestyle that the kidnapping and imprisonment had abruptly ended. But the hesitant, clumsy and tender aspect of adolescence—that she'd never experienced. She'd never had a high-school sweetheart and not even a bosom friend. After school, she would go back home, straight to her room. Her father was mostly absent and when he was there she used to avoid him. He'd remarried just months after her mother's death and then promptly divorced. Caterina hadn't even had the time to acquaint herself with his new wife and her children from a previous marriage before they disappeared. He'd had a series of partners, but never seemed to settle down.

They'd moved to Manhattan. She remembers the residence across from Central Park, where her father still lives. It was in those years— the last years she'd spent under the same roof with him—that he'd created the private collection of Etruscan art and funneled all his energy into it. It now strikes her as ironic that all those pieces, for which her father seems to feel such passion, came from the same general area where her mother was born and brought up. Unable to relate to the human Etruscan, he'd devoted the best part of his life to the ancient art of her region. Now, as she remembers those years, she's filled with sadness for herself, but also for that cold and impossible man who happens to be her father.

"He's a difficult person" she'd told Giuliano this morning, "a withdrawn and unhappy person, whose only real interest is Etruscan art."

"It must have been difficult for you to grow up like that," Giuliano had remarked, holding her hand. "It's a little hard for me to imagine that. I grew up in a large family. I'm the youngest of four. My siblings are all married and have children. I'm *a zio*. When we all get together for festivities there are so many of us. It's so noisy and joyful. We're a typical Neapolitan family, I guess—except for one thing. My father was a judge and was killed by the Camorra."

That's when her eyes had filled with tears of admiration. Instead of running away from danger, in spite of the fact that he'd experienced what it is like to be the victim, he was facing the Camorra and challenging it.

He had briefly mentioned that he was expecting to be included in a witness protection program and be transferred to some safe place soon.

What's going to happen to me, then? She'd thought but hadn't asked.

"We'll get you out of here before then." He'd read her thoughts.

Then he'd told her the most extraordinary thing.

"Do you remember your apartment mate when you were in Rome?" he'd asked her.

"Of course, I do." She'd felt almost embarrassed remembering how rude and distant she'd been to that friendly and cheerful woman. "She's a nice Sicilian woman who teaches at Santa Abelina University, just like me, but in a different department. She's a film specialist. Valentina Snupia is her name. She's a pretty brunette."

"That's her," Giuliano had nodded.

"How do you know her?"

"She's been looking for you ever since you've disappeared."

Caterina had pressed her hands against her cheeks feeling totally blown away. During the last month, she'd been feeling so completely isolated from the external world that the thought of people from outside being interested in her fate seemed preposterous.

He'd told her that Valentina and Fusco had witnessed her being kidnapped at the Leonardo da Vinci airport. They'd looked for her and followed her kidnappers to a country house near the Bracciano lake. They'd discovered her. The kidnappers had been alerted by their presence and fired a gunshot after them. They'd saved themselves by the skin of their teeth. The police had arrived at the location too late. She'd been moved to Marano, near Naples, where she was now. Listening to Giulano's tale, Caterina had felt overwhelmed.

"I can't believe it," she'd whispered. Then, the memories of her kidnapping and the first few days of her imprisonment had rushed back. It had been almost too much to take in.

"I met Valentina and Nick in a totally serendipitous way," she'd heard Giuliano say. "My mother's best friend, a retired high school teacher, had them over as her guests. They told her about their adventures with your kidnapping. They suspected that you might have ended up in Naples. Clelia mentioned my activity and they became interested in meeting me."

There is a world out there, the thought has kept repeating in her mind, *and I'm part of it.*

Now, listening to her boisterous jailers upstairs, she tries to quiet her mind and calm her anxiety, by revisiting that morning's breakfast on the imaginary grass of a fantasy park, where she'd flirted with Giuliano, her teenage sweetheart.

The hotel faces the park, Villa Borghese--a huge extension of wooded terrain covering a large section of downtown Rome. When he'd asked his secretary to make the reservation, Labauche had asked her to avoid the hotels in Via Veneto. In the past, he'd stayed there and found them filled with old world charm but too noisy. The street they're on stays awake all night, bristling with life and entertainment from various night clubs, restaurants and cafes. With jet lag and his present state of anxiety, he knew even before he left New York that he was going to need a quieter place. The Albergo del Parco is super modern and heavily air conditioned—a relief from the intense heat outside—somewhat anonymous, even though quite luxurious, and further away from downtown, built in the midst of a quiet upper class neighborhood. *Not too different from where I come from,* Labauche notices looking out of the window opening onto the park.

By the time he settles in, it's already evening. He has to meet the officials from the art department for dinner. He's suggested the hotel restaurant—a more private, quieter location than any other place in the nearby downtown. He needs to retire early. Tomorrow, he has a full agenda.

"I need to talk to you about your daughter," the man in gray from the *Questura* told him at the airport. Labauche knew that the Questura, which is under the jurisdiction of the Ministry of Interior, was the highest police authority in Italy.

The man must have seen his alarmed expression, because he'd added. "She's alive, and we know where they are keeping her."

After Labauche had retrieved his luggage and had gone through a perfunctory customs check, they'd gotten in an official car that was waiting for them outside the arrival terminal, and headed toward the city. The man in gray had then told him about Caterina. A police informant had found her. She was in the hands of a Neapolitan Camorra family. The Questura in Naples was planning a police operation to free her. They had to use caution.

"So is it the Camorra that kidnapped her?" Labauche had asked. *Why did they want the princess plate, then?* It was still hard to let go of his precious possession.

"We believe that her initial kidnappers were small-time criminals associated with some tomb raiders. Later, they must have sold her to a larger criminal organization."

"Why did they request the plate of the Etruscan princess as ransom?"

"There might be a connection…" the man in gray had been vague. It was clear he didn't want to give out too many details. "You're doing the right thing by returning the piece," he'd added with a reassuring expression. "You're taking that out of the equation."

They had then left the highway that runs around town tracing the round shape of a ring, the so called Circonvallazione Anulare, and they were now crossing a working class neighborhood.

"I'm concerned I might make it more dangerous for my daughter," Labauche had said after a short pause. He was hesitant in sharing his doubts with the police.

"I understand your concern," the man in gray had told him in his polite but distant tone. "This is why we're planning the police operation as soon as possible."

He had then asked Labauche about the return of the princess.

"It has been arranged," Labauche had reassured him. "I can give you all the details. I would like to have it arrive in Italy after my daughter has been released from the hands of the Camorra."

"I understand your concern," the man in gray had repeated. "I will relay your worries to the *Questore*."

Before they'd dropped him off at the *Albergo del Parco,* the man in gray had arranged for Labauche to meet with the *Questore*, his boss, the following morning.

With still a few hours to go before his final engagement of the day —the dinner with a sotto-segretario from the Art History Ministry— Labauche talks to Jacqueline Spiers on Zoom.

"They packaged the plate and brought it to the airport," she tells him before he even asks. "The red tape will take a few days."

"Hold it!" He now wants her to wait. He tells her why.

At the dinner with the sotto-segretario from the Art History Ministry, Labauche is diplomacy personified. He bargains and pleads for a few more days, providing all sorts of reassurance of his good intentions.

"We at the Labauche Collection were not aware of the whereabouts of the plate. We thought it was a legitimate operation. We're ready to return the piece and let justice take its course."

The sotto-segretario, too, is diplomatic, but he also stresses the necessity to return the piece as soon as possible. That's the only way to allow Labauche the immunity that he needs. The dinner ends on uncertain terms.

The following morning the phone rings and wakes him up. He picks up thinking that it might be some further communication from some Italian official.

"We know where you are," a gruff and muffled voice greets him.

"Don't play games with us. Don't you dare return the plate to the authorities! If you want to see your daughter alive, deliver it to us. We will contact you with instructions."

He hangs up.

Labauche sits up in bed, his head in his hands, and breathes heavily. He doesn't know whether he wants to see his daughter again, but he wants for her to be alive. A few minutes ago, he was still debating how to convince the Art Ministry officers that a short delay returning the plate would be the best strategy, the one that might save his daughter's life. Now, he knows that he has to stick to his guns and do it in the most public way.

The traffic on the *Autostrada del Sole*—the Sunshine Highway—is rather heavy on the last weekend of July. Even though Fusco and Valentina left Rome early in an attempt to beat both the summer heat and the vacationing crowds, the throng of cars thickens as they approach the Naples exits.

"Maybe," Valentina sighs impatiently watching the long lines of vehicles, "maybe, we should have followed Clelia's advice and left the car in Rome."

"Yes and no," Fusco argues. "There will be problems with the traffic in Naples, not only here. But there are also some advantages in having a car..."

"You're thinking in terms of our mobility with Giuliano's plan, I guess."

"Yes, that's for sure," Fusco nods. "I also didn't feel right in leaving the car parked in the street for days while we were gone. But yes, the car gives us some autonomy."

The details of Giuliano's plan, Valentina ponders as traffic inches along, are still unknown. The previous night's phone call had left so much unsaid and unsettled. The police still seemed unsure on how to proceed, and were in any case bound by secrecy. That's what Giuliano had told them. The few things he knew came from his so-called sources connected with the Neapolitan Questura—the highest police authority in the city. There were at least two different versions of the planned police operation. Neither one of them was totally clear, nor safe. Actually both versions appeared extremely dangerous for Caterina's safety. And then there was Giuliano's plan.

Are we doing the right thing? Valentina has been obsessing about it since last night. She has been tossing and turning, unable to sleep. Her cheerful enthusiasm is all but gone now. She turns to Nick, who is perusing a Naples street map. He seems so calm—serious, but calm. *Are we doing the right thing?* She's the one who's been campaigning for action from the very beginning. He's been the cautious one, the one who just wanted to have a fun vacation in Italy. Up until last night, those were their roles. And then there has been a role reversal. *Is that what is making me so uncomfortable?* Valentina wonders, while she drives through the *casello*, the highway exit for Naples. She also wonders why Giuliano's phone conversation with them has overcome Fusco's resistance. What has made him trust the journalist's plan? And why on earth has she lost her courage? She focuses all her attention on the heavy traffic as they approach the city. *What has ever pushed me into this mess? Why do I want to run away from it now?*

Even her body is reacting strangely to the stress. She's feeling nauseous and strangely tired and unfocused—very strange sensations for her. She's always enjoyed a good appetite, but this morning the thought of food feels totally repulsive. Her energy level, too, has changed. Her natural liveliness seems gone. *It feels like I'm trying to protect myself,* she notices. How strange! She even wonders if she should call herself out. And as that thought crosses her mind, she feels like a coward—very unlike herself.

"Are you all right?" Nick had asked her this morning. "You had such a hard time getting up and now you don't want to eat breakfast. What's going on, Baby?"

"Oh, I'll be alright," she'd said trying to sip on some tea. "I guess, I'm having some last minute jitters," she'd admitted.

She remembers now that her period is a bit late this month. If she didn't know that conceiving is basically impossible for her, she might think that her strange symptoms are due to a pregnancy. But she knows better than that. Unfortunately, she concludes, all this nausea and fatigue are simply stress combined with PMS. *That's it!*

"I'm so glad to see you," a very excited Clelia opens the door to Fusco and Valentina.

After the short ride on the highway from Rome and the longer than expected drive through the very congested Neapolitan traffic, Fusco finds Clelia's apartment a cool and pleasant oasis in the midst of chaos.

Clelia ushers them into her elegant and semi-dark living room. "Would you like some ice tea?" she offers. "Carmela has made a peach-flavored one that's quite delicious."

The ice tea sounds good and Clelia's chirpy mood is even more refreshing for Fusco.

"You've added a new dimension to my life," Clelia declares as she comes back from the kitchen with a tray filled with tall glasses of ice tea, and some homemade cookies too. "Even though I'm not really doing much, I feel like a character in that TV program with Angela Lansbury…you know that one who writes thrillers and is always solving crimes…"

"Oh, *Murder She Wrote*," Valentina laughs for the first time this morning. "That's the American title of the series."

"*La signora in giallo*" Clelia remembers. "That's how they translated it here. Just by relating phone calls and observing you three in action is so exciting for me. Before you two came into my life, I was feeling quite bored. The courses at the *Università per la terza età*, the university for old people, and the occasional canasta with my women friends are nothing to get one excited, you know?"

Valentina laughs again, sipping the ice tea carefully, but still refusing the cookie that Clelia offers her. "Well, Clelia, I don't believe your life has ever been boring," she points out. "You've always been so busy, so engaged in so many volunteer work and cultural activities. We may have just spiced it up for you a bit more."

Fusco notices with relief that Valentina is gaining back some of her usual liveliness. He's very concerned about her. He's noticed in the last few days that she's more tired. The worry about Caterina's survival, and the extreme heat, are taking a toll on her, for sure. But this morning she's been unable to eat and that's really unusual for Valentina. It's okay if she's scared of the ordeal they're themselves involved in. That would be quite understandable. It's just that there has been almost a reversal of roles. She, who was the one so gung-ho in pursuing the freeing of Caterina, is now more cautious. Fusco feels instead the usual adrenaline push that he's experienced so many times when action approaches and a case is just about to be solved. Not that this is my case, he has to remind himself, but still at this point he feels totally involved. Something happened after he read Giuliano's email and then talked to him on the phone. A still uncertain plan started to materialize in his mind. While they were driving on the highway, he was figuring out the details. Valentina instead seemed uncomfortable and very quiet. What a reversal of roles!

He overhears her talk to Clelia in the kitchen, while he settles down in the guest room right across the hallway.

"Could I have a cracker?" Valentina asks. "That might help me with the nausea."

"Nausea?" Clelia sounds very surprised. "Are you pregnant, kid?"

"Oh, I wish!" Valentina sighs. "No! I think it's just the stress of this situation. And my period is a bit late."

"Pardon my nosey question," Clelia continues paying no attention to Valentina's explanation. "But why don't you want to marry him? He's such a nice man and he adores you."

"I love him, too."

"If you want a family, the time to start it it's now. How old are you?"

"Thirty-eight," Valentina answers, "but I've never been able to get pregnant."

"What about now?" Clelia is relentless. "The nausea…"

"Oh, no! I'm sure it's just a false alarm"

So that's what's going on, Fusco reasons—a false alarm. I have to be extremely cautious in planning this operation.

"Let's listen to this," he hears Clelia say as the very low volume of the radio suddenly escalates.

Laurent Labauche, the well-known billionaire and father of kidnapped heiress Caterina Pedersoli, has arrived in Rome. Fusco hears the radio announcer blare now, as he crosses the hallway and enters the kitchen. Valentina and Clelia are sitting at the table, huddled around the small wireless radio and, as he walks in, they motion to him to get closer.

This morning, during a press conference, the announcer continues, *Labauche declared that, even though he is prepared to return the plate widely known as the Etruscan Princess to the Italian authorities, he will not do it until his daughter is released by the kidnappers who have been holding her for almost a month.*

"*I'm prepared to return the plate to the Italian authorities,*" Labauche speaks Italian with a French accent. "*But I don't want that to get in the way of my daughter's liberation. That's the most important thing for me.*"

"*Monsieur Labauche,*" an interviewer interjects. "*You seem to have changed your mind on this issue. You had previously declared that you were here in Italy to return the plate and clear your name. Why this reversal of position?*"

"*I can't comment on that now.*" Labauche sounds determined. "*I'm here to take care of my daughter's release.*"

There has been a rumor that the kidnappers might have been requesting the plate as a ransom, the radio announcer comments, *but there is no way to verify the rumor at this point.*

So that's where we stand now, Fusco reasons. He looks at Valentina and they exchange a knowing glance. They don't need to talk.

"When is Giuliano going to show up?" Fusco asks Clelia.

"At one thirty. He's coming for lunch." Clelia gets up. "I'd better let Carmela use the kitchen and prepare the meal. She doesn't want anybody around when she cooks."

At one thirty, the last details of the plan will be hammered out, Fusco decides, as they all move to the living room. Labauche's statement has changed a few things. *At one thirty, I will release my own statement.*

CHAPTER EIGHTEEN

SHE CAN'T BE PREGNANT

The cellar is dark, small and stuffy, but Caterina is determined to make the most of it. She plans to walk around its narrow perimeter fifty times several times a day. If she's going to stride out of her jail, she must be strong enough to walk and maybe even run. After a month of captivity, her legs are frail and her energy level very low. The first few weeks, she'd let herself go, lying on her mattress on the floor, napping or reminiscing, going inside, figuring out her messy life. There had been days when she felt she had no future, and holding on to her past had been the only way to keep some sense of identity. *I'm Caterina Pedersoli, previously known as Catherine Labauche, the one who did this and that.* Now, she has to reacquaint herself with her own body. No more idling around. She's never been particularly athletic. She never needed to watch her figure. She could eat a high carbohydrate diet and still be thin as a reed.

"Lucky you," Valentina, her apartment mate in Rome, had said one evening, watching her gobble up a pizza, "I would have to think twice. I gain weight so easily."

Now, she remembers the few times they'd spent together, during their first week in Rome. How unpleasant she had been to Valentina.

Why was I such a bitch? And to a person who appeared to be so friendly and so decent. *That's the first person to whom I'll need to make amends.* I still don't know how. As she walks around in circles inside her cell, Caterina imagines the world outside. The sky is clear, the air is clean and she looks more like the person she used to be. She wears clean and almost elegant clothes. Her hair is combed and a little longer than it is now. Even though the outside is not all that different from what it used to be in the past, her inner reality has changed. She sees herself walking up to Valentina. She's capable now of walking up to a person like Valentina and saying: "I'm sorry. I was a bitch. I don't deserve your friendship, but please forgive my rudeness. And thank you for caring for me and my survival."

The usual noise upstairs signals the presence of her jailers. Nunzio and Ciro exchange vulgar epithets and boast their sexual prowess.

"Hey, Ciro! I bet you can't fuck worth a damn."

"You have no idea how many women I fucked last night. I can last forever!"

Then they move to their criminal achievements.

"I sold so much coke and pills!" Nunzio boasts.

"I snatched five purses in one hour!" Ciro rejoins.

It's a miracle that they haven't done anything to me, Caterina sighs. My high commercial value and the sporadic, but oh, so important presence of Giuliano in the apartment upstairs have saved me from rape and other violence.

"What's going to happen to the princess downstairs?" She hears Nunzio ask. "Her father has arrived."

"He won't give the plate to the authorities," Ciro announces in his loud voice. "I bet he's going to give it to us."

"Where did you hear that?"

"On the radio this morning," Ciro is the one who knows things and he's proud of it. "He said it on the radio."

"What are they going to do with the princess?"

"Wouldn't you want to fuck her before they let her go?"

Oh, God, please don't do that! Caterina's heartbeat speeds up.

"No, not my type," Nunzio proclaims. "She's too scrawny."

Oh, good. My scrawniness saves me.

"Franco fucks her. He digs that type," Nunzio adds.

"That's why he buys her all that food. He's trying to fatten her up," Ciro comments. "He must be tired of fucking all those bones." And they both laugh at their own jokes.

Let them laugh, Caterina sighs with relief. At least, they don't lust after me. She rests before she starts a new cycle of exercise. I need to build myself up, she repeats. *I need to walk to my freedom.*

The familiar sound of Giuliano's scooter interrupts the exchange of vulgarity upstairs.

"I didn't know Franco was going to show up today," Ciro remarks.

"He wants to do a quickie with the *Principessa*," Nunzio laughs.

"Hey, you guys" Caterina hears Giuliano walk in.

"Franco, are you going to stay here this morning?"

"No, I have another thing," Giuliano answers. "Just a quick thing."

"I told you so," and Nunzio and Ciro laugh. "A quickie."

She hears all three of them laugh. For a moment, she's hurt by his joining their rough mirth, but then she immediately realizes that for her safety, for his own safety, he needs to have another persona—Franco who fucks the princess.

A few minutes later, he walks downstairs in her cellar. He kisses her on the mouth and then asks her for some information. Luckily, she knows the answer.

The Skype call comes unexpectedly in the early afternoon. The voice is reassuring. The accent is unmistakably from New York. He's a police detective from California, he says. He wants to help. He needs to talk to him as soon as possible. Even hours matter at this point, the voice insists. Your daughter's life is at stake. Let's meet this evening in a safe place.

Labauche knows his daughter's life is at stake. He knows even hours matter. The Questura assured him that they are preparing an operation, but they need to be cautious to avoid a bloodbath, which might involve Caterina. How can he trust this guy? Who is he anyway? Why does he want to help?

"My girlfriend was Caterina's apartment mate in Rome," the voice explains. "We saw her being kidnapped at the airport. We've been trying to find her ever since."

"How much do you want?" Everything has a price in Labauche's world. It's better to cut to the chase.

"Absolutely nothing!" the voice proclaims emphatically. "I'm calling to ask for your cooperation, not your money."

They settle it. They're going to meet in a few hours in his suite. Any other place would be too public and too dangerous for both of them. Now he needs a bodyguard. Who is this Fusco guy anyway?

Since his public statement this morning, Labauche has been under constant pressure. The Art Ministry has sent him an envoy, the same *sotto-segretario* who had talked to him the night of his arrival. During their first meeting, this youngish looking, trendily dressed man had been diplomacy personified. Of course, he understood his concerns. Of course, they could wait a few days. After two years of waiting, they could certainly wait just a bit longer. Of course, it had been just a big misunderstanding. They all knew that. Labauche must have been taken in by the tomb raiders and art thieves. Of course, they'd never told him that the plate had been stolen from the Etruscan museum in Tarquinia. Of course the Justice Ministry had been a bit too tough with Labauche. Of course, of course…

This morning the attitude had changed. The trendy clothes were still there, but the diplomacy had gone, replaced by a glacial tone.

"His Excellency, the Art Minister is none too pleased," the *sotto-segretario* declared sullenly and Labauche could tell that the young man's career depended on it.

"I thought we had a verbal agreement," Labauche tried his best to re-establish the diplomatic tone of the previous evening. "I thought we agreed that a few more days wouldn't matter, after such a long wait."

"A verbal agreement is one thing," the *sotto-segretario* kept up the glacial and nasal voice. "but to come out with a public statement is a whole different matter. You acted independently and that doesn't make us look good."

So it is a problem of public image, Labauche reasoned. He tried to be reassuring while still sticking to his guns. He wouldn't make any more public statements—not without consulting with the Art Ministry first.

Then, it was the turn of the Questura. What kind of a signal was he trying to send to the kidnappers? Del Chiaro, the gentleman in gray, who had been sent to meet him at the airport, had used a rather pushy tone with him today.

"We don't appreciate interference in our operations," Del Chiaro had stated. "Your public announcement was irresponsible. From now on, please restrain from any independent initiatives."

"You certainly know," Labauche had remarked, "that I received a threatening phone call from the kidnappers." Of course, his phone was tapped. He wanted him to know that he was aware of it. "I just wanted to buy time." As he said that he felt the pressure build in his chest.

The worst was the Justice Ministry. The public attorney who was prosecuting Jacqueline Speirs had called letting him know that unless the Etruscan plate was returned as soon as possible, he wouldn't consider dropping any charges. Worse, the inquiry against him would be picked up again and he had a good chance of being indicted. All in all, Fusco's Skype call had felt like a breath of fresh air.

Lunch had not been the usual relaxing and fun thing that a Neapolitan meal is supposed to be. Never mind that the *parmigiana di melanzane* –eggplant parmesan—was to die for and so was the spaghetti with clam sauce. Nick, Giuliano and Clelia had swallowed everything talking and plotting incessantly, paying very little attention to the food. Valentina had, instead, tried to keep down a few morsels of this and that, fighting nausea all the way and eventually had resigned to chew on some tasteless crackers. *What's the matter with me?* Valentina had wondered. She'd always been a good eater and now the sight of food wasn't the least bit appealing to her.

The worst was still to come. When coffee and babà—another one of those Neapolitan specialties her sweet tooth would have made her fight for--were brought to the table by the ever smiling Carmela,

210

Valentina couldn't take it anymore. She'd rushed to the bathroom, and before she'd been able to close the door, she'd barfed it all out.

"Nick!" she'd heard Clelia state in her loud voice in a semi-accusatory and partly triumphant tone. "You knocked her up. Take care of it, now!"

Nick had followed her into the bathroom. "I'm not pregnant," Valentina had shouted back, collapsing on the floor and still holding onto the toilet.

"All right, Baby," Nick had said in the tone he used when he didn't care to fight. "You're not pregnant, but then you're pretty sick."

He'd sat down on the floor and held her close to his chest. "You need to rest. Why don't you spend the afternoon taking it easy?"

That's how she'd gotten left behind. Stretched on her bed, feeling tremendously tired and just a bit disappointed, Valentina reviews the highlights and the low points of the afternoon.

Giuliano had arrived almost on time, traveling by bus from Marano.

"I got it," he'd told Nick.

"Got what?" She'd asked a bit annoyed that they'd left her out of the loop.

"Labauche's Skype contact," Giuliano had explained. "It's the safest way to reach him, avoiding his tapped phone."

If she hadn't been so nauseous, she would have thought about doing that on her own. They all moved into Clelia's tiny office and got on Skype. Labauche had picked up right away.

Once he'd finished talking to Caterina's father, Nick had said: "We need to leave in an hour or so to make it to Rome by six. We'll take our rented car and I'll let you drive it, Giuliano."

That's why the lunch had been more like a business meeting than a normal Neapolitan meal—a meeting for everybody else, except her. Nick had talked of a plan that the more she thought about it the more preposterous it seemed. Giuliano, much to her surprise, had not objected to it. He'd only asked a few questions: "Just to clarify this point…" he'd started every one of his inquiries. Clelia was brimming with excitement. "That's so great!" she'd exclaimed every three minutes. Valentina had fantasized Clelia with a gun in her hand shooting the kidnappers with overwhelming enthusiasm and shouting: "This is spicing up my life!"

Oh, well! As far as she's concerned, Valentina feels her only contribution to Nick's plan that she can think of, right now, is some well- aimed projectile vomit on the kidnappers' faces.

"It couldn't get any worse!" Laura Novak shouts on her Zoom connection to Prague, where her husband, Alistair Funklefinkel had to return to organize the summer courses of his exchange program. "Now the father is here. He was on TV and radio today."

"What do you mean?" Alistair is always trying to diffuse her agitation, but today it isn't working. "How would that affect you?"

Novak is ready to explode. How can he be so blind? Why doesn't he see the ramifications? He's always so literal. He never seems to get the subtext. One wonders how he's been working in academia for so long. Lucky for him that he got her to plot his career!

"How would that affect me?" she shouts even louder, hoping that the raised volume of her voice will convey more meaning to him. "Actually, the question to ask is: how would that affect us both?" Now she's said it and hopes he can see the light.

"What did her father have to say?" he asks. Well, at least she's engaged his attention.

"Oh, something about his willingness to return the Etruscan plate, which some tomb raiders stole for him from the museum in Tarquinia. He would do it, though, only after they released Caterina."

"It sounds fair to me," he comments in his detached voice. "I still don't see how that would affect us. Laura, you need to calm down."

Calm down? There he goes again, avoiding the issue. "Alistair!" she calls him by his full name, which she never does, preferring the shorter version, Ali. "She's going to be free soon!"

"What makes you think that?" he insists, trying to preserve his world based on denial. "There is still so much that can go wrong."

Always the optimist, her Alistair! "And what if it doesn't?" She's at her wit's end. "Have you thought of that?"

"Well, let's look at the worst case scenario," he continues. "The father pays the ransom and they free her, then what?"

"Then she would be interviewed by the press, and you know all too well what she would say…" The thought was too scary to contemplate. Novak had to catch her breath.

"Well, Laura, she might say that she'd talked to you a few days before being kidnapped and had expressed her fear…"

He finally got it. "That's right, Ali. She might say that. Actually, I can see her say it and even state that I didn't help her."

"It was not your job to help her." He doesn't seem to lose his cool. "You're not the police."

"That's the problem. I advised her against going to the police," her voice becomes teary, "I was afraid of the scandal."

"They may then ask her why she hadn't gone to the police,"

Alistair continues, still keeping his calm. "And I don't think she can answer that question."

"She can say that I advised her against it," *I'm lost whichever way this goes,* Novak feels. "I actually suggested that she should get a bodyguard."

"Not a bad suggestion, everything being considered," Alistair now tries to comfort her. "And why didn't she follow your advice, one might ask?"

"I doubt she could afford it."

"Let's not worry about what she could say," Alistair concludes in his usual conciliatory tone. "They haven't even released her yet and I have a feeling that might never happen after all."

What would I do, without Alistair? Novak feels relieved that there is at least one optimist between them.

CHAPTER NINETEEN

THE DAY EVERYTHING CHANGED

Some years from now, Labauche thinks, turning around in his hotel bed, unable to fall asleep, some years from now he will remember this day as the real turning point in his life—the day when he'd felt that giving up the Etruscan princess in exchange for his daughter was a fair deal. His bodyguard gone, the two strangers gone, he feels a deep sense of accomplishment.

The day had started with uproar and confusion. He'd called the press and requested to release a public statement. In a little more than an hour, TV cameras, radio and TV journalists, reporters from all major dailies and weeklies had assembled in the hall of the *Hotel del Parco.* He'd observed himself talk as if it had been another person. He'd always been a private person and had never been accustomed to deal with the press. He let his spokespeople do that job for him when it was needed in his financial enterprises.

Today, it had to be done and be done without delay. And he was the one who had to do it. He'd managed to talk without saying too much, to avoid stating what should not be said. He'd cleverly refused to respond to the many and bewildering questions the reporters had asked with insistence. What was he actually going to do with the plate? When was he going to deliver it to the Italian authorities? Why the delay? Was he going to pay the ransom? Whoever invented the expression, *no comment*, was a genius of diplomacy. Labauche smiles now.

The harsh reaction of the Italian authorities was something he'd expected. They must have felt taken for a ride. They'd even threatened to delay the police operation to free his daughter. At that point he'd started to question his plan and had considered backtracking on it. Maybe delaying the delivery of the plate was not such a good idea. Linking it to Caterina's release might not work, he'd reasoned—until his computer had signaled the arrival of the Skype call. He'd hesitated for a second, noticing the name of the unknown caller—a certain Clelia Palombelli. He couldn't afford to ignore the call. If this Clelia was some whacko trying to squeeze money out of him, he could get rid of her—nothing to lose at this point.

"Hallo," he'd said, speaking in his accented Italian. "Who is this?"

Much to his surprise, the man had answered in English with a New York accent. No, he didn't want any money. He just wanted to help, if he would just be willing to hear him out. It was then two o'clock. He'd set up a meeting for six.

There were two of them. One in his forties, mid-height, dark hair and intense dark eyes, a pleasant looking man—that was the American one—and the other one in his thirties, rather tall, with a short beard and curly hair, a gentle person, who spoke English with an Italian accent. They introduced themselves. The American was a police detective, a captain now working in California. He'd not met Caterina, but his fiancée was her colleague and apartment mate. The other one, the Italian, was one of her jailers.

They'd talked; they'd planned a strategy to free her; they even had dinner together never leaving his suite. By the time they'd left they'd agreed on every detail and had an appointment in Naples for the following day. His money would help in freeing Caterina, but not in the way he would have thought.

Now their words bounce back and forth in his mind. "The police operation has been delayed a few days," the Italian one had said. "That's what my police connections have told me. They're afraid you might change your mind about the Etruscan plate. They know you will not give it to the Camorra, but they still fear that you may not give it back."

"The Camorra may hope that you will deliver the plate to them," the American had remarked. "But I doubt they really trust that you will do that."

"From where I sit, Caterina is in danger," the Italian had rejoined. "Her jailers are young and unpredictable, trigger-happy and heavily drugged. A police operation might end up being a bloodbath."

Did I do the right thing? Labauche wonders in the early hours of the night. *Did I have any choice?*

Tossing and turning in her bed, alone for the first time in almost a month, Valentina knows that she will remember that afternoon as the time when she'd heard Clelia's story told in all its truth. No more adolescent myths about her favorite teacher, the fifty something teacher she'd met and adored when she was in high school. The seventy something woman, who'd sat right across from her, after Nick and Giuliano had left for Rome, and even Carmela had gone for the day, was another person.

As the hours went by, the nausea had lifted and her energy levels had bounced back. Maybe, I ate something that didn't agree with me, she'd reasoned—*l'insalata di pesce,* the fish salad, last night, that's it! She'd got up and wandered toward the living room in search of company.

"I'm here!" Clelia had hollered from the kitchen. "How are you doing?"

Valentina had found Clelia sitting at the kitchen table, playing solitaire. She'd sat right across from her. "I'm better," she'd reassured her.

"I'm done with this solitaire," Clelia had pushed the cards away. "How about some tea?"

They'd whiled away the afternoon talking. They hadn't done that in a long time—certainly not during this visit. Nick's presence and the Caterina issue had prevented them from being alone—just the two of them—and from opening their hearts and minds to each other.

"In high school, we all looked up to you," Valentina had confessed. "You were such a symbol of women's liberation, of uninhibited sexual freedom—so different from our mothers. The values our families passed on to us were so narrow, so traditional!"

"That's why you reacted by leaving for the States and finding your own identity," Clelia had served her some tea and cookies.

"I'm still struggling with it," Valentina had chewed on a cookie, feeling relieved that the nausea had subsided. "I guess I need to integrate the various parts of my identity."

"We cannot spend all our lives rebelling against the upbringing that was handed down to us." Clelia had rejoined. "Here I am playing solitaire when I would like to have grandkids to play with."

"Clelia, you have a very interesting life!" Valentina had protested. "As much as I would like to have a child—and I know it's not in the cards—I also know that motherhood is overrated."

Clelia had laughed. "You're probably right. But after thirty years in a long-distance relationship with a married man, I sometimes question my choices."

"Thirty years?" Valentina had tried not to sound as astounded as she was.

"For many years, I had relationships with younger men," Clelia had poured herself some tea. "Then during a trip to Spain I met this man, my age, so much in common, unhappily married. He seemed so eager to start over. Well, he wasn't then and he never was."

"Why did you stay?" Valentina had asked, feeling that she was being indiscreet, but couldn't help herself.

"I've asked myself that same question many times." Clelia had now attacked a cookie. "I tried to break it up many times and then I'd gone back. I tried other relationships, but they didn't work out. There is a very strong physical attraction between us, even now that we're both old."

"It's good to know that sex survives age," Valentina had joked.

"It gives you, younger people something to look forward to," Clelia had joked back and they'd both laughed.

"Just to change the subject," Valentina had started on another cookie, marveling at how hungry she was now. "Tell me honestly what do you think of Nick's plan?"

"Brilliant!" Clelia had sounded enthusiastic. "Much better than Giuliano's plan. That seemed so dangerous to me. Giuliano's a good journalist and a brave young man, but when it comes to planning a counter-kidnapping, he doesn't know what he's talking about. I can see why your Nick wouldn't go for that."

"I feel better hearing you say that because at lunchtime I was too sick to really concentrate and it all seemed preposterous." Valentina said.

"By the way, do you think Giuliano has some romantic interest in Caterina?" Clelia had asked with a twinkle in her dark eyes.

"Is he attached to someone?" *Oh, my*! Valentina had thought, *we're sinking into girls' talk. And why not?*

"Not that I know," Clelia had shaken her head. "His mother had made a comment to that effect not too long ago. She was worried that he wasn't ready to settle down."

"Oh, well," Valentina had commented sinking lower and lower into the gossip mode. "Caterina would not be much for settling down. She's such a bitch!"

"Is she?" Clelia had sighed. "Although a month of seclusion might have changed her…"

"It might," Valentina had agreed.

Later, Nick had called to let her know that he would be back very late that night. "So much more to arrange," he'd said. "But everything is working out. And how are you?"

Now, turning around in bed and unable to fall asleep, Valentina knows that everything has changed and will never be the same.

As he prepares to sleep, Valentina at his side finally resting, Fusco knows that, years from now, he will remember the day that just ended as the time when he changed his *modus operandi*. What had seemed impossible just a few days ago—such a breach of the protocol that had ruled his professional life—appears to be the most logical and inevitable outcome. His experience of almost twenty-five years served him well in planning tomorrow's action, but he had to step back from his allegiance to hierarchy and due process. Not that he considered himself a maverick. Without cooperation and coordination, a complex operation like this would be impossible.

"How do you plan to proceed?" Labauche had asked.

As he'd detailed his plan, Fusco had the feeling that he'd gained Labauche's trust. How had they reached that shift when mistrust, born of reasonable fear, had turned into curiosity and openness to possibility? Prejudice had been the mutual feeling they'd shared at the beginning of the session. Before meeting Caterina's billionaire father, Fusco had assumed that he would dislike him and disapprove of him. What could one expect of a man who had hesitated so long in swapping a plate—granted a piece of incredible beauty and perfection —for his own daughter? Fusco had expected to dislike him deeply. Never mind, he'd told himself, as they were driving toward Rome, Giuliano at the wheel negotiating swiftly through the traffic on the *Autostrada del Sole* (the highway of the sun). Never mind that I won't like him, as long as I can get him to listen to me and cooperate in freeing his daughter—after all it is his daughter's survival we're going to discuss. We don't have to be friends.

"What do you know of Labauche?" Fusco had asked Giuliano. "What has Caterina told you about her father?"

"Not much, except that he's a withdrawn and unhappy man," Giuliano had shared, never distracting his attention from the traffic approaching the Rome exit. "They have not spoken to each other in more than a decade. Her parents didn't get along. Caterina harbors a deep resentment against her father."

Withdrawn and unhappy—that's what he'd looked like at first sight. An elderly gentleman with light blue bespectacled eyes, fair skin, tall and thin—Labauche had invited them in and introduced them right away to his bodyguard. He wants us to be aware of his boundaries, Fusco had thought, feeling comfortable about that. He'd always been at ease around clear terms of confrontation. He'd prepared himself to show his own confines. He'd shown his credentials and invited Giuliano to do the same. And that's where the first snag had emerged. Giuliano had presented himself as Caterina's jailer. Only a few minutes later, he'd tried to mitigate the bad first impression by explaining his peculiar position as an infiltrated journalist collecting a dossier on the Neapolitan Camorra.

It hadn't taken them long to convince Labauche that Caterina was in danger and that waiting even a bit longer to free her—the Italian police's plan, from what they could surmise—might be a fatal mistake.

"By declaring that you won't release the plate to the Italian authorities until your daughter is returned to you," they'd explained. "you have sent an ambiguous message, which is buying you time. That's good, but it will not take much time for Camorra to understand that you're playing games with them and they won't like it."

Labauche had leaned forward, holding his head in his hands. That gesture of despair had revealed to Fusco his human side. From then on, the conversation had been much smoother. The plan had rapidly unfolded. Every single detail had been hammered down, while the other agents of the project had been called in and briefed. By midnight, Fusco and Giuliano were ready to turn back.

"Giuliano," Fusco had said, turning toward the young man again at the wheel, driving swiftly through the empty night roads. "If an indiscreet person were to ask you: deep inside what's your motivation for doing all this for Caterina? What would you answer?"

Giuliano had laughed. "Are you the indiscreet person, Nick?" and without waiting for his answer, "I would say that it's the reasonable thing to do—to help a person in danger. But deep inside, I must admit that I think I love her."

And so there you have it! Fusco thinks as he turns toward Valentina, asleep and facing him, when it's all done and said, deep inside, love is all there is—the great motivation behind all our actions. *And what wouldn't I do for this woman?*

As she turns around on her mattress on the floor, even more restless than usual, Caterina thinks that she will remember this cellar as the place where her life had turned around. As she contemplates the idea that this might be her last night of imprisonment, she can't help feeling relief. No more listening to the drugged up teenagers upstairs talking about their desperate lives, no more life threats, no more sudden flare-ups of moods, no more vulgar epithets, no more sleeping on a mattress on the floor of a dirty cellar, and no more filthy clothes. It's the end of that existence.

Is this going to be also the loss of a romance, an infatuation, maybe, which has sustained her during the last few weeks and allowed her to reach the end of each day with some hope? She can't delude herself. Once her freedom comes, she won't see Giuliano anymore. His life is driven by an all-encompassing commitment, which leaves no space for anything else. And even if he were able to make space for a little while for her, he wouldn't be allowed to by external circumstances. Her freedom is going to blow the cover off his own operation and the only thing left for him will be to run away forever, changing name and identity, hoping that the witness protection program will provide him with his survival.

Caterina knows that, even the end of her romance with Giuliano will not diminish the importance of the transformation that has occurred inside of her. So much has changed in such a short time, that she's afraid of not being able to walk out of the cellar and function in the world with her new identity.

This morning, when he'd come to see her, taking off the ski mask as he walked down the steps from the apartment upstairs, Giuliano had asked for her father's Skype address.

"Do you know it, by any chance?" he'd asked. "Your father is in Rome and he just released an interview. We want to contact him. His phone is tapped. So we want to avoid it."

Luckily, she knew it, even though it took her a few minutes to remember it—such a thing of the past. Not that she'd ever used it. They hadn't been in touch for so many years. But once, a couple of years ago, his secretary had contacted her to inform her that if she was gainfully employed, her father was going to terminate her financial support.

"Your father wants you to know that, should you still need some support, he's willing to extend it," the secretary had said in a rather distant tone. "Let me give you his contacts."

That's why she had received his email and Skype contact. For some reason, they'd stayed with her. Those were the contacts she'd passed on to Mickey Mouse on their aborted attempt at extortion a month ago.

"This may be your last day here," Giuliano had told her. "Tomorrow you may be free."

As he'd said that, she could see that the happy smile with which he'd announced her impending freedom had only lasted a second, immediately clouded by sadness. Even the passionate embrace that had followed—oh so very passionate!—was filled with a longing that could not be satisfied.

"Don't offer any resistance when they come to free you," he'd warned her before he'd climbed the stairs again.

She'd seen him disappear, feeling that this might be the last time. *To love and to lose* she tells herself, waiting for dawn to come.

CHAPTER TWENTY

A NEW BEGINNING

When she wakes up the day following her release, Caterina has a hard time recognizing the room where she'd fallen asleep the night before. How could this luxurious hotel room, actually a suite next to her father's, be the place where she's lodged? She gets up slowly, her body still feeling weak and her head slightly spinning. She approaches the window looking out onto a coastal road and to the distant islands of the Neapolitan gulf—all too blue and brightly colored. It all seems surreal—the room, the view from it—but not as unreal as the circumstances of her release.

"It will take you a while to adjust to this new reality," the social worker had told her at the police station. "Everything will seem somewhat overwhelming. You might even miss the awful surroundings of your cellar. They were horrible, but they were small. They allowed you to live inside your mind and to create a safe space there."

That's it—a safe space! She feels like a snail whose shell has been taken away and, yet, that shell was really no protection. It was her mind that had created that safe harbor. And Giuliano—that had been

226

the other anchor during the last few weeks. Now he's gone and the recognition of that loss makes her head spin even more and her heart skips some beats. She relives in her mind the moment she saw him disappear—her last glance of his back, his curly hair, his head stooping to enter into the back seat of the car parked in front of the car they'd made her get in.

"Where are they taking him?" she'd asked Fusco, who was sitting next to her in the back seat.

"To safety," Fusco had answered with a reassuring tone and no hesitation in his voice.

To safety. And safety for Giuliano means being away from her, maybe forever. I may never see him again and I have to accept that, she tells herself. She will never forget what he'd meant for her during the long weeks of her imprisonment. He'd been her lifeline. Even before they'd started to talk to each other, taking their physical as well as emotional masks off, his gentle presence had kept her alive. Now he has to survive and continue his work.

The light had started to change in the cellar as the morning had given way to the afternoon, when she'd heard his voice upstairs. It had surprised her because usually his presence was announced by the sound of his motorbike. This time he'd materialized from nowhere. He'd heard him argue with her adolescent jailers.

"They're going to let her go tomorrow," she'd heard him say. "Her father is going to give don Vito the plate."

"And that's why they told us to stay here all day and night," she'd heard them argue back.

"You can certainly leave for a short while and snatch a few purses, while I'm here," he'd insisted. "She won't do it, if you're around.

Come on, this is my last opportunity."

"Franco," Nunzio had teased him. "I really don't see what you find in that bag of bones. It's like fucking the dead."

She'd heard him laugh. "I have my own preferences." He'd said. "She may not be much to look at but she's good at fucking."

"She must be starved," Ciro had commented.

A few minutes after they'd left, she'd heard him say, presumably on his cell phone: "They're gone. Now!"

He'd come down with a pair of sunglasses and a hat for her. He'd handed them to her. But before she'd put them on, he'd hugged her tightly and kissed her passionately on her mouth. Then, he took her upstairs. That's when the men with the bulletproof jackets had come in and grabbed her.

"Go with them!" Giuliano had told her. "It's all over!"

Even though she was wearing her sunglasses and a sun hat, the light outside had seemed almost blinding and the fresh air had made her dizzy. The man sitting in the back seat of the car had told her that he was Valentina Snupia's partner.

As she sits now on her bed in the hotel room, her gaze down, she grabs her sunglasses to protect herself from this unearthly light of her new reality. She turns around and notices Valentina asleep in the bed next to hers. She climbs back to bed. The clock reads 6:30. The early morning light has woken her up. *Am I ever going to get used to this bright light?*

Valentina opens one eye and yawns. "Are you all right?" she asks and extends her hand toward her. Caterina grabs it and squeezes it.

Since yesterday afternoon, Valentina's hand has been her first anchor—first inside the office where Caterina was brought in to testify, and after that, in the social workers' room and all the way to the hotel.

"It's good for you to have a friend supporting you the first few days," the social worker had said. "She will be your first connection to the world." And then she'd asked. "Is your mother around?"

When Caterina had shaken her head: "No, my mother has been dead for twenty years." The social worker had continued. "Then hold on to your friend. Eventually, though, you will need to let her go. You will know when you're ready."

When will I ever be ready? Ready to be the person I was a month ago? Not that one—that woman is now a stranger to her. She actually needs to make amends for that one, she decides.

"Valentina," she says, still holding on to her hand. "I was such a bitch to you! So rude!"

As she apologizes for that Caterina whom she's left behind in the cellar, tears begin coursing down her cheeks grieving for the death of a person she didn't quite like, but nonetheless loved.

"It's okay," Valentina says. "I always knew you were better than that."

That's how she starts telling Valentina her story. As she explains herself to her new friend, she tries to make sense of her life herself.

Even though he does not consider himself a maverick, he's always trusted his gut feelings. And working that way, often in conflict with his superiors, he's been able over the years to solve complicated cases. *One has to trust one's intuition,* Fusco tells himself. And yet, one can't compromise one's career. In this case, he had to be careful every step of the way in the planning and development of the entire operation. And it worked.

He'd explained it first to Giuliano and answered all his questions. He'd also asked Giuliano questions about the logistics of the house where the Camorra had kept Caterina a captive for almost four weeks. He'd then explained the whole thing again to Labauche and further refined the plan. There again, there had been questions—useful questions. The last step of the planning had been with the group of private vigilantes, whom Labauche's bodyguard had helped them find in a matter of hours.

"You go in only after Giuliano has given us the green light from the inside," he'd repeated to them. Fusco didn't want anybody to do anything crazy. He didn't want any casualties on his watch. He would be out there in the car, directing the operation, but would not be physically involved. That's where he'd had to draw the line.

And Valentina of course, always on his mind. She was the only one who had not asked him questions. She'd looked all consumed by her inner thoughts, which she'd not shared with him.

Still not feeling well that morning, she'd said: "No coffee for me, please.," She'd made herself some tea and chewed very slowly on some plain crackers.

He'd noticed without saying anything, just wondering whether she wanted to be part of the operation. Before he could ask her, she'd asked him: "So where do I come in?"

"You'll be inside your car, parked in front of the police station," he'd explained, feeling relieved that she'd wanted to be included and that he had a role for her. "You'll come out as soon as we arrive and you will meet her. Even though you were never close" the thought of their unfriendly apartment sharing in Rome making him smile, "you're still a familiar face, actually the only familiar face for now."

"What about her father?" she'd asked. "Is he going to show up at some point?"

"Of course, he will." He'd poured himself some coffee from Clelia's Neapolitan coffee maker, and noticed Valentina's disgusted expression. "Labauche is probably already here in Naples. He's booked a suite, next to his own, for her to stay at night. He will come to the police station, as soon as they call him."

It had worked. After Giuliano had called, they'd moved the car in front of the *villetta*—a small single occupancy dwelling. The team of four men had entered the house. A few minutes later, two men had emerged escorting Caterina. To Fusco sitting in the back seat of the car, she'd looked quite different from the tall blonde young woman whose face he'd seen on several magazines during the last few weeks. Her hair covered by a sun hat, the face hidden under wide dark sunglasses, she was wearing discolored jeans, a t-shirt too big for her emaciated body and flip-flops on her feet. Appearing confused and dizzy, she'd walked hesitantly toward the car.

"I'm Captain Nick Fusco." He'd smiled at her, while the men helped her sit next to him. "I'm Valentina Snupia's partner. You're safe now."

She had not shown any reaction—too confused and bedazzled to react.

Right at that moment two more men had emerged from the house, accompanying Giuliano to the other car and to his new life. Fusco had noticed Caterina's emotion being aroused as she watched her friend— her only friend for those life threatening weeks—being taken away. He'd felt then that Giuliano's feelings for her were returned.

Assembling his few belongings scattered around Clelia's spare room, Fusco prepares to leave to return to Rome. Tomorrow morning he's flying back to the States, back to his life in Santa Abelina and to his work. Valentina will follow him in a month.

"Clelia," he tells their host. "Thank you for everything. Without you, Caterina would still be in a dark cellar."

"What are you talking about?" Clelia smiles happily. "Don't flatter me. I was just the connection. Happy to be useful! You took care of everything. Bravo!"

The phone rings. Clelia picks. It's Valentina. She wants to talk to him.

"Come and get me. I'm driving to Rome with you."

"Are you sure?" As much as he wants her to spend their final night in Rome with him, now he worries for her health. "It's a lot of driving. You need to rest."

"I'm fine," he hears her say and knows she's lying. "I want to spend this last night with you and have a little vacation in Rome," she jokes.

Right! A little vacation!

Unfounded optimism never helped anyone. That's how Laura Novak feels now. She's been glued to the television ever since last night's announcement of Caterina Pedersoli's release after 29 days in captivity. She's watched every *Telegiornale*—that's what Italians call the TV news—taking only a short break at night to sleep, expecting her impending demise. But no, no mention of her, just a cursory mention of the Exchange Center, where Caterina had worked for the month previous to her kidnapping. Today's media though has tentacles. The TV and the newspapers are only a fraction of it. The internet is where most of the information gets spread around. She can already see the news of her miscalculated moves appearing in a blog and from there climb their way to every form of social networking until one day the entire academic community knows about her faux pas. Her only hope is the notorious tendency of academics to only read what can advance their research and their careers—ignoring any lower level information. That's what Alistair has told her each time during the last twenty-four hours that they talked on the phone or Zoom.

"As you can see, she hasn't mentioned you at all," Alistair had first pointed out.

"Well," Laura had rebutted. "Don't you think that she's too busy with other things right now? But wait and see!"

"Wait and see what, Laura?" he'd sounded quite exasperated. "What would she gain by dragging you into this story?"

What would Caterina gain from it? Laura has been wracking her brain trying to imagine any possible advantage that would come to Caterina from total disclosure. And then, of course, it had come to her.

She'd called Alistair and told him with the triumphant tone of one who has made a major discovery. "She could use my advice—you know, when I told her not to go to the police—as a way to justify the fact that she actually did not go to the police."

"Brilliant!" He'd commented and this time he sounded sarcastic. "That would really work. Laura, she's not a five year old and you're not her kindergarten teacher. She cannot use you to cover up her own mistakes."

"Oh, yes she could!" A sudden thought crossed her mind. "By the way, why do you think she'd avoided the police?"

"Now, you're talking! Don't you think that she had something to hide?"

"Like what? The drugs, maybe?"

"Maybe! In any case," he'd continued this time with a serious tone. "She must know the rules of the game. Like us, she comes from the Ivy League. She knows that if she wants to stay in academia and have a career, she has to avoid ostracizing her senior colleagues. What happens among us has to stay among us."

And isn't that true? Laura now thinks. Alistair is a real prize winner. She'd bet on the right horse when she'd made his career her priority. He plays by the rules. She now feels that everything is going to work out. Caterina is a bit unstable, but she's ambitious and knows how to play her cards.

She's so much calmer that when the phone rings, Laura picks it up without screening the call. The man's voice catches her off guard. He's a journalist from one of the major Rome dailies. He wants to interview her regarding Caterina Pedersoli's kidnapping.

"Never," she shouts in the receiver and hangs up.

Two hours later, by the time she gets to the Exchange Center, a throng of reporters has already assembled in front of the door. They take a few shots of her as she covers her face with her briefcase. She has a hard time fighting her way. She rushes, breathless, upstairs. The secretaries are on the phones fending off incoming calls.

"No," she hears them say. "She's not in. We don't know when and whether she's coming in today."

She gestures frantically to them. No, she's not in. She slams the door of her office and crashes on her desk chair. *How am I going to survive all this? What am I going to tell them? Alistair, where are you?*

My daughter slept next door last night, under the same roof. The thought crosses Labauche's mind as he wakes up and then again throughout the morning, as he busies himself with all the arrangements for the next week. He has the plate to bring back to Italy and deliver safely to the Italian authorities. He has a daughter whose life he has to protect now. And he has his own life to plan—his pending judiciary problems in Italy, the future of his collection and his return to New York.

Only a door separates his suite from Caterina's. He doesn't dare open it, or even knock on it to demand permission to enter her rooms. He can only hope that she will emerge from her suite and start a long overdue conversation. He's afraid they might start on the wrong foot —a series of accusations, trying to establish who's the guilty one in a doomed race to the bottom. Did he actually mistreat her mother? Did she try to swindle him? The only way out of their predicament should be to ignore all those past misdemeanors and start anew as if they'd never happened. He knows, however, that is not what is going to happen.

"This is going to be a time to rebuild broken ties and to heal all wounds," the social worker had warned him at the police station. "Be patient! It may take time and you may need professional help."

They had called him from the police station as soon as Caterina was brought in. He'd been waiting in his hotel room, pacing nervously and fearing the outcome of the operation. *What a fool I've been to trust this guy, this Fusco!* He'd been telling himself. *Why didn't I shop around a bit more?* A minute later, another inner voice would argue that Fusco's operation was the right course and there wasn't really any other choice. *Wasn't I totally desperate before Fusco and Giuliano called me and showed up with their plan?* Then the call had come. Caterina was at the police station.

"She's safe and sound. She'll be able to talk to you in a little while," a police woman had reassured him. "A social worker will talk to you and tell you what to expect."

It had been a long wait inside shabby offices, followed by a number of interviews with officers whose names he couldn't remember and whose faces all looked alike. When Caterina had finally emerged from yet another office, she looked very different from the skinny, angry and rebellious teenager he'd last seen, leaving for college--to never come back. She was also different from the stylish young woman whose face he'd contemplated on magazine pages during the last week. Even though she bore some resemblance to the desperate and furious woman on the DVDs—the same hair cropped to the skull and emaciated body and pale face—she'd looked more disoriented and frail. She'd walked hesitantly holding on to another woman's hand. The other one had been introduced to him as Valentina Snupia, his daughter's colleague and former apartment mate. She'd exuded warmth in the way she was leading Caterina. At that moment, his daughter had reminded him of her mother—not at her age, still at the height of her exuberant beauty and splendor, no, later, when she'd been facing her untimely death.

"Papa!" Caterina had exclaimed. And then as it had really mattered given the circumstances, she'd inquired about his wellbeing. *"Comment vas-tu?"* She'd addressed him in French as she used to when she was a child.

He'd felt his heart skip a beat and his throat close, unable to utter even the slightest sound. He'd hugged her—her thin body quivering. In the confusion of the moment, that's all they'd done.

And now, he wonders whether he should knock at her door and start their conversation, maybe, by pointing out the many practical things that need to be decided and arranged. The big and important things may have to wait for a later moment.

A soft knock and then Caterina's face emerging from the door slightly ajar takes him by surprise. *"Bonjour Papa!"* she says and then takes him by the hand and makes him sit next to her on the sofa, *"Il faut parler."*—we need to talk—just a few simple words. That's how they ask each other for forgiveness.

Labauche looks at his daughter's eyes and for the first time recognizes the exquisite beauty and the ineffable poetry that has captivated him for the last few years. It is there for him to contemplate in flesh, even more resplendent than in effigy.

"When I was a child," Caterina had started while they were still in bed, "I used to spend summers in my grandmother's farm in Tuscany. I've never been as happy in my life as I was then. The light has never appeared as bright to me…"

Valentina has listened to her for a good portion of the morning—just listened, holding space, not interfering in the process with comments. Her intuition tells her that what's requested of her now is to bear witness. At times, it has been difficult to keep her mind steady and attentive when her body distracts her—the morning sickness coming in waves and no crackers available among the many enticing delicacies the hotel room service offers for breakfast.

Caterina has noticed that she's not eating. "You're not hungry in the morning, are you?"

Valentina has to explain: "Actually, I'm usually a good eater. During these last few days, I've been slightly nauseous in the morning."

Caterina smiles. "Are you pregnant, by any chance?"

Valentina shakes her head. Why does everybody have to ask that question—everybody except Nick, who knows better? "No, actually, I wish I were," she shares. "But no, that's not the case," and trying to steer the conversation back to Caterina's predicaments, she adds: "It will pass, I'm sure."

When, after a while, Caterina talks about the pain in her relationship with her father, Valentina interrupts her silent witnessing with a comment. "Your father is there," and she points to the door, which connects their two suites. "You may not be able to repair the past, but this is your chance to improve communication and re-establish your ties with him."

At first, Caterina hesitates. "No, I can't," she lowers her gaze. "I tried to swindle him."

"And he damaged you in so many other ways," Valentina insists. "You both need to confess and forgive each other."

After a while, Caterina knocks at the door, and disappears into the next suite, as if she's been swallowed by her past. It is right then that Valentina, too, feels that she needs to let go of Caterina for awhile and reconnect with her own life. Nick leaves tomorrow morning, the thought strikes her mind like lightning on a clear sky.

"Come and get me," she phones Nick. "I want to go to Rome with you."

On the highway to Rome, she glances at Nick at the wheel for a change and notices how tired he looks— dark circles around his eyes, a certain paleness even on his tanned face. She has been so taken by the events of the last two days and her own morning sickness and exhaustion that she hasn't paid attention to almost anything else.

"You'll be glad to be back home and be able to rest," she remarks. "No more Caterina, no more kidnapping, no more Camorra, no more Valentina nagging you to save the world…"

"Actually, I wish I could stay a few more weeks and enjoy Italy without all of the above mentioned concerns, except the nagging Valentina whom I would keep," he smiles, "but I owe, I owe and back to work I go."

In Rome, their tiny Trastevere apartment exudes tranquility. It is the beginning of August and the Roman traffic has noticeably subsided. Most inhabitants have left for vacations at the seaside or the mountains, or they are at least resting at home, with shutters closed to fend off the brutal summer heat. As she helps Nick assemble his luggage, Valentina feels a tinge of sadness for the little, too little time, left for them. *Where did this whole month go?* As much as she regrets not having more time to spend just with Nick, she also feels a sense of accomplishment. We saved a life, she repeats to herself to let that awareness sink into her consciousness. Yet, she knows that the life they saved is not only Caterina's—it's their life as a couple.

Later that night, as they prepare to spend their last night together, the windows wide open to let the *ponentino* breeze sweep through the apartment, Valentina glides under the sheets. Even before they kiss, she holds up her hand to gesture to Nick to wait.

"Remember that question you asked me," she begins her eyes deeply entangled into his eyes. "And I answered with a not yet, why

239

change things, what for…"

"Yeah? I got the picture," he answers a bit perplexed. "And it's okay."

"No, it isn't!" she shakes her head. "That answer has changed. The answer now is yes."

He smiles, and actually laughs, with an abandon she's never seen before.

CHAPTER TWENTY-ONE

AN UNEXPECTED ARRIVAL

"We will arrive on Wed. at 3 pm," the email reads. *"Can you come and get us?"* Fusco reads it twice. It's not the time of arrival that perplexes him—three pm is when the flight from San Francisco gets into Santa Abelina airport. It's the use of the plural "we," which he finds puzzling. What does Valentina mean by "we"? Is she alluding to the baby they're expecting or to a traveling companion—a full grown one?

A week after he'd left, Valentina had announced the big news during a Zoom conversation.

"Now, sit down!" she'd started the call.

Fusco was seated in front of the computer, but the command to sit made him feel very self-conscious. *Is she afraid I'm going to faint? How bad can it be?*

"I'm sitting down," he'd said, his heart pounding a bit in his chest.

"I found it hard to believe, but I'm pregnant," she'd said and he could hear the joy in her voice.

Not bad news at all, but life transforming, yes! He immediately thought of his age—not old, but not young anymore—with a grown daughter barely out of college. Oh, well! One can't plan everything and this baby wasn't planned.

"This is fantastic," he'd immediately responded. "We will call her or him Itala or Italo, to remind us of the Italian vacation that we were supposed to have and didn't quite manage to, except for a few asides."

It had taken him a whole day to absorb the news, but he had, and then felt very excited and touched by the strange way in which life had given them an unexpected gift.

Instead of writing back, he decides to call her now, partly to find out about the "we" she's alluding to, but especially because he wants to hear her voice.

"Caterina and I are arriving at three pm, on Wednesday." Valentina immediately repeats the information. "Can you come and get us?"

"Of course," he immediately answers. "How are you, Sweetie? Still nauseous all the time?"

"Uh, yeah! Mornings are the worst. I can't keep the food down. That's why Caterina changed her plane reservation and she's coming back with me. She says she wants to help me with the luggage. Isn't that nice of her?"

"Yes, it is nice," he tells her. *Although*, he thinks, *schlepping your luggage is nothing compared to saving her life.*

"You know," Valentina sounds excited. "We've made plans to teach a course in tandem—something like Italian novels made into films. I would do the film part and Caterina would teach the novel."

"When would you do that?"

"We don't really know," she sounds more realistic. "With our baby arriving in March and Caterina's relationship with Giuliano, our plans are vague at this point."

Plans, who can afford plans? He has a piece of news to share, too. He feels just a bit awkward.

"Sweetie," he tries. "Remember that you always said that getting married on top of the Court House tower is very romantic?"

"Yeah, it is..."

"Well, two weeks from Wednesday, that's what we're going to do —on the Court House tower..."

"Are you out of your mind?" her scream crosses the transatlantic distance which separates them. "We don't have to get married just because I'm pregnant!"

"Just because you're pregnant?" he yells back. "Valentina, what are you talking about? I proposed four months ago, and you finally accepted a month ago. We didn't have a date yet, and now the baby has set the date. Why don't you want to marry me? What did I do?" He's feeling offended and wants her to notice.

"I do want to marry you," Valentina now is speaking with a calm tone. "I just didn't want you to feel that we have to do it now, so soon. But it's okay. And the tower is good. What about the reception?"

Good, Fusco sighs with relief, *if she's worried about the reception, everything is cool.*

After he hangs up, he leashes Pippo, who's been nudging him for the last fifteen minutes.

"Okay, boy," Fusco pats his dog on the head. "Let's go!"

As they cross the street, he announces: "You're going to get a little brother or sister!"

The dog responds with enthusiasm, wagging his tail. After a month at Franca's, Valentina's best friend, Pippo is happy to be back at his home, without a cat to contend with. Then he suddenly remembers that he has to call Franca. *The reception, right, the reception!* It will be at Franca's restaurant. Valentina requested that and he's agreed. He also has to ask Franca and her husband to stand as witnesses. Yet, as hurried as all this preparation for the wedding feels like, it's almost relaxing compared to his Italian vacation and its climactic conclusion.

As he strolls through the green and shady alleys of his neighborhood, with Pippo on a leash—his nose sniffing every blade of grass—Fusco reviews the events of the last month. The cooperation with Giuliano Materassi, the courageous Neapolitan journalist undercover in the Camorra, and Giuliano's surprising and unusual romance with the woman he was supposedly jailing for organized crime—nothing less than Caterina. Valentina and Fusco had persistently searched for her, even though initially, they didn't care much for her. And then, after her release, she'd appeared as a changed person. It was as if the imprisonment had worked as a visit to an ashram—a purification, a transformative experience. A snotty preppy had turned into an Etruscan princess.

A few days after her release, Caterina had returned to Rome and had chosen to share with Valentina the same apartment they'd inhabited before the kidnapping—except that now they were getting along just fine. Her father had requested that Caterina be accompanied by a bodyguard, who ended up also sharing the apartment.

The unresolved issue in Caterina's life is of course her blossoming romance with Giuliano. After a few weeks' silence, he'd been able to reach her by email (oh, the wonders of the Internet!) and they'd been able to stay more or less in touch. It is still unknown where he has started a new life, with a new name and a new job as a front to protect his identity. Only the future will tell whether they will be able to develop what seemed like a promising love affair. Valentina has shared with Fusco that Caterina seems very committed to Giuliano and very much in love with him. They suspect that they've moved him to a South American country. The problem is that, for Caterina to join him, a series of security measures will have to be enforced. Whichever way you look at it, their lives are going to be complicated, Fusco sighs.

And what about all that mess with the stolen Etruscan art? Labauche, Caterina's father, is still under investigation for that. The plate of the Etruscan princess—the centerpiece of Labauche's collection and the object of his obsession—had been returned to the museum in Tarquinia, where it belonged. The Italian justice system and the police would have to solve that issue. *We can't take on everything*, Fusco chuckles as he reaches for his cell phone and dials Franca's number. *And now let me organize my wedding to my princess.*

Author Bio

Maria Marotti is a retired academic, hypnotherapist and alternative health practitioner who lives in Santa Barbara, California. She is the author of essays, collections, academic books, short stories, screenplays and novels. Besides <u>The Etruscan Princess</u>, her novels include <u>Memoirs of a Scoundrel Dog</u>* (a humorous dog autobiography) and <u>A Question of Class</u>*.

Her website is mariamarotti-author.com.

* <u>Memoirs of a Scoundrel Dog</u> is available on Amazon. <u>The Etruscan Princess</u> is the second—but not the last--novel in the Captain Fusco Cases series The first novel in the series is <u>A Question of Class</u>. Its publishing house is no longer in business, but it will be republished on Amazon soon. If you would like to read it or any of Maria's future books, feel free to send her an email (mariamarotti@gmail.com) and she will let you know when they are available.

Author's Notes and Bonus

Thank you for reading my book. I hope you enjoyed it. As an expression of my gratitude, I would like to give you "The Crying Game," which is one of my best short stories. Just email me at mariamarotti@gmail.com and I will send it to you

I have a favor to ask: would you please leave a review on Amazon? Your doing that will make it possible for more people to enjoy my book.

You can find the book by doing a search for Maria Marotti The Etruscan Princess on Amazon, or you can find a link to it on my website: https://mariamarotti-author.com/booklinks.

Thank you!

Made in the USA
Columbia, SC
10 July 2021

41583470R00155